RADIUM HALOS:
A NOVEL ABOUT THE RADIUM DIAL PAINTERS

Shelley Stout

Kim -
Enjoy the journey!
Shelley Stout

First Printing—2009
Second Printing—2010
Third Printing—2010
Published in the United States by LibriFiles Publishing.

FOREWORD
SEPT. 2009

Five years before I was born, my father, Leonard J. Grossman, represented women from Ottawa, Illinois in litigation against the Radium Dial Corporation seeking not merely damages but also recognition of what had been done to them. I grew up in the shadow of the Radium Dial case, a landmark in workers' rights in this country. I was deeply proud of my father and infuriated, as he was, by the injustice inflicted on these women. I am sure this background is one reason I became a government lawyer enforcing workers' rights. So when I came across *Radium Halos* by Shelley Stout I was very excited.

Sometimes fiction can speak truth in ways that the bare facts cannot. Ms. Stout has found a unique voice in which to tell the tragic story of the Radium Dial workers and at the same time to say much about life in this country. The story goes beyond the Radium Dial case and reflects much about our attitudes toward work, women, mental illness and aging. Along the way it speaks of fear and loyalty and truth itself.

CHAPTER ONE

Young folks these days complain too much. When I was young, they taught me to never complain about nothing. If the boss asked you to work a extra hour, you done it without saying a word. If you had a bellyache, you suffered through it until you got home, when you could curl up in bed with a hot-water bottle.

I don't mind the hospital. I don't never say one bad thing about it. By and large, I'm happy most days. Happy about being here at Mannington, because it's home. I don't never mind the banging, hissing radiators in the winter. I sleep right through the racket most nights. On the hottest summer days, I survive the heat, with only huge, clanking fans to swirl around the stifling air.

Some of the girls here don't like it when the nurse makes them get up so early. They don't like to be told to work hard. They whine and carry on. Not like when me and my sister Violet was in our teens and we worked at the Radium Dial in 1923. Course, we was told we could make better wages if we was to work hard. Our supervisor Mrs. Peltz told us if we took pride in our jobs and saved our earnings, we could have us a nice life.

Mrs. Peltz was a older lady, with long eyelashes and deep maroon-colored lipstick. She had only her four front teeth, then gaps for the rest. I couldn't tell for sure, but it looked like as if she'd painted beauty marks on her wrinkly cheeks.

Me and Violet was in the hall waiting for our interview at the Radium Dial. We had our friend Clara Jane to thank. She already had her a job at the factory. Some of the other girls was outside the office in the hall with us, and a couple of them talked about somebody who begin work last month, only to quit after four days. They said ever single morning at ten o'clock she got sick to her stomach. At first, they thought she was in a family way, but it turns out she just didn't like the taste of the paint. She had to go and find her a different job.

I set and stared out into the big factory room where the girls was painting. The ceiling seemed to go up to three stories high, just like the auditorium back at Belmont High in North Carolina, where we was from.

After a few minutes, Mrs. Peltz invited Violet into the office first, and then me behind her. We set in the chairs across from her desk. She had her some pretty roses in a vase, and she held up the cards we filled out before we come for the interview.

"I understand you're new to Ottawa. Even new to Illinois."

Just like always, I let Violet do the talking. She could talk better because she studied elocution harder than me in school. "Yes ma'am, we are."

"Well, we hope you'll stay with us for a long time to come."

"Thank you," we both said together.

Mrs. Peltz smiled at me, with her gaps for teeth. "Now girls. I'm sure Clara Jane has told you what the job entails, has she not?"

Violet crossed her legs and pulled down the hem of her dress. "Yes, she told us about the watch dials."

"Oh. Well you girls won't be graduating to *watch* dials just yet." She rolled her eyes when she said it, like as if we was too dumb to understand. "You'll be starting off with the *clock* dials. You'll have thirty days to show us how well you do. Then, when quality control says you're ready to graduate up to watches, we'll let you give them a try."

"I see," Violet said.

"Now, have you girls had a little taste of the paint yet? Some girls aren't fond of the taste, and we can't hire them."

Me and Violet turned to each other and giggled. I held a couple fingers over my mouth, because we was both recollecting the same thing. Violet told on me. "Helen here, when she was a baby, she used to eat the paint chips off the sideboard. I was about four-and-a-half, and my job was to keep her away, because she would get these red marks on the edges of her mouth from the red paint. Then, one day, I tried one of them too, and, well, we *both* became fond of paint chips. After that, our daddy gave us both a whipping." Mrs. Peltz smiled, but I could tell she didn't think it was all that funny. "Good," she said. "Then you shouldn't mind working here at all."

She pursed her lips and then opened her desk drawer, taking out a little jar of pale bluish-green paint and three skinny brushes. Before she even opened the jar, she stuck one of the brushes between her lips, to get it wet. "Now, I'll teach you to do your tipping."

"Tipping?" I asked.

"That's how we get a sharp point on the brush." She stuck the tip of the brush in the paint, then back again in between her lips to make the brush more pointed. "The taste isn't bad once you get used to it. If you want to achieve specialist, you'll *need* to."

"What's specialist?" Violet asked.

"That's the highest you'll achieve as a dial painter. First, you'll start off as apprentice. Then, when you've received your certificate for expert, you'll be able to do the watch dials. Later, if your production quota exceeds our standard goals, you'll be rewarded with an *Excellence in Training* plaque, and you'll be in our specialist category. Those girls have special privileges they've earned, by working hard and producing more than the others. And they make more money too, of course. You'll be paid by the piece."

It was all too much to take in at one time, and I hoped Mrs. Peltz would change the subject.

She opened a different drawer and give each of us a bare clock dial to practice on, and give us each a skinny brush too. I went first. I took a deep breath and stuck the dry, tickly brush between my lips. Then, I stuck the tip of the brush into the paint. "That's right, Helen. Now, hold the clock face in your other hand."

Violet watched me, blocking my light, so I nudged her out of my way.

"Don't forget to do your tipping," Mrs. Peltz said. "You need to kiss the brush between your lips. Make it a nice sharp point, so you can paint the tiny numbers."

"Yes ma'am," I said, worried I would make a mistake. My hand begin to shake, but I knowed I had to try. I stuck the tip of the wet brush between my lips, and kissed it. Soon after that, the paint slipped to the back of my tongue and down my throat. I swallowed it, and it tasted and smelled like a gritty medicine. All of a sudden, I wished I hadn't come to Illinois.

"It feels sandy, doesn't it?" Mrs. Peltz said.

"Yes ma'am. It does." I just stared at her, trying to suck the sandy feel off my tongue. I didn't want to kiss the brush no more. I tried to paint the number one on the dial, but Mrs. Peltz said to do the number eight first, because that was easier. Round I went with the brush, and I only made one teeny mistake. Mrs. Peltz told me I was a *natural*. After a while, Violet tried too.

Violet wasn't near as good a painter as me. She tried real hard that first day, but more often than not, she lost her patience.

I heard a expression once—"The good die young." But you couldn't rightly say that was the case with my sister Violet.

#

I reckon most folks know what's real and what isn't. Like if they have them a bad dream that wakes them up in the middle of the night while their fists is still squeezed and their heart is in a gallop. Nightmares can be like that. Now and again, I have me a bad dream about Violet. She's been dead since 1934.

Usually that nightmare don't bother me for long. I might go right back to sleep after or get me a smoke and go up to the nurse's station for a light. I can do some of my best thinking late at night when everbody else is asleep. I set in the dark, thinking of the dream and recollecting my sister when she was still alive.

It's easy to tell it's a dream because the ward is quiet—no radiators clanging or slippers shuffling across the tile floor. What happens first is I'm setting on the floor of my room at Mannington. My legs is bent to my chest, and my hands is resting on the tops of my knees. Suddenly, the air turns so cold my bones chill, then my heart races and my breath comes in sharp, painful bursts. I'm still cold, but I turn myself over to push up from the floor.

Through the doorway, the light is a faded rose color. Like a gunshot, the rose colored light changes to bright white, and I squeeze my eyes shut and cover them with one arm. I listen for the sound of Violet humming "Little Ella," her favorite song from when we was girls down in Belmont. The humming gets louder, then Violet turns up in the doorway, and the brightness goes back to the rose color.

The vision I see next is Violet from 1933, just before she got sick and passed. Violet's fair skin takes on a blush, and she hasn't aged at all, the way I have in the past thirty-nine years. She wears a flowery robe tied at the waist with a wide, yellow sash, and she carries a box in her hands. "Helen, don't be scared," she says to me. But I already am skittish as a ground squirrel.

Next comes the part that always makes me wake up. I tell my arms to stay by their sides, but they don't listen. I can't control my fingers as they lift the lid on the box. And I can't control my eyes neither, as they peer inside at the black emptiness. More than anything, I want to look away, because nobody needs to tell me what I'm about to see. I wait, and then something fades in. It's a skeleton head with a broad grin of overlapped teeth. I have one of those screams trapped in my throat, and I taste blood on the back of my tongue. Then finally, the scream finds a way out and I wake up.

I don't know how many times I've had me that dream. It gives me the shivers even now to tell it. But last night was different. When I woke up from the nightmare, I wasn't in my bed. I was flat on a gurney with orderlies all around me. My wrists was strapped down. Somebody's sweaty hand clutched my last free ankle, buckling it into the leather strap. Because I was screaming, a orderly snapped, "Quiet down, Helen."

We left the room on the gurney through the double doors of the ward. Along the way from the corner of my eye, I took in the smirking faces of other ladies on the ward. Also some of the nurses. With my wrists and ankles so tight inside those leather straps, all I could do was wiggle my spine trying to escape before we reached the underground tunnel. I hate the tunnel. "Give it a rest, Helen," the orderly said, in a firecracker voice. "You're only going to the infirmary."

Above my head, the ceiling changed from those tube lights to the arched brick ceiling of the tunnel. The floor dipped as we went under the building. Spider webs and dust clung to the faded bricks like Spanish moss. The rolling gurney wheels scraped against the cement floor, with the dead, damp smell all around me like a fog. Ever few feet overhead, a bare light bulb blinded me, while the wheels jolted the gurney, driving over stray stones below or cracks in the cement. I was still screaming because any time I'm in the tunnel I feel like as if I'm in a tomb and it's smothering me.

"We're almost there." I knowed the orderly was meaning to calm me down, but instead, the voice startled me, and I sucked in a breath.

At the other end of the tunnel, a door opened and I had to squint at the bright infirmary lights. Somebody grabbed my arm and then a needle jabbed my skin. I turned my head to tell them to stop, but instead the room faded to nothing.

#

When I opened my eyes next time I wasn't screaming no more, and I wasn't scared, neither. I wondered if maybe I hadn't fell to the floor and they'd scooped me back up, because ever part of me hurt—my neck, my arms, even my back. It felt better to be still. I knowed they give me something, because I could smell formaldee-hyde and my mouth was pasty.

For some reason, my wrists and ankles was still strapped down, only now I was on a bed, alone in a empty room. Then Dr. Winslow come in, followed by the new doctor, only at first, I couldn't recollect his name.

"Helen, do you remember Dr. Stokes?"

Dr. Stokes. That was his name. Dr. Stokes had him a bird's beak for a mouth and dark rimmed glasses.

"Ye- yes..." My voice crackled like split logs. The insides of my cheeks was stuck to my gums, and I couldn't get my tongue to form a word.

The two doctors talked about me to each other like as if I wasn't there, about my name, which is Helen Waterman, and my age, which is 65. They talked about my mental illness.

"Helen, we're going to remove your restraints. Can we do that? Will you sit up for us?" Between my toes and the end of the bed was a long distance, since I hadn't never growed past five-foot-nothing.

"Wa-ter," I said, hoping somebody would give me some.

"We'll go ahead and get you out of these while we wait for the nurse, all right Helen?"

Everthing with Dr. Stokes is "we." "We will do this, or we'll do that." Like as if he was a group of people instead of just one doctor. I like him anyway. He has a youthful, sweet-smelling breath. Not like some of the other Mannington doctors whose breath stinks of garlic or cigars. When me and Violet was younguns, we had to put up with our daddy's cigars, but that didn't mean we enjoyed smelling them.

But Dr. Stokes is nothing like me and Violet's daddy. Our daddy was one to change his mood often—at times in good spirits, and at other times, down in the dumps. On occasion, he was mighty strict about certain things. Us girls had to make things up, or leave out information so's he wouldn't know what we was up to. Other times, he would allow us to do as we pleased.

Just then, a nurse come in with a metal tray on wheels. I recollected that nurse from last time I was in the infirmary. Nurse Barnes is from New York, and she's always making a fuss about being from *Upstate* New York, like as if that makes her better than everbody else. Better than all of us from North Carolina, with her fancy talk. At least now and again I try to talk like folks do on the television, but it don't always come out just right.

Nurse Barnes was wearing a nurse's dress, which is uncommon. Ever since it got to be the 1970s, most ladies don't dress up much no more. They go out in slacks instead of dresses.

"Nurse Barnes, please bring Helen a cup of water." Dr. Winslow finally got me out of the straps.

I decided right then and there, I wouldn't say nothing else until I had me a drink.

Once my hands and legs was free, I rubbed my wrists. The straps had made my skin raw, and the leather had left the smell of stale sweat.

Dr. Winslow said he was leaving me in the care of Dr. Stokes. On his way out, Dr. Winslow passed Nurse Barnes, and I managed to raise my shoulders and head, gripping the water cup with both hands while I tried to drink it. Most of it went down my throat, but some soaked into my gown. At least now I could try to speak without my tongue sticking to the insides of my mouth.

Across the hall, a man was cussing up a wild streak, stringing words together in new ways I hadn't never heard before, and a few I had. First, there was filthy names of private body parts in the same sentence with words like suck and shove, or combinations of "Jesus H," then a foul word between, followed by "Christ." I didn't never like it when somebody used the Lord's name that a-way.

Next there was a loud crash, like as if somebody kicked a wheeled cart and all the items on it shattered to the floor.

I reckoned that man must be crazy.

When they finally got the noisy man to quiet down, I waited while Dr. Stokes pulled up a chair next to the bed. "Helen, we understand you had a bad dream."

The dream was now just a far away memory. A trifling memory like dozens of times before. Dr. Winslow knows all about my dream, but I hadn't never told it yet to Dr. Stokes. Course, there's some things neither one of the doctors knows, like how me and Violet worked at the Radium Dial factory.

"We're going to try some new medication," Dr. Stokes said, "so you'll sleep better and we can eliminate some of those disturbing images."

I nodded, recollecting images I seen over the years. When I was a young girl, sometimes I might see a kind of cloud around a person's head. A soft cloud with blurry edges to it. One time, I seen a cloud around a old woman's head. One other time, I seen it around a boy's head we used to go swimming with in the pond back in Belmont. His name was Jerrod. Me and Jerrod looked like we was twins, even though we wasn't. We was sad to learn just a few weeks after the start of summer he come down with the diphtheria. He died before he was nine.

I chewed on my lower lip, reaching for the sleeve of the doctor's white coat. "I... I don't want to leave Mannington. Please don't make me go live with Pearl."

Dr. Stokes smiled and patted me on my arm. "Let's not worry about that now, Helen. We'll see you tomorrow in our session, and we can discuss it then, okay?"

I let out a breath, and told him it would be fine. Whenever I was worried, Dr. Winslow always had a way to make me feel better, by talking real gentle to me. Dr. Stokes most likely would do the same. Also, Dr. Stokes has got him a sense of humor. One time, he come in to see me and my roommate Neely, wearing a funny straw hat that could light up like a Christmas light.

I cracked a smile for him, because I knowed they would soon return me to my room. I knowed we could talk about me going to live with my niece Pearl at our session in the morning. The first time Pearl mentioned the idea, she said right in front of me, "It's embarrassing to have a relative up there at Mannington." Plus, the doctors are sending lots of folks home now, specially the ones who aren't so bad off.

When Pearl was a little girl, things was different. I brought *her* up. Now that Pearl is forty-three and has her that personnel job in Gastonia, she thinks she knows everthing. If I do go live with her, she will probably make me feel as if I'm a great big burden.

Oh, I know all about burdens. Keeping a secret hid is a kind of burden, and I've kept plenty of those since I was young. Things I never told nobody but my husband, and he's been gone years.

Thinking about Pearl has stirred up some memories from that 1923 summer when me and Violet lied to our daddy. Memories about the first girls who died from the radium, like Bess and some of the others. About how they was so sick, I didn't want to visit them.

Nobody can make me talk if I don't want to. I hold fast to my secrets, specially the ones me and Violet and Clara Jane promised never to tell.

CHAPTER TWO

It's hard to keep some memories quiet. Like memories of my husband, Jesse, before he was killed in the war—the second one. I still can't get over the fact they have had so many world wars they have to keep count.

Since I can't recollect everthing, I rely on the photographs Pearl keeps closed up in her dining room hutch. Photographs of Jesse, short for Justice, in his uniform, all starched and pressed, with those fancy ribbon medals.

Sometimes, when things get specially bad, I long for my husband. I don't never like to think about the terrible way he died. If anybody ever asks, I just don't answer them.

I can barely recollect now what it was like to sleep pressed up next to Jesse's warm body, the soft, curly whiskers on the back of his neck and how he could be inspired in a instant, just from sneaking a glance at me under the covers. I cried ever month when I discovered again there would be no baby.

Our first night together, I giggled all night long like a school girl, but by the time he went off to war, we'd been married and I'd been barren for seventeen years. Violet was more lucky. She give birth to Pearl. Along with Pearl there was a twin baby brother named William, born just after. He didn't live but a few days.

When I think about that first day I seen Jesse at the factory, I never dreamed I would marry him. Never met nobody more clumsy and dim-witted. At least I thought he was dim-witted, but it turned out he was just shy as a snail.

When me and Jesse got our first home together, it was nothing but a room over a fabric store in Cramerton. We had lots of ladies always coming to the store, and Jesse would tease me about how he had a constant stream of lovely young ladies to gander at, but *my* supply of good-looking gentlemen was bone dry. I told Jesse it was all right for him to gander all he wanted, but he wasn't never allowed to *touch*.

Jesse had got him a job as a fry cook at a diner. He worked nights and weekends and ever space of time between. Finally, after he had been working there for a few months, they give him a day off here and there.

I recollect one day me and Jesse was taking a walk through town, when we run into Frank MacDayne, a boy I had dated once when I was still in high school. Jesse clung to my arm, while I made introductions. The two young men shook hands, while Frank kept looking up at tall Jesse and back down at me, over and over. Up, down, up, down. I told him if he didn't stop, he'd get a crick in his neck. After that, he only stared at me.

Frank said he worked at Pharr Yarns, in the hosiery department.

After he left, Jesse teased me about it, and said I'd probably be leaving him for Frank. He pushed me away from him, so's I was standing a few feet away, while he winked.

I pretended I was shocked, and asked why would I leave.

Then Jesse explained it. He said with him, all I would get was a room over a fabric store. With Frank, I would get a lifetime supply of hosiery.

I just smiled nice at my new husband, and told him it wouldn't matter where we lived. With Jesse, I would've been happy living in a junk yard or a palace, so long as he was there with me.

We was out of money most of the time, but we was happy. By the time Violet and Grady was married, they was able to save up a little before Pearl come. After a time, I thought it didn't bother me no more that other girls around me was having babies and I wasn't. I would smile nice meeting them on the street, seeing their little bellies poke out from their shirtwaists, and seeing how their skirts would ride up in the front, showing their knees, while the back of the skirt hung down to their calves.

When other young mamas was at the market with their new infants, I would watch the baby's little noses and mouths, wishing I had a little mouth like that nursing up on my breast. Jesse once told me I had enough love for two or more, so he wouldn't never be jealous of a baby.

I told him the same. But I didn't really mean it.

Nobody back home knowed how I first met Jesse at the Radium Dial factory when I was 16, because nobody besides me and Violet knowed we had worked there with Clara Jane Hart in the summer of 1923. I recollect the day Clara first told me and Violet about it.

I had been working my shift at the Belmont Five and Dime, and I set at the kitchen table rubbing the soles of my feet. After that, I set us a loaf of bread to rise in the oven. Me and Violet waited on the front porch for our friend Clara Jane. I couldn't wait to see her again. We hadn't seen Clara Jane since her family moved back home to a town near Chicago, when her daddy took that job to be a stock broker.

In Clara's last letter, she said she had her a surprise.

Violet stuck a hair pin into the side of her wavy, coffee-colored hair. "Could be a new suitor, or maybe she's decided to move back down here. She always said she liked North Carolina better 'n Illinois."

When a friend dropped Clara off, I couldn't barely wait for the Chevrolet Coupe to pull up in the gravel drive. I just started in right away hollering out *hello*. "She's here!" I opened the automobile door for her. "Clara Jane. Oh, Clara. You look wonderful."

Everthing about Clara Hart made me feel plain, with her tropical sea blue eyes and her shiny hair, inky black and straight, then curved under at her chin. She was dressed in a blue beaded wool suit. A pair of rose gold earrings hung from her ears. Around her collar was a fox fur stole. "Thank you. Oh, Helen and Violet, it's so good to see both of you," Clara said.

All of us girls hugged each other, like as if we hadn't been together for the past one hundred years. Our daddy waved from the back where the chickens was, but he was frowning at us. Felix Meisner didn't believe in keeping idle when there was work to be done. Soon, he left the chicken coop and walked toward us, wearing his faded denim pants and a ragged checkered shirt. He took off his work gloves and tossed them to the ground.

While he was on his way to us, Clara whispered in my ear. "What kind of mood is he in today?" I whispered back to her that it didn't matter, because his mood could change at any moment like the weather. Just the night before, he was singing to a phonograph record, when out of the blue, he started in crying and shaking his head to and fro like a lantern in a breeze.

When Daddy reached us, he held out his hand for Clara to shake it. Then, he changed his mind and hugged her a little instead. "My, don't you look fancy? How's your Momma and Poppa, Clara?"

"They're fine, Mr. Meisner. They send their hellos."

"They let you come all the way down here by yourself? On the train?"

Clara fixed her fur collar. I reckoned she was perspiring in the heat. "Yes sir. After all, I *am* seventeen years old now."

Daddy just scratched next to his round nose and rolled his eyes. "How could you be that old already? I remember when you and my girls used to play with rag dolls on the porch."

I was glad today Daddy was in one of his good moods.

Instead of spending more time with him, we excused ourselves and left for the bedroom me and Violet shared, where we could all be alone. While Clara slid the fur from her neck, I stroked the smooth softness with the back of my hand. Violet snatched it from me. "Let *me* feel it."

That made me cross, and I made a little squeak sound.

Clara set on my bed and peeled off her shoes. "These are new, too."

"Where'd you get enough money for shoes like these?" I asked, wishing I had Clara's eye-catching legs. I knowed Mr. and Mrs. Hart was just like us as far as money. Not poor, but I was pretty sure they didn't have lots of extra money neither.

Clara set straight on the side of my bed, knees together. She said part of her surprise was she didn't live at home anymore with her family. She lived in Ottawa, Illinois. It was a different small town outside of Chicago, and her mama had been forwarding her mail.

"Where do you live exactly? Do you share a room?" Violet asked.

Clara stood from the bed. She was the kind of young girl who had to touch everthing as she passed. She picked up Violet's bottle of toilet water and set it back down. Then she opened one of the drawers on Violet's dresser and shut it again. Clara said she lived in a kind of a big boarding house with rooms to let, but the lady who owned it didn't charge her a nickel, because she did errands for her and took her children to church on Sundays. "And since just after Christmas, I've been working at a new company."

Violet picked something from her front tooth. "I thought you were going to secretarial school."

"Things just didn't work out for me there. My folks don't know yet."

Clara was just like me and Violet. We had to keep things hid from Daddy, in case he was in one of his cranky moods.

Violet winked at me, but continued talking to Clara. "So you lied to your mama and daddy? I thought you were a good Catholic girl," she said. With a little shrug of her shoulders, Clara appeared like as if she was fixing to explain, but she kept quiet.

Violet checked her teeth again in the wall mirror and asked Clara the name of the company.

"It's called The Radium Dial Company, but everybody just calls it the Radium Dial." She paused to peel off her white gloves. "We paint the numbers on luminous watches and clocks."

"Luminous?" I asked. Then I recollected..."You mean like on one of these?" I reached to the nightstand for my wind-up alarm clock.

"We probably painted those very numbers at our factory."

"Huh," Violet snickered. "Helen here once scratched up the face on a grandfather clock. She got sent to bed without supper for it."

Clara dropped her chin and frowned at me. I didn't say nothing, but I was recollecting what I done wrong. I was only seven years old when it happened. I scratched up that clock with the sharp end of a hay hook.

Next, Clara told us how the paint was made of radium powder which was why the clock dials glow in the dark. She said they work at the old high school building, setting at desks upstairs in the auditorium. She called it the "studio."

It was beginning to sound more interesting as she went along. While I listened, I was busy wishing our daddy was more than just a bee-keeper and a chicken farmer.

"You'll never believe how much they pay," Clara continued.

"How much?" Violet asked.

Clara crossed the room to the window. Folding her arms, her eyes got big as sunflowers. "Instead of making five dollars a week at the bakery, where I used to work, guess how much I made my first week."

I was about to burst from waiting. "Tell us."

"I made seventeen-fifty."

Violet stuck her hands on her hips. "Applesauce! Nobody can make that much at a factory job."

"I make even more, now. Most weeks, I bring home about twenty-five to thirty dollars."

I didn't believe a word of it. "You telling the truth?" I asked, beginning to grin.

"Ab-so-loot-ly," Clara answered. "Just look at my clothes. She fingered her fox fur stole.

I set before the mirror at the dressing table, deciding whether to brush my thick blond hair or straighten my wayward eyebrows. Staring at my own self, I wondered what it would be like to have so much money. I was fond of my job at the five and dime, but I didn't make enough there to fill a cold cream jar.

Clara snuck over to the door to make sure it was closed tight, asking if we had us any plans yet for the summer.

"No, we don't," Violet answered, fixing her blouse collar.

"What if we ask your father? Maybe he'll let you work at the Radium Dial. Think of all the money you'll make. You'll come home rich."

Since I quit high school just last month, and Violet was already graduated, maybe we could stay longer than just for the summer. It would be the perfect plan, except for one thing—one *person*.

I stared at Violet. "What about Daddy?"

Clara got a confused look in her eyes. "Can't you just try to catch him when he's in one of his good moods? Like he is today?"

"It won't matter what kind of mood he's in. He don't want us to work in any kind of a factory," I said. "Because of what happened to our mama."

Clara nodded, with a frown. She was recollecting what me and Violet had told her, years ago.

"I'm sorry. I didn't think about that." Then Clara set still and didn't speak for a minute. "You think they'll ever find the man who did it?"

Violet made a little *huff* sound. "Not this many years later."

I have no memory of my mama. When I was in the sixth grade, Violet told me what had happened when we was both just babies. How when our mama worked at the textile mill, a man had beaten and raped her. After that, she was so distressed she couldn't live with herself, so she took her own life. I seen a photograph of my mama from when she was a young woman, only she wasn't distressed then.

Going away for the summer wouldn't be the problem, since last June we went together to South Carolina for two weeks and stayed with our cousins just outside of Clover. I only thought Daddy wouldn't want us going to work at a *factory*.

"Don't be such a worrywart, Helen. Why would he have to know?" Violet asked, while trying on one of Clara's new shoes. "We can just tell him we're going up there to Illinois, and we can make something up about what sort of work it is. He'll be happy we're earning so much. Then, we can spend some of the money on things he won't know about like new face powder and getting us a permanent wave. Bring the rest home."

Violet was always coming up with ways to sneak around and not get caught. Ever since we was younguns, I was the one to lag behind. Violet would invent the ideas, and I would shrug and follow.

For the rest of the afternoon, we planned our summer. Everthing was decided. How we would get there, which room in the boarding house would be ours, train rides to Chicago for all our new clothes, handbags, scarves, and gloves. We talked about which things we would tell our Daddy, and which things we would keep quiet.

"But Clara, don't we have to be a certain age to work there?" I asked, picking fingerfuls of blond hair from my brush. I reminded her she was seventeen. Violet was eighteen and a half, but I was only sixteen.

"Of course you're old enough. We've got lots of girls there your age. Some even younger."

After that, I settled down a little more. I got to thinking about Madam Langlie. She was one of those ladies who sets in front of a crystal ball and you give her a quarter and she could tell you what would happen in the future. I only wished I had saved up enough to go see her before we left for Illinois.

CHAPTER THREE

The night we told our daddy the first lie, Violet pulled me outside onto the porch. She whispered so's he wouldn't hear. "You think now's a good time?"

I told her I reckoned it was a perfect time, which was after supper and after Daddy had already finished the apple tarts with fresh cream I baked for him. Also, it was only a few days until the start of summer, and we wanted to wait until closer to the time, so's he wouldn't have too long to think about it.

We brought Daddy out to the porch to set with us, and he puffed on his old smelly cigar, but I smiled nice anyway, listening to Violet. "Daddy, Clara Jane told us of a way to make lots of money this summer."

"Oh?" He blowed smoke away from my eyes and nose.

"Yes sir. She says she makes more than twenty dollars ever week."

"My God, girl. Where does she work? In a bordello?" His voice drowned out the chorus of crickets just off the porch.

"Oh, no. Of course not. She's working at a music store in a town outside of Chicago. One of the biggest music stores in the world. They sell sheet music, pianos, violins. Even flutes and clarinets. Just about any instrument you want. She makes a commission."

"Is that right?" Daddy reached over to pick a teeny chicken feather off his pants leg.

"Yes, and she says she can get a job for me and Helen if we go up there in a few days. Then, we can make all that money and bring it home to you. We can get that new ice box you want. From the Belk's Department Store in Charlotte."

Our daddy asked us all sorts of questions, and Violet had her a answer for each one. I just set still and listened to her make things up as she went along, while Daddy nodded and said hmmm. Violet said we wouldn't need to pay rent at the boarding house since we would help Clara with Mrs. Yearsall's children, and we would write home once a week to let him know we was all right. "And if things don't quite work out, we'll come straight home."

When Daddy said he needed more time to think about it, Violet said if we didn't let them know right away, they would give the jobs to somebody else. I wasn't sure how I would feel if he said no. Maybe me and Violet would just sneak onto the train anyway. He said the subject was closed, and he didn't want to hear nothing more about it.

A couple of days later, our ice box started to drip and smell bad. Daddy got into one of his moods and after supper we all set again on the back porch, while he grumbled about not having enough money for things. As he set in the rocker, one knee bounced quick-like, and he rubbed his chin with his palm. After a minute, Daddy set and stared off into the yard, not saying nothing. Then, his voice turned dead quiet. "I believe if your mama was here, she woulda wanted you to go."

That was the best news we could of got. We cheered and hugged our daddy, hoping and praying all that night that we could get on the train before he had him a chance to get into one of his sour moods again and change his mind.

#

This morning at Mannington, a dreadful thing happened when my great-nephew Tony come by. Nurse Wilson called me up to the nurses' station. "Pearl's boy is here to see you again. He's in the visiting room."

I thanked her, then when nobody could hear me, I said, "What's *he* want?"

All last fall, Dr. Winslow told me I needed to work on my behavior around my family. I told him if my family ever started behaving normal around me, I would be glad to oblige.

I was right about Pearl's first marriage to that Puerto Rican boy, Enrique. I knowed they wouldn't be married long. She still keeps his last name, which was Velasquez. Ever week, Dr. Winslow tells me, "At least Pearl's trying." Pearl says she has plans for me. What bothers me is I can't figure out exactly what sort of plans she has in mind. I only know whatever it is it can't possibly be nothing proper.

But that didn't make no difference. I still didn't want to see Tony. The only reason my great nephew Tony Velasquez ever comes by is when he's in the area to get his marijuana. He sees some man he knows and they enter into their business.

Sometimes he brings his girlfriend, Adrienne Connaway. I only wish Tony would bring her more often. Adrienne's real nice. She's a nurse, and she's learning to be a midwife.

For once, Tony didn't show up empty-handed. "Here, I brought you this."

He give me a flower bouquet in a pink wicker basket, about the size of a loaf of rye. The flowers was made of plastic, and they smelled like motor oil. I could see they wasn't real, even though my eyes aren't as good as before. Not near as sharp as when I used to paint at the factory. "Thank you," I said, turning the basket over to look at the price tag. Two dollars and thirty cents. That dark-haired lady on the television had one exactly like it on *Let's Make a Deal*.

Once we reached my room, Tony's face begin twitching, like always. He shrugged and then he threw hisself stomach-down across my bed.

"Don't do that!" I screamed. "You'll jimmy my hospital corners."

After that, Tony set up straight, with his knees spread, feet pointing out. "Sorry. I'm tired. Don't you ever get tired?"

Since I didn't feel like answering him, I kept quiet. Tony tugged up a sleeve on his uniform shirt. He's been working for Scott's Auto Body for the past four years, since 1968. Ever time I see him, his hair's longer than before. Sometimes, I can barely make out his face under that beard and mustache. I guess he's still handsome under it. He used to be. The only way I'm sure I'm looking at Tony is because of his strong shoulders. He can do one-arm push-ups, and one time I seen him lift two ladies up, one on each arm. For a while, I feared Tony would have to go to war too, like Adrienne's brother did. But he has him a trick knee.

After a minute, I asked, "You didn't bring Adrienne with you today?"

"She's parking the car."

Tony stared at Neely's bed. "Where's that other girl?" he asked.

"Neely's with Dr. Stokes. He's new."

I didn't like the way Tony's hair was different lengths. Ragged in the back and the front. Not like Dr. Winslow or Dr. Stokes. "You ever think about seeing a barber?"

"Adrienne trims my hair for me. And my beard. Look, if you don't want me here, I'll split."

All of a sudden, I couldn't help thinking of Tony as a boy. He's twenty-seven now, but when he was little, the older boys would beat him up, just because his mama Pearl and his daddy Enrique divorced before Tony was even old enough to take his first step. I know what it was like to grow up with one parent gone. With me and Violet, it was our mama who was dead at a early age. We got raised by our peculiar father. But Tony had the sour luck to be raised by Pearl.

I set on the side of Neely's bed, across from Tony. "You don't have to leave. You smoke one of them cigarettes before you come here today?"

He give me a crooked smile. "What if I did?"

I could smell it on his clothes. "I tell you time and again drugs is bad for you. I should know. They had me on Thor'zine for fourteen years." I shook my finger at him, like as if I was scolding a child. I pictured him smoking with the smoke above his head in a cloud, like some of those images I used to see as a young girl. Whenever I would see a cloud like that, it always reminded me of the grandfather clock I scratched up. Papa Noone was a drinker and he always smelled of a bitter perspiration. I reckon he didn't know to use Mum Deodorant under his arms. He worked hard repairing grandfather clocks and cuckoo clocks from the 1800s, but the one I scratched had the face of God behind the clock hands, just like that painting from Michelangelo. Ever since that day, I have tried again and again to paint a face just like it. But I can't never get it right.

Tony didn't like me scolding him, so he jumped off the bed, grabbed my finger, and squeezed it. "Look, get off my case, all right? It isn't just for me. I sell it sometimes, but only to my friends. You know, I came all the way up here to see you, but I didn't have to."

"Then why *did* you come here?"

"Because I brought something... important."

I wondered what it was, and when would he give it to me. Tony let go of my finger and brushed his dark brown hair from his eyes. He sniffled through his nose, making that clogged up sound like when you need a handkerchief. I wanted to scream, but instead, I pinched myself on the back of my hand, and that made me feel some better.

Finally, Adrienne come into the room. She give me a nice smile, which I always liked about her. She had her pretty light brown hair pulled back into a big clip. "Hi Helen." Then, she leaned over and give me a little hug. She never wears a brassiere, but she should because she's got two healthy bosoms up top. Course, if you're only twenty-six, you don't always need a brassiere.

"I'm sorry it took me so long," she said. "They made me park down by the commissary. Plus, Saturdays are always crowded."

She pulled out my wooden stool and set close to me by Neely's bed. While she was still smiling, Adrienne took a glance down at my arms. She reached over and held one of my arms up to the light. I don't mind whenever she checks to see if I been scratching again, because she don't yank me or talk ugly like some of the nurses we have here. She holds my arm soft and talks to me gentle-like. I wish she worked at Mannington.

"Guess what, Helen," she said.

"What?"

"I'm going to my first birth soon."

"You are?" A smile spread across my lips.

Tony interrupted. His face was twitching again. "That woman better not go into labor on the twenty-fifth."

Adrienne stared at Tony with a scowl in her eyebrows. Then, she recollected and explained to me. "Oh, that's right. We have tickets to a concert that night."

"Well, honey," I said, patting her on the shoulder. "You can't never count on when a youngun comes into the world. They have a plan all their own."

Tony took a folded piece of paper out of his pocket. "Mom wanted me to ask you about this letter." He unfolded it and read it to hisself. "It's to Violet from the Argonne Laboratory in Illinois."

I blinked, trying to understand what Tony was talking about. As I tried to reach it, he held it tight, crumpling it, just away from my hand with a crooked smile. Then he give it to me, and I straightened it. When I started to read it, my stomach got hard as a rock. The letter said they wanted Violet to "report for testing." They wanted to see if she would go to Illinois to be in a science study. Instead of reading the rest, I just glanced at the words. Something about federal funding, and the "Radium Dial Company."

Ever since that summer, me and Clara Jane and Violet promised we would never tell we worked at the factory. Now they wanted to speak to Violet. How did they know where to send the letter?

Tony and Adrienne asked me what it was all about, but I didn't want to answer them. I folded the letter and give it back to Tony. He growled at me. "Mom says to get you a day pass and bring you home. She wants to talk to you about it."

I clamped my lips together and crossed my arms, staring at Tony. "I don't want to."

Then, he blocked the doorway of the room, giving Adrienne a mean look. "I'm going to get the pass. *You* talk to her." Then Tony was gone, and Adrienne reached for the letter. "Would you like me to read it aloud to you, Helen?"

I didn't want her to read it to me. I already seen what it was about. Adrienne looked at it again, asking me questions. "Did you work at this factory, Helen? You and your sister?"

To keep from answering her, I twirled a piece of my hair, just behind my ear.

"It says here if Violet has already passed away, you would need to provide a copy of her death certificate," Adrienne said, pointing to the letter. "And they asked if you know the whereabouts of any of the other ladies listed here at the end."

Adrienne started in reading the ladies' names aloud. I recollected one or two. Some, I already know died young, just like Violet. Instead of answering Adrienne, I just kept my tongue.

I done a good job of keeping my secret all through the years. Me and Violet knowed our daddy didn't want us to work at a factory, and we went right ahead and did it anyway. But that wasn't the only reason we didn't never tell we worked there. The other reason was because of something bad we done one night that summer which caused a terrible accident.

I reckoned Tony and Adrienne could get me the day pass and they could take me to Pearl's if they wanted, but that didn't mean I was going to tell them nothing I didn't want to tell.

CHAPTER FOUR

On the way to Pearl's, I set in Tony's car, chewing the inside of my lip. I was recollecting more of that summer. About the very first day me and Violet went to see the Radium Dial, and we had to stand outside the supervisor's office to wait our turn for a interview. I hadn't never been to a interview before. Not even for the Belmont Five and Dime. I got that job cause my friend Maravelle knowed the manager.

Ever since me and Violet arrived in Illinois, I felt guilty about the lie we told our daddy. I started in biting my nails more than usual. Violet kept slapping my arm, and telling me he'd never find out. She asked me, "How will he ever know we're not working at the music store? He knows only what he needs to know, that we can make more money here than back in Belmont." I was doing my best to forget it.

Mrs. Peltz, the supervisor, begin to talk to us about our paperwork, but out the window behind her desk a flock of ladies was gathered. Below us, down on the front lawn, some of the other workers was gathered around a delivery truck. Mrs. Peltz's face got riled up, specially around her eyes. She pushed herself from her chair. "Girls, would you please excuse me a moment?"

"Yes ma'am."

Once Mrs. Peltz was downstairs and outside, many other girls rushed out behind her, frantic about that delivery truck. Soon Violet took off too, but I stayed in the office. I wondered what all the excitement was about, but I shrugged and reached to touch the vase of golden colored roses on Mrs. Peltz's desk. I wanted to stick my nose in the roses and smell the perfume, but they was on the other side of the large desk. Sneaking myself around to the other side, I leaned in and sniffed. The flowery sweet smell reminded me of being back home in Belmont and the thick sweet honey Daddy would bring in from the hives.

Suddenly, everthing got real quiet out in the main work room. The studio. I looked out the window and listened. Down there on the front lawn, Mrs. Peltz was doing her best to keep order. The girls was jumping up and down, laughing, and jabbering away about the new furniture for the employees' lounge. Going back to the roses, I slid one from the vase. I looked up at the doorway, and just at that moment, the custodian boy was rolling a cart of boxes down the hall. He stared at me as he floated by, and I had to stick the rose stem back into the vase.

The custodian boy's name was Jesse, and Clara Jane had said to stay away from him cause he didn't have the sense of a doorknob. Me and the boy locked eyes for a time. He was tall and thin, with a healthy sized Adam's apple. He stood in one place, holding the cart still, then when the girls started to file back inside, he started that cart up again. The whole darn time, he never took his eyes off a me.

Up until then, I hadn't never had much luck with boys. I'd only had me a few dates back in Belmont. Violet had already necked with a boy, maybe even more. I wasn't sure. Clara was the careful one. She was a flirt, but also, she was so beautiful I reckon she scared most of them off.

Soon, Mrs. Peltz and Violet come back into the room, and the custodian boy was gone. Instead of waiting for Violet to fill out her papers, I was thinking about how I could get to talk to Jesse some time. But only if we could be alone somewheres else, instead of inside a factory with a hundred other girls.

#

I wasn't happy about being at Pearl's. I just set on her living room sofa with my arms crossed, while chewing the inside of my lip. I knowed she was fixing to ask me about that letter, but all I agreed to do was to go in the car with Tony and Adrienne. Nothing else.

Adrienne was in a sour mood. At least until she excused herself and come out of the bathroom later. After she took her a pill. I know she takes drugs because she told me once. I've seen where she keeps her pills. She keeps them in her handbag, inside a old Bayer bottle. After she takes them, she gets cheerful and full of pep again, so I don't mind much when she does it.

Adrienne once told me that something about being in Pearl's house makes her *need* to take pills, but the main reason she started was her parents, when she was sixteen, out in Denver, Colorado. That was when she started smoking marijuana with her friends. One time when she was visiting me at Mannington, she told me about her parents. "I could blame them for a lot of things," she said. "For being forced to leave home at such a young age, and for the wrong reason. For starting nursing school so late. Although I can't blame them for graduating second to last in my class."

I just told her we can't *all* be first.

She said almost ever day, she argues with herself about why she's still with Tony. I reckon she does have one more reason to be out of sorts. Her brother Ron is in the war, and he got him a injury in his leg, and now the doctors say he might not walk again. Adrienne is fretful about him because he still isn't back home. She said she hadn't seen him for more than four years.

Pearl's fiancé Donald Schaeffer was already there before we drove up. After he spoke to me, he went back out to Pearl's porch to do what he always does—holds a cocktail glass in one hand, with a folded newspaper in the other. He's got him some deep lines on his face. Like as if he's had lots of excitement in his life. He has the type of face you might see on a television commercial or in a magazine. Like a Marlboro Man. Only not as handsome.

From where I was setting on the living room sofa, Pearl's voice carried into the room. "Y'all come here. I want to show you these letters."

Tony walked into the dining room where Pearl was and asked her if it would take long, because he needed to use the bathroom first. "Oh, go on then," Pearl answered. "Helen. Come in here and sit at the table."

I pretended I didn't hear. I just set still staring at her potted plant. The poor thing was dry as old wood, and some of the leaves was crinkled on the carpet underneath. After about half a minute, Pearl marched into the room. When she seen the dead leaves she frowned, picking them up and tossing them into the waste basket. Then, she stood in front of the Hi Fi with a hand on one hip. She clucked her tongue at me. "Aren't you coming?"

I told her we had to wait for Tony anyway. Then, Donald come in from the porch, and Pearl turned all sugary, flipping through one of her bridal magazines. Whenever she's around Donald, she doesn't talk the same. She tries to talk like a person from up North, instead of like somebody born and raised in North Carolina. Donald and Pearl stand near the same height. They're both tall, and neither one of them is very nice to look at. Specially not Donald. But somehow, he got people to vote for him.

Donald leaned next to Pearl, while she pointed to a picture of a pretty table all set for a wedding banquet. "I just love these napkins, here," she said, pointing to the bottom of the page. "And I want to use these pew bows. What do you think, darling?" She smoothed up her bee-hive hairdo.

Donald scratched his head and wrinkled his eyebrows. "You do have a knack for planning and organizing these things. I defer to your expertise." Then he made him a little gesture of a bow, turned to me, and winked. I just grinned.

When Tony come from the bathroom, Pearl asked everbody to set around the dining room table, so's she could read the letters aloud. I got into my chair, but I didn't say nothing. She reached to the top shelf of her hutch and took a folded letter from a envelope. "I got these letters in the mail, both of them, and I wanted you all to hear them at the same time. I'll start with this one."

At first, she just read what the letter said. It was the letter to Violet, written to her like as if she was still alive. They said if Violet was already dead, they could dig up her bones and test them, but Pearl said she wouldn't have it. Instead, she broke down in tears until Donald had to take her outside. Then me and Tony and Adrienne was alone in the dining room.

Tony leaned back in his chair. "What's *her* problem?"

My foot twitched below the table, and then Adrienne answered him. "I guess it's the idea of it. I mean, having them open the casket after so many years. Wasn't it back in the thirties, Helen? Pearl was only a little girl when..."

Tony interrupted her. "Here they come."

Donald and Pearl come through the kitchen door. Pearl held a hanky over her face, then took it away and folded it into a square. She sniffled, then set again at the table. "I'm sorry. This brings up a lot of sour memories." Then, she stared at me. "Helen, don't you know anything about this? About Mama working at this...this factory?"

"Me and Violet wasn't together ever minute, you know."

I reckoned that was a good enough answer. But it did make me recollect things I had wanted to forget. Like the day Violet's baby son passed on. Born four minutes after Pearl. His name was William, and he was sickly. I got frantic when he passed, since I couldn't have babies of my own.

Pearl kept on with her sniffling, but her face got squinched up, and she snapped at me. "I bet you know more than you're saying." After that, she got that sugary sound to her voice again, and she dabbed her nose with the hanky. "Donald, tell Tony and Adrienne what you told me on the porch. Donald knows people in Washington."

Donald stayed standing behind his chair, gripping the back of it. "I told Pearl I would find out what I can about this."

Then Adrienne asked about the second letter. I was glad she did, because then maybe Pearl would forget and not ask me any more about the Radium Dial.

Pearl opened the second letter. "This one is from a man in Atlanta. He said his mother passed away, but he got the same letter from the laboratory, and now he wants to talk to me about it because his letter had the names Violet and Helen at the end. His name is Benjamin Reed, and his mother's name was Clara Jane Hart. He says he remembers you, Helen, but he couldn't find you."

When Pearl read the names out loud, I knowed right off she was talking about Clara Jane, and her little Benjamin, all growed up. The one thing me and Clara Jane had in common was we both become mamas because of somebody else's misfortune. I got little Pearl because Violet died when she was twenty-eight. Clara Jane got her little Benjamin because when she married her husband James, he was a widower with a child.

I remember what a darling boy Benjamin was. Always so clever and he knowed so much for a youngun. He knowed a lot about insects and birds and lots of other things. One time when I visited, I think he was only about seven or eight, he showed me a clay model of a owl he made, with the feathers and wings so real-like. When I told him how much I liked it, he give it to me. I reckon he growed up to be a fine gentleman.

Sometimes I wish I'd ended up with a youngun like Benjamin instead of with Pearl, because she give me and Jesse a lot of trouble.

Tony snapped up in his chair, talking to Pearl. "Didn't you know your mother worked at this factory?"

"No, I knew nothing about it," she said, shaking her head.

Pushing away from the table, Tony stood, laughing. "Maybe they can finally do that lobotomy on Helen. *That* should help her remember."

Adrienne snickered and said something about what a lobotomy was *really* for, then she followed Tony to the front door, which he held wide open to let Pearl's cat out. Adrienne got mad. "Tony, Pearl hates for you to do that."

"I know."

After Tony left for the car, Adrienne returned to me and give me a little squeeze. "Sorry we can't stay. Call us when you're ready and we'll drive you back, okay?"

I told Adrienne Pearl would call her after supper. Maybe I could just eat and not talk. And maybe Pearl would keep on being sugary sweet to Donald, and just leave me alone.

CHAPTER FIVE

Nurse Dubois told me to get in line, so I did. When it was my turn, she handed me my tokens, then I thanked her and left for the commissary.

Thank goodness Pearl hasn't been worrying me much over those letters. And since I started on my new medicine, I've been feeling more like myself. Ever week, I earn more tokens than anybody else on Ward Six-A. People always see me first out of bed in the morning, and for that, I earn five. Just by making my bed, I can earn three more.

After counting out the tokens from my sweater pocket, I paid Barbara Flynn, the commissary worker for a orange soda and a pack of Salems. Miss Flynn dropped the tokens into a small metal box, then held up a Butterfinger. "Helen, how many you got left?"

Dipping into my sweater pocket, I jingled the rigid plastic tokens, listening as they clanked and slid together. "I'm saving the rest."

I looked away from Miss Flynn as fast as I could, because she has her a deformity on her face. Most of the time, I'm not scared of people. The only time I get scared is if I *suddenly* come across somebody with a boil or a scar on their face, or if they're wasting away from a disease. I have to be warned ahead of time before I see them.

With the cold drink pinned against my inner elbow, I left the commissary and crossed the road to the cement steps. Across the way, a sheriff brung in a man in a long coat. I sucked in a breath. Whenever I see any kind of police I get jittery inside, because I always think they have found me. I don't never want to be found.

As I climbed the steps, I held tight to the railing. Most people in their sixties can't climb stairs without help or walk without a nurse assistant. But then, lots of chronics can't be let out to walk around by themselves, anyhow.

Once I reached the top step, I stopped a moment to catch my breath. The soles of my feet ached, but I only had me a little chest pain. I thank God ever day for my strong heart. With my free hand, I smoothed some of the fly-away hair a breeze found on top of my head.

Across the grass, some patients was out for a walk. Others was setting up in a rocker. A few of the patients was smoking and visiting next to the full shrubs at the corner of the Avery building. A few weeks ago Dr. Winslow explained we wasn't patients no more. Now we are *residents*. Myself included. Course, I prefer *patients*.

Just like me, the other patients look exactly like average folks—a neighbor, or like somebody's son or daughter. Some who had frightful things done to them when they was younguns. Some like me was raised all right, except for that dreadful thing that man done to our mama when me and Violet was babies.

Still, sometimes I can't close off parts of my mind. The parts with things I seen over the years at Mannington. People tied face down to bare metal bed frames without no clothing, or old men forced into cold water up to their necks. At least I'm one of the lucky ones. They never done that surgery on me, where they take part of the brain, but I seen plenty of other patients after they had *their* surgery. One day, I might be talking to a person and they answer me just fine. The next day, they might give off the blank stare of a bronze statue.

There's other parts of my mind with memories of me as a young person. Good and bad. In my memories, one special weekend always stands out. It's the weekend in 1923 when I won first prize for my painting of the Ottawa, Illinois public park on a summer's day. I done my best to give it bright greens and blues that was pleasing to the eye. It was only a water color, but I'm more proud of that painting than almost anything. It had a blue ribbon on it and I painted it from memory, once me and Violet got back home to North Carolina.

One day I tried to describe it to my roommate Neely, but since she's blind, it was a waste of time. Like trying to describe a radio song to a canary.

Instead of joining the others on the porch, I just stood still as a board while these two young people held hands and walked together toward the corner of the building, gazing into each other's eyes. The girl was short and reminded me of me, years ago—when I was Helen Meisner. Before I got gray hair and liver spots, and my waistline got to be nearly the size of my hips.

On my way back to the Avery building, I stopped to hold the orange soda against my cheek. First one side, then the other, cooling my skin. With my eyes closed, the only sound was a rustling from the bushes beside the building. When I opened my eyes, the rustling kept on. After thirty years at Mannington, I've been witness to ever manner of smut and sin at least once. They call it *bush therapy*, but if they really wanted to, people could find places to be alone all over the hospital grounds, and besides, there wasn't enough nurses or orderlies to keep track of everbody.

I unwrapped my cigarettes and stuffed the cellophane into my sweater pocket.

By the time I got to the day room, the other girls was waiting, already slouched in their seats, and the channel was set on *Search for Tomorrow*. Eight or ten years ago, before they started sending so many people home, the day room never had enough chairs, and if you wanted to watch *Queen for a Day* or *Love of Life*, you had to get there early.

I waited my turn for the nurse to light my cigarette, then I inhaled. The smoke burned a stretch of my throat, but I tried to ignore it. I swallowed it down.

Quick-like, the nurse grabbed me by the wrist, checking for scars. She was rough with me, not gentle like Adrienne. "You haven't been scratching yourself again, have you, Helen?" she asked, frowning a nasty frown. I told her I hadn't. Not since before winter. These nurses have to keep on, like as if they don't believe me.

Soon, the familiar music of the program begin, and I settled in to watch. I hoped Pearl wouldn't come before the program was over. I was supposed to go in Pearl's car to Lawton for some shopping, but I didn't want to go nowhere with her. Pearl and her bee-hive hair and little-girl bosoms. Pearl and her politician fiancé.

At least she was leaving me alone about that letter. I still didn't know how they found the address to send it to Pearl. And how did they know Violet and Clara Jane worked there? I reckoned soon there would be a letter for me too. All this talk about the Radium Dial was reminding me of the accident we caused, which always makes me feel sick. I feel sick because of what we done that night. Hurt feelings caused us to make a bad decision. Then our plans went all out of kilter, and the unspeakable happened. But we never meant for nobody to die. Mostly, it was Violet's fault.

Violet was often getting me into trouble. Always fixing to get into mischief, like when she yanked me into the basement of Mrs. Yearsall's boarding house. We had only been painting at the factory for four or five days, and here Violet was already breaking the rules. "Look at what I snuck home."

In her hand, Violet held her a jar of paint. I recollected it right off. It was that gritty radium paint we mixed from powder ever morning at work. Violet slid a skinny brush from a tangle of her brown curls. She possessed a wicked look in her eyes. "How about a little fun?"

I already knowed. In my belly, I felt a tingle of excitement, knowing what was about to happen. We done our share of sneaking. Lying to our daddy about why we was in Illinois, lying about our paychecks. We done a good job of talking him into letting us go, too.

"Helen, go get Clara. It'll be the cat's pajamas."

Charging up the stairs, I found Clara setting by the sewing box, her dark silky hair falling forward, and just ready to thread her needle. I put my lips next to her ear, "Violet has got her some paint."

In a instant, Clara's eyes turned sparkly and dark, like the navy blue of her dress. "From work?"

"Mm hmm."

Clara's lips curved into a grin. After she stuck the needle into the pin cushion, she peeked into Mrs. Yearsall's setting room, making sure she wouldn't suddenly come down and surprise us. "Let's go," I whispered, smiling. "She'll never know."

I thought it might be our only chance. The only days we had off was Saturday afternoons. Sunday mornings, we all took Mrs. Yearsall's children to church, and then on Sunday afternoons, we had to wash our underthings and get our dresses and blouses pressed for the next week at work.

In the basement, us girls met behind the door to a small dark room with a wash tub and wood shelves. Violet held up the brush and a hand mirror. "We'll have to take turns. I only brought one of each."

I held my hand over top of my giggles. "Violet, if they find out, you'll get fired."

"No I won't. I heard after a week or two, they tell you to take it home anyway. For practice. Isn't that right, Clara? I was talking to Lynette, she said she even painted her dog's toenails."

I snickered.

Opening the jar, Violet carefully set the lid on the wood counter top, next to the clothes pins. "Everbody paint something different. Don't tell what you're gonna do. That a-way, it'll be more of a surprise."

Clara stuck her hand on her hip. "Are you sure it's all right? It won't hurt our skin?"

"Don't be a Dumb Dora," Violet answered. "Everbody knows radium's good for your skin. Haven't you ever noticed how all the European girls have clear, healthy skin? They've been painting since during the war."

At work, I seen a couple of girls from Paris or Italy. One of them did have pretty skin. Smooth and perfect. Even though our family went a ways back to Germany, nobody guaranteed *me* more of a healthy glow. Instead all I got was a plain face and hard to manage hair.

Facing away from each other, each of us finished painting. I thought about painting my teeth, but I still wasn't quite used to the taste of the paint. It was one thing to be careful with the brush and not paint outside the lines on the clock dials, but something else altogether to stick the brush between your lips to get a sharp point. Everbody at work said you could paint better if you did it that a-way.

Once the lights was out, it was pitch black in the room except for the glowing eyebrows and teeth on Clara, and bright nostrils, a mustache, and pointed beard on Violet. I had painted my cheeks, my lips, and the edges of my ears. Clara laughed, grabbing my arm. "Oh my land, Helen, you look like a kewpie doll."

Then I stared at my sister. "Violet, you look just like John Wilkes Booth." While us girls kept on laughing and scrunching our faces in the dark, I watched, hopeful we wasn't making too much noise.

After a moment, I heard only whispers, and I couldn't see the other girls. "Clara? Violet? Where are you?"

Suddenly, their glowing faces flashed in front of my nose, startling me. They both blurted out "Boo!" at the same time. Once I caught my breath, I seen something strange. "Violet, did you paint your hair, too?"

"No. Of course not."

"Then how come there's a halo around your head? Like there's paint in your hair?"

"How should I know?"

I recollected all those times when I was a young girl, and I seen a cloud around a person's head. The cloud or a halo with shadowy edges. But Violet's hair wasn't the same. It wasn't so much a cloud as it seemed like a electricity lamp.

Then the room filled with light. It was little Frank Yearsall, all of eight years old. Violet yanked him inside and closed the door tight. Just before it went dark again, she clamped her hand over Frank's mouth. His eyes went wide as two big "O's," and he was hollering right through Violet's hand. We told him to shush, and after a little minute, he did. I think he was more scared than anything, not saying a word at all, but at least he stopped trying to get away. Soon, Violet set him free, and he just giggled like the rest of us. "What's on your faces?" Frank asked.

Violet told him to shush again, and she would paint his nose so he could glow in the dark too. Then, after Frank's nose was painted, we started to get silly again, but he opened the door to try to escape. He run right smack into his mama.

Mrs. Yearsall stood in the doorway, holding her a basket of dirty clothes and a new box of Chiffon Flakes. "Frank? What are you girls doing in here? And Clara, what have you got on your eyebrows?" Frank had already darted up the stairs and out to the porch. For a second I recollected being back in school, getting a demerit. Then, I giggled because I reckoned Mrs. Yearsall wouldn't notice Clara's teeth until she answered the question. "We were just having a little fun, that's all."

Mrs. Yearsall set down the basket and took off her spectacles. She swiped them with her apron. She was a big woman, with pinched eyes and the kind of lips that showed her gums when she talked or smiled. "Someone could get hurt. And aren't you girls a little too old to be playing in the dark?"

Me and Violet backed out of the door, while Clara grabbed the jar and brush. "Sorry, Mrs. Yearsall. Do you need help with the washing?"

"Please."

"I'll be right back," Clara said, "After I get changed. I don't want to muss my dress."

Me and Violet went to wash our faces and change out of our work dresses too. No sense in getting wrinkles before the next work week.

On the way out of the laundry room, something caught my eye. It was hanging on the wall, and I stared at it a minute. It was a hay hook like the one I used when I was a child. I used it to scratch the grandfather clock. I recollect how sorry I was at the time for what I done, only by the time I was sorry, it was too late.

Once we was alone in our room, I had me a question for Violet. "Do you think Daddy got our letter yet?" Along with the letter, we sent him some sheet music and told him it was from the music store.

Violet unbuttoned the top of her dress. "If he did, he's likely not thinking what I'm thinking."

"And what are you thinking?"

"How at the end of the summer his two daughters are going to come back home to Belmont, North Carolina, each with a suitcase full of furs, and handbags stuffed with twenty dollar bills."

After a moment I took off my work shoes and rubbed my feet. "Violet, there's something I want to ask you. I was too embarrassed before now, but the last couple of days, did you notice anything unusual when you... moved your bowels?"

While Violet grinned, she arched her eyebrows to ask me a question. "Didn't you pay attention that first day? They told us the paint would pass out of our bodies. They said we might see it the first time we went to the toilet. No wonder you failed all your classes at Belmont High, Helen. You never pay attention."

I didn't like to think about extra things inside my body. Things that didn't belong, like radium paint. But if most of it was expected to pass out of me, maybe I shouldn't worry so much.

"Violet, do you think Daddy'll find out where we're really working this summer?"

Violet shimmied until she slipped out of her dress. "Not as long as you don't never tell him."

#

Me and Neely was talking about Dr. Stokes. "What did he look like?" Neely asked.

"Like somebody I used to know." I wasn't sure how to describe the new doctor in a way Neely would understand. Neely probably don't even know nobody she could compare him to. So I just explained that Dr. Stokes was nice, and Neely seemed fine enough with that.

Whenever I tell Neely something, like what our room at Mannington looks like, or what fog is, the only thing Neely can do is imagine them. Neely has to imagine those things in her mind because that's the only way blind people can see—in their minds.

Even a sighted person can see things in their mind. Like what's happening inside me. The cancer. How it eats away at everthing. Inside my organs and tissues and bones. The cancer's been there since me and Violet was girls; hiding, sneaking around in my blood, like a worm that never sleeps. The doctors have tried, but they haven't come across it yet, and even if they never do, it still gets me to itching sometimes.

Opening the chifforobe I share with Neely, I took out the award I got at the Radium Dial that summer in 1923. My *Excellence in Training* plaque. Somewhere, maybe in Pearl's attic, there's the water color painting I did, the only water color left from that summer. I hope she didn't give it away.

I also took out a couple of my old dresses. One is a golden brown lace dress, made of silk, with scallops at the hemline—one of the most beautiful dresses I ever owned. Clara Jane was the one who helped me to pick it out. I bought it with the money I earned. The other is a winter dress, the color of fresh milk, now with creases that won't never iron out, but at least the fur collar still looks like fur. It still has the original beads on it, too. The shape of leaves. Between the beads is teeny ribbon flowers.

"Neely, do you remember if anybody ever bought you a brand new dress? I mean, when you was a child?"

Neely's face got sad and she stared past me like always, frowning, like as if she hadn't never been asked such a question before. "They must have. I know they did. I just *know* it." Tears dribbled down Neely's cheeks, and I stepped toward her to dry them with my palm.

I'm forty-two years older than Neely. It's my duty to look after her. I help her get dressed in the mornings and get her into bed at night. I help her get her needle started when she does her yarn pictures. More often than anything, I dry Neely's tears.

With a jolt, the new nurse, Flora, marched into our room. I don't recollect her last name, but it's too hard to say anyway, so we call her Nurse Flora. I *do* recollect her last name starts with a P.

Nurse Flora's fat, with too much dark hair on her arms. She's nice enough, just like most of the other nurses, but she can turn without a warning. Nearly all of the nurses and staff is white, but once in a while we get us a colored one.

Years back, I worked in the nurses' office. They asked me in one day, and I set in a chair at a table for nine hours, stuffing envelopes and licking them. I didn't mind though, cause after I was done, they give me a pack of cigarettes. They said I worked so hard that day, I would be asked to come back again, and sure enough, they did ask me. Quite a number of times.

I liked working in the nurses' office, cause after a while, the other nurses forgot I was there, and they talked about the other residents and the doctors and all. About rumors that I figure was mostly true. A young woman resident who pleasured a doctor with her hand, and a commissary worker who used to steal Thor'zine and hide it. I found out Nurse Dubois had her a patient in Ward Seven with a extra knuckle on each of her thumbs. Also, one of the former orderlies in the chronic ward liked to eat raw meat.

Over the years, I seen all types of workers come and go. Once, in the 1950s, one of the new nurses wanted to peroxide everbody's hair on the whole ward. I said, "No thank you." It's been many a year since my hair was last blonde. And I was born that a-way.

I reckon it would be useless for Neely to bleach her hair. She hardly has any of it. Neely's hair is wispy and full of static. She has a skinny nose the shape of a thin triangle, and bony elbows, but the main reason is a blind person don't need to worry about how their hair looks anyhow.

"You ladies going down to the movie tonight? They're showing *What's So Bad About Feeling Good?*"

Nurse Flora perched her fists on her round hips and waited for somebody to answer.

When me and Violet was girls, we used to go to the picture shows all the time. Of course, that was before the pictures even had sound, and you had to read the words. At times, I couldn't keep up.

I recollect the "Bad About Feeling Good" picture from last fall, when they showed it the first time. It's funny, and it stars one of my favorite all-time movie actors, Dom DeLuise. I just love him. He makes me laugh, just from the way he looks, even without him saying one word. Thelma Ritters is in that movie too, and she's one I also really like.

"I'm going," I said, hanging my dresses back into the chifforobe. "You going this time, Neely?"

"I don't think I will."

If I could get Neely to change her mind, I was certain the actors' funny lines in that movie would cheer her up, if only for a while. I like having somebody to cheer up. A person to care for. Even if it is only a blind, twenty-three year old depressed girl from Gastonia.

Suddenly, Nurse Flora yanked the sheet corner out of Neely's bed. She pressed her big lips together, until her cheeks made dimples. "People in the south don't know shit about making a bed."

She makes me so mad. I worked really hard on Neely's bed this morning. Sometimes I see Nurse Flora staring at me like as if I'm stupid. Of course, I don't think I'm stupid. There's a big difference between being just plain old unschooled like me, and being like some folks who forget to use the brains God give them.

While Flora tore up the bed and re-did it, she kept making a tsk tsk sound with her tongue. Tsk tsk tsk.

After Nurse Flora tucked the last sheet corner, she spun around and grabbed tight to my wrists, checking my skin. I drew my arms back, but she yanked on me again. Tony was the one who found me the last time. He come into my room here at Mannington way last fall and seen my scratches. Just by chance, Adrienne was with him that time, and she called for help. I recollect that day like it was yesterday, because Adrienne wanted to stay with me, but Tony made her leave.

Nurse Flora kept on making a tsk tsk sound. Over and over. I wanted to scream, so I did. I pinched my eyes up tight and give a shrill, earsplitting scream, echoing down the halls of the ward, until Nurse Flora grabbed my face hard and told me to shut up. She said she had to get along to a Ward Seven A.

It wasn't until after I was finished screaming that I scooted into bed next to Neely and held her in my arms. I rocked her to sleep, worrying over Pearl wanting to know more about her mama, Violet. I reckon Pearl would want to know something cheerful, instead of her own memories of her mama wasting away and dying.

CHAPTER SIX

Pearl had already picked me up in her car and drove me to her home. "Helen, quit your complaining. I need you to help me find it." She dragged me by the hand up the steep attic stairs to help her look for Violet's death certificate. Pearl had on a scarf over her fancy hair-do. She's always styling her dark brown hair more than she needs to, piling it high on her head, with curved bangs in front, and pulled back away from her ears. She curls the ends around her shoulders, with small sideburns that curl to the back. After that, she soaks her whole head in hair spray. Not too many young girls wear this hairstyle no more. It's about eight or ten years out of fashion.

"You *know* I don't like coming up here alone," she said, yanking on my arm. Pearl had to stoop to miss the ceiling.

I'm not keen on going into the attic any more than Pearl is. It reminds me of the tunnels at Mannington, all full of spider webs and dead bugs. Nothing like the rest of Pearl's house. She's got everthing in its place.

Pearl made me set in a dark green wicker chair, while she found her a old box of papers. Some of the papers was eaten partial by rodents or bugs, with droppings on them. The air up there was like a incinerator.

"Don't you remember anything about where you and Violet worked? I mean, I know Grandpa Felix was a bee keeper and he raised chickens. Did you help with that?"

"We did sometimes, but he always had him a worker. Me and Violet had to stay inside and clean house and set out meals."

"What about after you left home? Before you got married?"

I had me a way around Pearl's questions. I didn't have to lie. All I had to do was keep the answers general. We just had normal jobs. Both me and Violet got married when we was young. Violet give birth to Pearl and baby William. Violet's husband Grady left and never come back, and we heard he died in 1960. Jesse got killed in the war. Keep it general. When I sniffled, my nose filled with dust. I was starting to get me a sinus headache.

I hoped Pearl wouldn't stumble across my water color painting. Even though I would love to see it. Ever so often I paint at Mannington, but I don't never let nobody see it, because all I'm trying to paint is that face of God from the grandfather clock. I paint it, but when it's not right, I tear it up, even before it's dry.

Maybe I don't want Pearl to find my water color after all. That might get her to asking even more questions. Behind a box of old phonograph records, Pearl finally found the death certificate. She brushed it off, and stared at the words. "Here, see? It says Mama died of…"

Pearl didn't finish her sentence. She looked at me, while her face got rigid as a brick wall. "It says she died of a brain abscess and familial insanity."

"Is that a fact?" I said. I hoped Pearl couldn't tell I was hiding something. Ever since Violet first got sick in 1933, I was the only one in the family who knowed the true cause of death. That doctor from Gastonia just flat out had it wrong. And now, Pearl was worried about something that wasn't even right.

Pearl held the paper in the air, facing me. "I always thought she died of pneumonia. Did you know about this?"

"Well, I…" I scratched a itch on the tip of my elbow.

"Helen!"

I felt like screaming again, and took in a long breath.

"Don't you dare scream," Pearl said. "This is upsetting enough."

She stared at the certificate again. "All this time I thought you were the only one with…mental problems."

I reminded Pearl about my pass from the hospital. Only a day pass. Soon, Pearl got fidgety, searching more papers. She shoved some other boxes around, and a torn paper sack of old books.

"Tell me again about that letter from that man in Atlanta," I said.

Pearl froze and give me a scowl. "You were there when I read it. He wants me to call him."

"What about that other letter?"

"You mean the one from The Argonne Laboratory?" Then she slid a different box across the floor. "I wish I knew more about these people."

I didn't know nothing about the laboratory neither, except they sent that letter, saying they wanted to dig Violet out of the ground and test her bones. If not for that letter, Pearl wouldn't be bothered right now about what it said on the death certificate.

Pearl continued staring at the words. "This can't be right. Brain abscess?" Her head was just nodding back and forth. "Familial insanity?"

Folding the paper with jerking hands, Pearl got lines in her forehead, between her brows. "You know, *familial* means I could get it too. And, if Donald ever found out about this he'd never marry me."

I set up straight in the wicker chair. "Maybe he won't find out."

"He will eventually. It's a matter of public record."

Pearl was the type who couldn't leave well-enough alone. Even though Donald Schaeffer already was in a political office in Charlotte, Pearl would want to get all her ducks in a row before he ran for congress. Before they was married.

I never dreamed it would take all the way until 1972 for Pearl to find out about the death certificate. Until now, only I knowed what really happened.

#

After Sunday dinner, Pearl drove me back to Mannington. On the way, she kept on fiddling with her left side sun visor. I stared out the passenger side at a cattle farm as we drove by.

If Pearl hadn't started again about that certificate, I wouldn't be chewing the inside of my lip. She steered the automobile into the next highway. "Was she ever in an institution?"

I stuck the tip of a finger in my mouth to chew my nail, but Pearl scowled at me. "Stop chewing, Helen."

I didn't stop, and I didn't apologize, neither. Sometimes I have to wait in line behind six or seven other people to get my nails trimmed. It's quicker to chew.

"Your dinner was good," I said, wanting to change the subject. "I hate the hospital's vegetable soup. They make it from the whole week's leftovers."

"Answer my question. Was my mother ever institutionalized?"

Soon, I begin chewing on my lip again. If I set quiet long enough, maybe Pearl would stop asking her fool questions. I didn't want to say one more word about the subject of brain abscesses, or insanity, or why Violet really died, because I spent most of my life trying to forget the truth. That was how I kept secrets. Because I knowed I wouldn't accidentally say the wrong thing, if I pretended I couldn't remember none of it to begin with.

But I was only pretending. Most of it I remember real good, like some of the early days at the factory. After a week or so at the Radium Dial, Mrs. Peltz told me to follow her to the office on the second floor so's I could sign my new punch card. I should've signed mine a few days before, but I got mixed up that day and stood in the wrong line. "We're very happy indeed to have you here at The Radium Dial, Helen. You've been increasing your production nicely." I thanked her for saying that.

"Have you been practicing your tipping?" she asked.

"You mean when I stick it between my lips? Well...it tastes sort of... funny."

Suddenly, there was a loud, mean voice, yelling at Jesse. "Boy, get your lazy backside in that main room and finish polishing them floors."

When he said that to Jesse, I felt sorry for him. There wasn't no reason for Jesse's supervisor to be that a-way. Hateful as a old vulture.

Mrs. Peltz had a funny look on her wrinkled face. She motioned to me with her finger to come closer. "Nobody likes that old man. Andrew Calder is his name. He doesn't shave but once a week," she said.

I peeked out the door and took a look. White stubble over pasty skin.

"Yes ma'am."

Mrs. Peltz then handed me a card to sign. "Now, I want you to take this card and keep it inside your locker until tomorrow. Then you'll be using the new punch machine. The other girls will help you."

Just then, Violet showed up at the door to bring Mrs.
Peltz some papers from the employee lounge. Mrs. Peltz said
thank you to Violet, and we headed out the door together.
Suddenly, we both slipped on the shiny floor, and I twisted
my ankle a little. Old Mr. Calder laughed at us. At first, I
started to giggle too, but Violet clenched her teeth and glared
at Mr. Calder. He snickered.

After that, I pulled Violet by the sleeve and got her to go
downstairs with me, so's she could cool off. Later, we
watched while Mr. Calder got his keys for his automobile and
took off for the parking lot. I heard Violet whisper she would
"fix *him*." That was fine if she wanted to, but I wasn't mad at
Mr. Calder. I was excited, and I felt like as if sunshine was
glowing out of my eyes and fingertips. A real job in a real
factory. I couldn't wait for my first paycheck. I decided when
I got the money, the first thing I planned to buy me was a
dozen golden roses.

#

At the end of me and Violet's first week at the Radium
Dial, I slipped again, but this time I was on my way to my
locker. One of the girls, Bess, with straight brown hair and
plump cheeks was setting in the lounge, filing her
fingernails. She kept on looking close at her nails, then up at
me. "You're new here, aren't you?" she said.

"Yes, I am. Me and my sister Violet is just here for the
summer."

Out of the blue, Bess and a couple of the other girls just
broke up into laughter. "You talk so funny," Bess said. "You
sound like a country bumpkin."

To me, the girls from Illinois all sounded funny. They
said their "R's" real strong.

"And, you're clumsy too. Just like Jesse. He's always
tripping over his push broom, and knocking things over."

I just shrugged. I hadn't seen Jesse knock nothing over,
and I'd been watching him ever day.

"Where are you and your sister from?"

Since Bess had already made fun of the way I talk, I didn't
want her to know where we was from, so I just said, "We're
from south of here."

"Hey," Bess said. "Come over here a minute."

I inched my way closer to her and she had her a watch. "You won't paint one of these until you've had more practice with the regular size clocks, but I've been here for a long time now. Look at what I did."

She held up the watch and flipped it bottom side up. It was a man's watch. In teeny letters she had wrote her name and telephone number. "If some lucky fella wants to call me, we can go out. Or if he doesn't live around these parts, well, we can just be pen pals."

I shrugged again, but tried to smile too. Just then, Jesse was right outside the door to the lounge. Bess grabbed me by the arm and dragged me over to stand me next to Jesse. "Make way for the bride and groom. Mr. and Mrs. Pinhead." Bess laughed and giggled, and her round cheeks and stomach jiggled, like as if it was hard to stop laughing.

While many of the other girls snickered, making me feel like I wanted to cry, Jesse stared into my eyes, and I could tell he understood. I never believed he was stupid, like Clara had told me. What I truly believed was there was something behind his eyes. He had thoughts and feelings like anybody.

At the end of the shift, Violet waited for me to get my handbag from my locker. "Come on, Helen. A whole group of us are going to a picture show. You don't want to be late, do you?"

I didn't feel like joining the group, but I also knowed I had to find a way to fit in with the other girls. I told Violet I'd be along soon. Then I reached inside my locker and snapped my hand back. "Ouch." Reaching inside again, I pulled out a long stem golden rose. I had to be careful of the thorns. As I stuck my sore finger into my mouth to stop the bleeding, I had a strange feeling somebody was behind me. I turned around, and standing about ten feet away was Jesse. He stopped sweeping, and leaned the broom handle against the wall.

I held the rose to my nostrils, and breathed in. Then, I stared into his eyes. "I hope Mrs. Peltz didn't see you stealing one of her roses, Jesse."

He twisted around to make sure nobody was nearby. Then Jesse come over and pulled me by the hand, out the door of the lounge, into the studio, then down the long stairs outside to the back of the building. He kept right on pulling me around the corner of a wood building, which had tools hanging from one wall, and one of those climbing vines on the other side.

A maze of L-shaped brick walls hid me and Jesse from anybody who might've been watching. A wood shelf was at the end, with farm tools. A hay hook leaned against a old tire, and my mind went right back to that day I made Papa Noone angry at me. He was my mother's daddy. He had him a temper, and when he seen what I done to his grandfather clock, he said a curse word. Back then, most folks didn't say curse words, especially when there was two little girls in the room.

At the center of the maze, Jesse stopped and stepped aside, so's I could see what was in front of us. My eyes got big as two moons, and I gasped a breath.

A whole rose garden, all different kinds and colors covered a long fence. "They take my breath away, Jesse," I said. I made believe the rest of the world had vanished, and only me and Jesse was left. I gazed up into his eyes. Close to him, I seen how much shorter I was than him, and I also recognized that along with his slender body, long lanky arms, and healthy-sized Adams apple, Jesse had moss green eyes, and full, soft looking lips.

I swallowed, realizing I hadn't never felt these feelings before. I felt like as if somebody just strapped me upside down from a tree limb, then set me right side up again.

From a distance, Violet was calling my name. "Helen! Get a move on. We're waiting." Clara called, too.

Suddenly, I recollected I needed help getting back out of the maze of brick walls and buildings. "Jesse, which way do I go?"

He took my hand again, and I felt safe following him out to the back of the main building. With a quick flip of his hand, he waved good-bye to me, and disappeared back into the maze. I turned and run to catch up with Violet and Clara.

"What took you so long?" Violet scowled at me, with her hands on her hips.

"I'm sorry. I guess I went out the wrong door."

"Helen, sooner or later, you're gonna get lost, and no one will ever find you."

With a quick shrug, I joined her to the picture show. All the while, I kept thinking about Jesse. About his warm hand, and mostly, about his lips. Now, I knowed what grown-up love was all about.

CHAPTER SEVEN

Even though we worked in a old school, there wasn't no cafeteria. And we couldn't go home in the middle of the day to eat our lunches, so we just put our paint and dials off to the side into our trays, and ate at our desks.

Ever since Mrs. Peltz told me I was a *natural*, I tried my hardest ever day to do more clocks than everbody else. Sometimes, the other girls would just get to talking about this and that, and while they stopped work to do all their chattering, I took the time to work harder on my tipping. I found me a way to do it without letting so much paint go down my throat. I would *kiss* the first time, but that was all. Just make a sharp point on the very tip. Then, I would make sure I tilted the paint jar, so's there was plenty of paint left on the edge. After that, I would twist the brush real fast, and it made a sharp enough point to paint the numbers just fine.

After only a couple of weeks, I learned to paint fast and sharp without never putting the brush between my lips at all. So I would just set and listen to the other girls talk while I worked. I didn't believe everthing I heard, since most of it was just silly.

Bess told us Mrs. Peltz once had her a love affair. With a married man. He was a undertaker, and he used to secretly meet with her in the funeral parlor. But the wife found out and boxed the undertaker's ears back.

I knowed it was a silly story, but I enjoyed listening. Still, I kept on painting. Soon I filled my tray with finished clock dials.

Some of the girls was talking about a reporter who was visiting from Chicago. He was with a good-looking photographer, and they was doing a article about the Radium Dial—about factories with mostly girl workers, and our factory was exactly that.

The whispering across the aisle was about how handsome the photographer was. "I wouldn't mind waking up to that ever morning," said Violet. "All those muscles." Clara agreed. Then, Bess said, "There he goes with Mr. Calder."

When Bess said it, her voice sounded dismal, like as if Mr. Calder was the worst person she ever met. "What's wrong, Bess?" Clara asked.

"You mean you don't know?"

Clara said she didn't know what Bess was talking about, and I sure didn't neither.

"There's a rumor most girls at the Radium Dial like to tell about Andrew Calder."

"What is it?" I asked, beginning to chew the inside of my lip.

Bess whispered real quiet. "We used to have a girl who worked here, named Jeanette Levane. She didn't come to work one day, and nobody could ever find her. But the last person to see her was Andrew Calder. The rumor is he killed her and stuffed her limp body into the old school furnace."

Violet put down her paint brush. "That's nothing but a cock-and-bull story."

"Well," Bess went on. "They still haven't ever found Jeanette."

Then, we all stopped talking, because the photographer from the newspaper was busy taking a picture of Mr. Calder standing next to the furnace room door.

That story might of been a lie, but I believed ever word.

#

Later that day, Mrs. Peltz come into the studio. She shushed everbody and said she had her a special announcement. Then, she called my name and told me to come to the front of the room. I tugged at my collar and shifted the waist on my skirt. By the time I made my way there, everbody's eyes was on me. Specially Clara and Violet's.

Once I was at the front of the room, Mrs. Peltz put her arm over my shoulder, then waited for two girls in the back to hush. "Girls, I want you all to know someone has broken a new record here at the Radium Dial. Helen Meisner here has broken the old record for daily production and will be advanced from apprentice to expert. Quite an accomplishment after only three weeks, don't you agree?" Then, Mrs. Peltz clapped a little and said "Congratulations, Helen."

I was expecting everbody in the room to stand up and cheer, but nobody did. Instead, a few girls clapped and the rest whispered among theirselves. Clara was the happiest, and clapped the loudest with a big grin. Then, Mrs. Peltz give me a nice wooden plaque that said, "Excellence in Training" on it in fancy letters. I hadn't never earned a plaque before. Back at Belmont High, I nearly won a attendance award, but Pauline Nann won it instead.

As I set down again in my seat with my new plaque, I stuck it under my desk, so's I could get back to work. We was getting settled, when suddenly, Mrs. Peltz interrupted us again. "Ladies, I hate to do this, but if you wouldn't mind, Mr. Barry here would like to take a picture of all of you hard at work at your desks."

While the other girls started giggling and touching up their hair and their lips, I just set still, thinking how we wasn't going to get our work done with all the interruptions. The photographer set his camera up on the three legs and told all of us girls to set with our hands folded on top of our desks. Mrs. Peltz reminded everbody to press their knees together and tug their dresses over them, toes pointed in front.

After the photographer was finished taking the photos, he come right up to my desk and leaned over. "I understand you won an award today, young lady."

If I ever turned red in my life, that was the day. He was the most handsome man I ever seen.

"Yes sir, I did."

"Would you like me to take a photo for your scrapbook?"

All around me, the other girls was giggling and teasing me. "Go on, Helen. Let him take your picture." Then somebody said, "You can send it down south, so they can hang it on the wall." And a third girl added something else. "That's right. On the wall. In the outhouse."

All the girls around us just broke up into laughter, but I just wanted to take my plaque and go home. Suddenly, Violet got out of her seat and told the photographer we didn't need a photo to send back home, but thank you very much. The handsome photographer then asked Bess if he could take *her* picture.

When we got home that night, Violet wanted to see my plaque. I handed it to her, and she stared a minute then give it back to me.

"What's wrong? Aren't you proud of me, Violet?"

She just stared at me, sort of biting her lower lip. "You're gonna make me look lazy. Like I can't do my work as fast as everbody else." She left for the parlor. I took my new plaque and set it up on the dresser. Then I set down to write Daddy a new letter. I wanted him to know all about my award, only I couldn't say it was for clock dials. Instead, I told him I had learned to play the organ.

#

As Nurse Flora lit my after-dinner cigarette in the day room, I recollected when Violet first showed me how to smoke. I had tried it once before, when I was 13, but I never told nobody. In Belmont, there was a shoeshine boy who rolled a dozen or so cigarettes each morning, then smoked them all during the day. One day he offered one to me which I took, then I thanked him and left for home. I snuck a couple of matches from Daddy, and tried smoking one of them rolled cigarettes, but I coughed so hard, I upchucked my lunch.

The day Violet showed me how, we was off work a half day from the Radium Dial, because of the Independence Day picnic. We went to the Ottawa Public Park, where they had a lake with ducks and a outdoor theater with a giant shell over a stage. Violet asked if I wanted to learn to roll a cigarette, and I said yes. She had the papers and tobacco there in her handbag, so she took it out and showed me what to do.

"Where'd you get these things?" I asked Violet.

"From Myra Peck. Remember that day when you had to do that ironing for Mrs. Yearsall, and I had me a visitor at the boarding house?"

I told her I recollected it, but I wondered why she didn't say nothing before now. It was like as if my sister Violet had a secret life I didn't know nothing about.

"First, you need a good flat surface, like the top of a desk or a table."

Since we was outside, we used Violet's handbag, laying on its side. I watched everthing she done. Once we had finished rolling it, she even had her a matchbox in her

58

handbag, so I tried the cigarette. I took me a little puff, and blew the smoke out. It felt warm and smelled funny, but it didn't bother me none.

"What a dumb Dora. You have to take it all the way into your lungs. Not just into your mouth." Of course, when I tried the next time and took it into my lungs, I choked and coughed like all get-out, and then Bess seen me from across the way. Violet motioned and hollered for Bess to join us, and soon they was both giggling at me cause I was coughing so much. Violet patted me on the back, and Bess did too, only she patted much harder.

After that, Bess snatched the cigarette from me and took her a few puffs too. "See? Nothing to it." Bess jabbed Violet in the ribs and they kept on giggling with each other. Then Bess said something ugly to me. It still hurts today, just recollecting it. She said, "Helen, don't worry if you can't smoke. Maybe you're just not cut out for it. You know, you can't expect to win an award for *everything*."

#

Just as the sun was behind the trees, I was the last one left on the Avery building porch. All the other residents was inside, since it was medication time. Soon, I would have to get up out of my rocker and get in line for mine.

Suddenly, I reckoned my eyes was playing tricks on me. Standing with one foot on the cement sidewalk, with his other foot in the tulip bulbs, was a curious-looking man with a hat, wearing a pair of ragged overalls with a brown sports jacket over them, Since I was setting alone on the porch, I could see everthing he done.

First, he tipped his hat to me, but his lips wasn't in a smile. It was almost like as if he was just tipping his hat without really meaning to. Next, he took a small piece of paper like the size of a wallet out of his jacket pocket, and stared at it. Then he stared at me. Back to the piece of paper. Back to me. I reckoned it was a photograph. I started to get twitchy.

Then, I jumped when Nurse Flora appeared next to me and yelled in a loud voice. "Helen, you know you're not allowed out here after sundown. And it's almost time for the ward meeting."

I turned my head to answer her. "I'm sorry. I thought the meeting was tomorrow." Flora pinched her lips flat. "You know it's always on a Tuesday, Helen. Come along. The rest of them are waiting."

As I pushed myself out of my rocker, I looked all around for the peculiar man in the overalls, but he was gone. There wasn't nobody anywhere, not on the sidewalk that goes to the parking lot, not on the grass. No where. I recollected all the ladies in our ward who see things and people that aren't really there, and Dr. Stokes said if I ever seen people that wasn't there I should let him know. He said he would give me a different dose of my medicine.

#

When we was in Ottawa, me and Violet was together most of the time, but once in a while, I went off by myself too. After work one day, Mrs. Yearsall asked Violet and Clara to go to the shoe repair, and she didn't need me for nothing, so I went for a walk to the end of the street. The sun was beating down, and a drip of sweat fell into my eyes off of my eyebrows.

After a little ways more, I come to a large old oak tree, next to a patch of other trees in a dark forest. On the other side of the oak tree was two boys—a white boy and a colored boy, both about nine or ten years old. They was pulling a rope and giggling at something on the back side of the tree. As I tiptoed closer around to see what they was up to, the boys seen me and got a startled look in their eyes. Down on the ground was a sight I will never forget. The rope was tied to the back legs of a little brown and black dog. In the front, he only had one leg. The poor little thing was yelping and trying to bite the boys. As soon as they seen me, the boys let go of the rope and the little sad creature limped off into the dark woods, trailing the rope behind him.

The next thing I seen I will never forget neither. Before I could say nothing to those boys, a man come out of the dark patch of woods, carrying that little three-legged dog. I didn't know many men in Ottawa, but I recognized this man. It was Mr. Calder from the factory. He wasn't carrying the dog in a nice gentle way. He had it by the scruff of his neck, and he held the dog out away from his body.

Mr. Calder didn't see me right off. Instead he started in fussing at the boys. "Let 'im get away from ya again, didn't ya?"

Then, Mr. Calder finally seen me, and he give me a wicked smile. He set the dog down on the ground, and took a knife out of his pocket. Then, as I was about to cover my eyes, Mr. Calder leaned over and cut the rope off the dog's legs. Then he give him a little kick of his dusty boot and laughed real evil-like.

After the little dog limped off, the boys run off too. I was glad the little dog got away, but then there was nobody left but me and Mr. Calder. He just made a funny sound in his throat like as if he needed to cough something out. He leaned into the grass and hawked it up. I just crossed my arms and asked him about that poor little dog. His answer wasn't very nice.

"Piece a shit stray dog. World's got too many of 'em."

Mr. Calder had more to say. I wanted to run away, but I stayed and listened. "Whole town's overrun with defectives. Seen a squirrel with a split tail, birds dying before they're outta the nest. It's best to put 'em outta their misery."

Instead of answering Mr. Calder, I just kept quiet, cause I couldn't think of nothing nice I wanted to say. I just left and made my way back to the sidewalk. All I wanted to do was get back to the boarding house so's nobody would see me get sick to my stomach.

#

While me and Clara and Violet was finishing up our mixed berry pie, Mrs. Yearsall said she seen our picture in the paper. She left the table for a little minute, and when she come back, she had her a article from the Chicago Tribune about the Radium Dial. It said we was "an industrious factory," offering "incentives for increased production."

Under the article was a picture of Mrs. Peltz setting behind her desk with her vase of roses. In front of her was a row of clock dials. Then on the next page, our group picture was below a different part of the article. It said how much we make in our paychecks. Mrs. Yearsall said she wasn't aware we was paid so high. After supper, she allowed me and Violet to cut out the article and save it for a scrapbook.

Then, the next night, me and Violet was ironing our things. Mrs. Yearsall asked us to join her and Clara in the parlor. Once we was all seated, she said she had something important to tell us. "Girls, I'm afraid I can't afford to allow you to live here without paying me a little something."

Violet tapped her fingernails on the side table. "How much would we have to pay?" It would ruin all our plans if we had to pay Mrs. Yearsall ever week.

Mrs. Yearsall had her a answer, which made me think she had already give it some thought. "I'll have to charge you six dollars per week. In advance."

Violet and Clara knowed more than me about rent. "That's awfully high, Mrs. Yearsall," Violet said. "We'll have to think about it."

Later, in our room, us three girls had us a talk. Violet held up the newspaper clippings. "You know what happened, don't you?"

"No, what was it? I asked.

"She saw this article, and decided to get a little something for herself."

Clara agreed. She said if Mrs. Yearsall hadn't never read that article about our paychecks, she might not have knowed what she was missing.

The next day, Violet got out the city directory, and telephoned all the other boarding houses in Ottawa. They was all charging five dollars per week, except one that was charging six. "Do you have any girls from the Radium Dial living there?" Violet asked. The man said yes, he did. After that, Violet said we should all just stay where we was, but she said if we was paying rent, we shouldn't have to help around the house so much. So that would give us more time for fun.

CHAPTER EIGHT

The first time me and Jesse spoke in a real conversation was one evening after he put a poem and a new rose in my locker. The poem was one he wrote hisself. Course, this time, first, he sliced the thorns off the rose stem with his pen knife. I know because I didn't get stabbed with a thorn like before, and because he told me he did.

He spoke to me after work on a Friday night. All us kids was lined up by the Ottawa Dairy Company, which was a diner with a lunch counter in the shape of a U, and the waitress would stand inside the U so's we could give her our order. For some reason, the lunch counter was full of old people that night. Grandmothers and hunched-over folks with canes, with the shoulders of their clothes hanging forward. There was a alleyway between the diner and the place of business next door, which was a grocer's and general merchandise store, and the air smelled like fried potatoes and meat loaf. Jesse was waiting alone in the alleyway.

I was with Violet and Clara. When I seen Jesse, I snuck away from the girls and smiled at him. He was dressed in a suit, only it was two or three sizes too large, like as if somebody had maybe loaned it to him. His shirt collar was yards too big, and he wore a bow tie on it that made the collar set up in a jumble of creases. I stood next to him and studied him a minute. "Hello Jesse. Thank you again for the gifts."

When he answered, he hardly made a sound, but his voice was as deep as a quarry. A voice like that just didn't belong with a tall, skinny, backward custodian boy. I got to thinking maybe that was why he didn't talk much to other folks. Maybe he was ill at ease, or didn't want to stand out as different.

I told him his poem and the rose was nice, and he smiled. When I heard his deep voice the next time, he told me about the roses. "I tend to them. Trim them back. It's my job."

I scrunched my eyebrows at him, tilting my head a little. "How come you don't talk to nobody else but me?"

First he stared ahead, way across the road, then he lowered his eyes and looked at me, like as if he was confused. "Don't know yet."

I may not be the smartest person that ever lived, but I can tell when it's hard for somebody to choke out the words.

Soon, the group of old people begin coming out of the diner. Some of the kids our age wasn't behaving that night, and started in teasing the old folks, calling them names and such. I didn't think it was proper. One of the old people was Mr. Calder. Jesse cleared his throat and swallowed at the same time, while he squinted his eyes. When I studied Jesse's face, it had changed, like as if he was recollecting something awful. "He hurt me once."

"What do you mean, Jesse?"

"I was a boy. He hurt me. Broke my thumb."

"Why did he do that?"

Jesse told me the story of how Mr. Calder used to work in the old general merchandise and grocers' in Ottawa. One day, Jesse and his little friend John was returning from grade school and stopped in for a piece of candy. The boys each picked up two pieces, but Mr. Calder thought they was trying to steal it. He grabbed each boy by the wrist and pulled them behind the counter. John broke free and ran, but Mr. Calder still had hold of Jesse. Then he forced Jesse's little hand into the till drawer and slammed it. Broke his thumb.

"To this day, I don't know why he did that." Jesse just shook his head.

"Why do you work for him then?"

Jesse leaned closer and whispered. "Who *wouldn't* want to work in a factory full of girls?" I reckoned that was a good reason. But he had him one more reason too. "Also, one day soon, I'm gonna make things right. Make *him* hurt somewhere."

Me and Jesse just stared at mean old Mr. Calder as he passed us by in the alleyway. He was with the other old folks, only he wasn't acting like he was enjoying hisself too much. Soon, he was walking alone back down the street, with a toothpick between his teeth, and he stopped to spit it out so's he could get him a pinch of tobacco. Jesse held tight as a belt to my arm, and told me to shush. I held my breath until Mr. Calder was gone down the street.

Out of the blue, Violet and Clara showed up, and startled me and Jesse. Violet spoke first. "That man makes my skin twitch like the last lonely feather on a plucked chicken." Then, she sort of stared up at Jesse, like as if she was trying to decipher what he was thinking. "You like my sister, don't you, Jesse?"

Even in the low light, I was pretty sure me and Jesse both blushed a shade or two. For a little minute, I hoped he would declare his feelings for me, but then I reckoned it would be better if he kept quiet, so's I would still be the only one who knowed he could talk. Instead, Jesse answered for hisself. "She's nicer than most."

Violet giggled and poked Clara in the arm. Then Clara rubbed herself where she got poked.

Violet got this wicked look in her eyes again, and then gathered the four of us together in a huddle. "I got me an idea," she said, in a quiet whisper. "Jesse, you know where Mr. Calder lives?"

Jesse nodded his head yes, then his hand sort of clutched onto his chin, and he slid his palm around back of his neck. "On Clairemont. Way at the end, by the railroad tracks. In a two-story house. I've been past there more nights than I care to count."

At first, I was surprised because I hadn't never heard Jesse speak that many words to nobody before, except to me. Then, I was scared about what Violet was planning to do. Clara saved me the trouble of asking. "Violet, what's going on in that twisted mind of yours?"

The sun was already down now. I smacked a mosquito on my arm and listened to Violet and her idea. "Jesse, you remember a while back when you polished the floors, and a couple of us girls almost slipped and fell on the tile?"

"Yes, I remember. I remember because Mr. Calder laughed at you."

Then Violet got closer to Jesse, so's she could whisper to him. He bent forward to hear her. "Can you get us some of that floor polish? Maybe sneak into the supply closet and we can pour it on his porch? Then we can holler at him to come outside. Maybe honk the horn or something, and watch him slip and splatter."

Now, I knowed Violet was just mean, but at the time, it sounded like a good way to spend a evening with my friends. Also, I wanted to avenge Jesse, and that poor little brown and black dog. It just felt proper.

Since Jesse had his daddy's old Tin Lizzy, we let him drive us to the Radium Dial. He used his keys to get inside the building, and in a minute or two he come out of there with two cans, one in each hand. After he handed me the cans in the front seat, he turned the automobile around and we headed back toward Mr. Calder's house. I could tell the cans was different. One said, "floor polish," and the other said, "motor oil." I reckoned Jesse made a mistake.

"Did you know you give me two different cans?"

He nodded a moment, then added, "I sure did. The two of them together should be slick as goose shit." Then he bowed his head and said in a low voice, "I'm sorry to have been crude in your presence, Helen." I told him I was not offended in the least.

It was dark, and the house was on a deserted road that wasn't too far outside of the town. Mr. Calder only had one light on in his house, and I could tell cause of the way the light flickered it was a oil lamp, not a real electricity lamp. Jesse stopped the Tin Lizzy under a tree, and we snuck to the porch, all four of us.

Since it was summer and Mr. Calder had his windows open, ever sound he made traveled into the night. He coughed up phlegm and hawked it somewheres. Maybe into a cup or down the kitchen sink. A breeze kicked up, but the air was still as hot as daytime and a dog barked in the distance. It just made me that much more jittery.

Just to be safe, I whispered we should go back into the yard where it was dark.

Violet snuck to the automobile and got the two cans. She handed one to me. It was the motor oil can. "How are you gonna get yours open, Helen?" She was chuckling at me, in a evil voice.

"Here, Helen. Give it to me," Clara said, snatching it from my hand. She searched around for a sharp stick to punch into the top. Then, she picked up a rock from the grass, but the sharpest part on it was too rounded.

Jesse and Violet tried to figure out a way to get the other can open. They fussed over it, trying to use a sharp stick and a rock, or a different rock with a sharp point.

Finally, they got the floor polish open, and Jesse handed it over to Violet. Yanking on his shirt, Violet asked, "Ain't you gonna help me?" Her voice was deep and scratchy, so's she wouldn't be too loud.

Out of the blue, I got to shaking. I said I didn't want to get in no trouble, but the others could go right ahead and break the law if they wanted. I hurried over to the automobile.

That's when Violet said she was shamed of me. Clara was quiet. I think she was shamed of Violet, because she decided to join me by the Tin Lizzy. We leaned our backsides up against the rusty door, and watched in the dark.

Jesse twisted his head back toward me and Clara. He stared at us for a time, then put his hands in his pockets. He wouldn't answer Violet. He just kept quiet and still. Then Violet run to the porch, poured some of the polish all over it, and run back to me and Clara at the automobile. She held the can up in front of Clara's nose. "Your turn."

Clara took her a breath, and stared at me. "I think that's enough polish, don't you, Helen?" I told her it was plenty. Me and Clara whispered about Mr. Calder, and I told her about what he done with that little dog. She said it come as no great surprise to her.

"I have to do *everthing* myself," Violet said. Then she poured the rest of the polish out in the grass and tossed the empty can into the back seat of the automobile. She reached inside to the wheel and pressed non-stop on the horn. Me and Jesse and Clara all climbed into our seats and Jesse started the engine. Just as we was commencing to drive off, Mr. Calder come running out of his house with the lantern in his hand. Jesse jammed his foot on the brake.

Mr. Calder slipped on the mess and went down, and the lantern rolled a good five feet away from him. We waited for him to get up and hold his aching back or holler "who done this?" but he just lay there and didn't move. Then the oil lantern made a spark. It made a poof sound, and flames spread like a flock of birds from a pond, whooshing over the sides and top of the porch.

Next thing I heard, all four of us screamed and we all got out of the automobile and run in circles, while we seen Mr. Calder's clothes catch, then his porch was lit up hot like a gas furnace. The flames flickered to the sky and there wasn't nothing we could do.

We got back into the automobile and drove away without uttering a word, past the train tracks and parked with the lights off. We set still, listening to the gasping sound of our breathing, to the sound of vehicles on the highway screeching their tires, and fire trucks coming to try and save what was left of Mr. Calder.

CHAPTER NINE

On Sunday, Tony come to get me again to go to Pearl's. This time, Pearl wanted me to help her look through old pictures of me and Violet, to see if I recollected anything about the Radium Dial. We was setting in her living room, and she brought one album after the next of old family pictures from her dining room hutch. There was a stack a mile high next to me. "Keep looking," she told me.

She left me alone and went to her room to get her reading glasses, when the telephone rang. Since I was setting right next to the extension, I picked it up, and at the same time, Pearl did too, from her bedroom.

Now, most of the time, I'm not one to listen in to somebody's private telephone call, but this time I did. I held my mouth real quiet and tried not to breathe heavy, so's nobody could hear me.

The man's voice asked if he was speaking to Pearl Rodgers Velasquez.

"Yes, this is Pearl Velasquez. Who's calling?"

It was Benjamin Reed calling. Clara Jane's boy who sent the letter from Atlanta. While him and Pearl talked, I felt like as if I was listening to a radio program about a couple of families who had been through a tragedy. Benjamin said his mama had died just a short while ago, after she had her a stroke and a bad kind of jaw cancer. And now, Benjamin thinks it was from the radium poison. Me and Clara had lost touch a long time ago, and I was sad the same thing happened to her that happened to Violet, only Violet was a much younger woman when she died. About the same time that Violet passed, I even heard of one girl who had her arm to swell up and burst, and the doctors had to amputate it. I shivered, thinking of skeleton bones and cancer.

Pearl asked Benjamin if he wanted to have his mama's bones dug up to test for radium, but he explained Clara's body couldn't be dug up because it had been cremated.

"Oh, I'm sorry," Pearl said. "You know, I don't care for the idea at all. I barely remember my mother, but I believe once a person's body has been laid to rest, it shouldn't be disturbed."

"A difficult decision, I'm sure. Something you and your family will need to decide together."

"Fortunately, I can make this decision myself."

"Isn't Violet's sister Helen still alive?"

"Yes, but you see, my Aunt Helen is... well, she's incapacitated, and I handle all her affairs."

"Has she told you anything about having worked at the factory?"

"Not a thing. Believe me, I've tried, but she refuses to discuss it."

Then, there wasn't no sound, except for Pearl breathing. Then, she asked, "Do you know much about exhumations?"

"Enough to be dangerous," Benjamin answered.

Pearl kept silent, then she started in talking again. "Do you further know... I mean, if there was more than one reason to test a person. Could they perform multiple tests?"

"I imagine as long as the pathologist was informed ahead of time, he could perform an additional test."

"I see. Then I think I will give my permission. I believe the cause listed on my mother's death certificate was false. I need to know."

Benjamin said he thought they could of made a mistake. He told her to get the right answer.

"Oh, believe me, Mr. Reed. I intend to find out everything I can."

Benjamin started in talking about a trip he took to visit Clara's cousin, Jean, but she didn't know nothing about the factory. Then, he told Pearl they used to use radium when people was sick, having them to drink it. I recollect times when no matter what sort of ailment, even blemishes and goiters, folks would drink radium water hoping to be cured. Or sometimes when folks had the chronic bronchitis or the constipation, the doctor give it to them by a enema.

"Snake oil, Mr. Reed. I guess we've all been deceived by outrageous claims at one time or another."

"Very true."

Then, of course, Pearl had to crow all about her engagement and how Donald was from one of the oldest families in Charlotte. A minute later, Pearl asked Benjamin if he would like to come to Belmont. "Maybe you could come for the exhumation. Perhaps talk to the pathologist about the findings."

"And perhaps I could also talk to your aunt."

Pearl was silent, then answered, "You can try. Helen and I haven't gotten along in years. Ever since I was in my teens. You see, when my mother died and my father abandoned me in 1934, I was only five years old. Helen and Uncle Jesse took me in. I had no where else to go."

#

I thought it might be nice to see Benjamin again. To see how he become a fine gentleman. I didn't think I would tell him much of anything, even though now, it seems him and Pearl already do know a lot about radium and the factory.

For days after that fire at Mr. Calder's, Violet told me to keep away from Jesse. She said she didn't want nobody to see us together. We should've been cheerful since we had began saving from our paychecks, but ever since the fire, we wasn't cheerful at all. The girls at work wasn't neither. Some of them was depressed about Mr. Calder, sniffling into their hankies. Violet said we should do the same, so's it would look like we cared, too.

"Just try to fit in with everbody else," she said. "Go about your business."

In the ladies room, I seen a girl crying and when I asked her what was the trouble, she stopped long enough to answer me. "No one I've ever known has died before." I didn't know the girl's name, so I asked her. She said her name was Glenda, and she was fourteen and a half.

"You mean you never lost nobody in your family, or a neighbor, or nobody like that?" I asked.

"No. No one I've known personally." Glenda had her a little turned up nose, and it was red and wet from crying.

She sniffled some more and wiped her eyes. "I know the other girls didn't like him, but Mr. Calder was always nice to me."

Just then, Bess come into the ladies room and stood in front of the big mirror to put on lipstick. As she seen Glenda behind her in the mirror, she spun around to talk to her. "What's wrong?"

Glenda said she was still trying to not get so tearful when she thought of what happened to Mr. Calder. Bess went on with her lipstick, leaning close to the mirror, and still talking to Glenda's reflection. "If you ask me, it's no great loss."

In a instant, Glenda rushed to Bess, and punched her in the back. She was hollering too. "How can you say that? He was a nice, Christian man. You're just evil, Bess. You're an evil person for saying that." Then, Glenda kept on crying and carrying on, like as if she lost her best friend.

I didn't like being in the middle of a fight, but since I was already there, I wanted to see how it would end. After Glenda punched Bess in the back, Bess dropped her lipstick on the wood floor, then turned and lunged for Glenda, backing her up against the wall. Her voice was calm, but her eyes was angry. "Don't ever do that again, Glenda. There's no reason to hit me. I'm entitled to my opinion, just the way you are."

After that, Bess let go of Glenda, and marched out the door. Me and Glenda hugged each other for a minute, because I think we was both just as scared as could be. Then, I stood just back from her. "You all right?"

"I think so. You know, she should have more respect for the dead," Glenda said, motioning to the door. She was right. The dead deserve respect as well as the living. Specially when it wasn't really their turn to die.

#

A day or two later, me and Violet was at the dress shop in Ottawa to spend some of our money. We had just got new paychecks, and the lady at the Ottawa bank had cashed them for us. First, we went over to the Ottawa Mercantile and I got me a new hair brush and some new hair ribbons, and Violet got her some Ivory soap.

After that, we went to the dress shop. While we was there, a old woman with a blue hat was talking with the cashier about the fire. She said Mr. Calder's funeral filled up the church with his great big family of children and grandchildren.

Me and Violet stared at each other. The lady also said the sheriff was going from house to house seeing all the girls from the Radium Dial, to ask them questions.

After that, I didn't feel like buying no new dress. I got this funny feeling inside me, like as if there was something crawling under my skin, and I got itchy all over. I rubbed both hands over my arms and shoulders. Violet dragged me to the back of the dress shop, and got a angry look in her eyes. "Stop it, Helen." Violet didn't want me causing a fuss. "The last thing we want is to draw attention." The itching didn't go away until a few hours later.

That night, me and Clara and Violet set out back of the boarding house whispering about what to do. Clara sort of sucked on one of her knuckles. "Nobody suspects any of us. How could they? Since Violet threw the floor polish can in the back seat after, and the only thing we left in the yard was the can of motor oil, and anybody could have that in their yard."

Then I added, "And nobody seen us around there."

When there was a noise inside the house, we all turned around behind us. Mrs. Yearsall called to say we had us a visitor. It was Jesse. We invited him to join us. Violet grabbed his arm and we all stepped farther away from the house. Mrs. Yearsall called out, "You girls know I don't allow members of the opposite gender inside past dark."

"Yes ma'am," we all answered. Clara leaned down and got her a stick from the grass, tapping it in her palm. "Has anybody suspected you, Jesse?"

He shook his head, then said, "No. Not so far."

Violet gathered us together. "Remember what we all promised that night. That none of us would ever tell."

As Violet stared into each person's eyes, we all nodded yes. We wouldn't never tell. Never.

After a few minutes, Jesse said he had to get back home. His mom was waiting up for him, and she wasn't feeling well. He asked if I would walk him to his automobile. I did. On the way there, we stopped at the side of the house. "Last night, I didn't get any sleep."

"How come, Jesse?"

"I had a bad dream. I dreamed they came and took us all to prison. They locked us all up together and they wouldn't let us have any food. They would hold the food just past our reach, outside the bars of the cell."

He grabbed me and hugged me tight. My ear was pressed against his chest, and inside it, I felt the thumpity thump of his heart. He was breathing a little fast too, but I didn't think it was because he was in love or nothing. I knowed his heart was thumping because he was just as scared as I was.

#

On the morning of Violet's exhumation, Pearl drove me in her car to the cemetery. On the other graves there was flowers, tall and colorful, but when the worker men got Violet's grave ready, they had left a mess of crushed grass and patchy red clay. I said me a silent prayer.

Memories come back to me about how Violet's hair shone in the dark from swallowing too much radium paint, and how it looked like as if she had a halo around her hair. The same thing happened to some of the other girls too, specially when they went out with their young fellas at night.

The reporters come to the gravesite and so did some local Belmont folks. The preacher from Pearl's church come and said a few words, while little beads of sweat collected on my arms and soaked my collar. The worker men's throats and arm muscles bulged as they lifted the casket with those thick chains.

After the men set the casket into the rear of a big van, a man in a nice suit was standing off to the side, maybe one of the reporters but just watching from a distance. Soon, the reporters gathered all around Pearl, and she shifted her weight, like as if she was impatient for a train. I pressed my hand across my unruly hair and gnawed on my lower lip. Inside, I was feeling lots of different feelings. Confused, and sad, and worried. I had both my hands in a fist, and I held them together against my mouth with my elbows to the side. But then watching Pearl made me forget my troubles.

Even when Pearl was only a young teenage girl, she was always trying to be in charge of everbody else. Just like now. She was a good actress, too. She held a hanky to her nose, and her eyes was red and weepy. Then, she told the reporters she was waiting to talk to somebody else—the man in the nice suit. I reckoned he was Benjamin, and I wanted to meet him too.

He held out his hand for Pearl to shake it. "Hello, I'm Benjamin Reed." He drove all the way from Atlanta.

She sized him up good before she answered. "Hello Benjamin. I'm Pearl, and this is my aunt... Helen Waterman." He said hello to me.

Pearl's shoulders was rigid, while she scowled at me. I know that look of hers. It means for me to don't dare say a word. Then, she turned back to Benjamin and got all sugary again. "I wish we could have met under different circumstances, Mr. Reed."

"Benjamin. Please call me Benjamin."

Pearl lowered her voice. "May I speak to you privately?"

"Of course."

"Just one moment." Grabbing me by the arm, Pearl pushed on me and made me set on a stone bench. "Don't get up until I come for you."

They moved away, and Pearl tried to whisper, but her voice traveled easy in the morning quiet. She wanted Benjamin to try to get me to talk to him about the factory. They looked in my direction, but I quickly stared at the ground. I knowed they was talking about me. Sometimes I feel so small.

When I looked up next, Benjamin was standing in front of me. "Mrs. Waterman?" He smiled at me a little, and held my hand between both of his for a moment.

"You may call me Helen."

"It seems my mother knew you and your sister Violet many years ago."

"Clara Jane Hart. And I remember you from when you was little. Me and my sister come to visit your family once or twice."

All I could do was twist the strap on my handbag. He held onto my arm then let it go. I scooted over on the bench. "Won't you sit down?"

"Thank you."

For a moment, I set still, just blinking my eyes. Then, I took a glance over at him. "Do you recollect me? When I come to visit your mama?"

"I do," he said, smiling.

"You have the same eyes. Like when you was a boy. With crinkles when you smile. You're the same build, too. Of course bigger. Not tall, but you're built powerful. And I recollect your baby sister. What was her name again?"

"Iris."

"Oh, that's right. Iris was her name. I imagine she's a grown woman by now."

"She is. She has a thirteen-year-old daughter. She and her husband make a good living as dog breeders. King Charles Spaniels."

"How nice."

"Would you mind if I came to see you at the hospital? So we could have a longer visit?"

"No, I wouldn't mind."

"Good then. Pearl will arrange it with you. I'm looking forward to our next meeting."

He scooted from the bench, and more of them reporters was still waiting to speak to Pearl. She stood with her back board-straight, almost to the point of bending backward. Some of their questions was just alike, even from two different people. "Mrs. Velasquez, what do you think the tests will show?" And "Do you plan to make the test results public?"

After a few minutes with the reporters, Pearl come back to me on the bench. She opened her handbag and handed me a envelope that was already opened. "I forgot to show you this. We received a letter for *you* now, too. I've already told them I'll make sure you go to the laboratory."

When Pearl told me that, I squeezed my fists so tight, my fingernails dug into my palms. I knowed darn well, I couldn't go get that testing done, because they might ask me why I never said I worked at the factory. They might ask me if I knowed anything about Mr. Calder. What would I say?

CHAPTER TEN

At my last session, I set in Dr. Stokes' office talking about that peculiar man in the overalls. He asked me about it. "Tell me what you saw, Helen."

I took a puff of my cigarette. "I was setting on the porch in a rocker. The sun was almost down, and I couldn't hardly see, but there was a man. He was a older fella, but not quite my age. He was dressed in a pair of overalls with a jacket. Like a sports jacket."

"What else did you notice?"

"Well, he took something from his pocket. It was like the size of a photograph. He held it in his hand and stared at it a minute, then looked up at me. Like as if he was comparing to see if I was the same person in the photograph."

Dr. Stokes leaned back in his chair. "Were you alone on the porch?"

"Yes."

"What else did the man do?"

"Just then, Nurse Flora come out on the porch, and I spoke to her and when I turned back around, the man was gone. And I couldn't see where he went."

"Did the nurse mention she saw him?"

"No, but I didn't ask her."

"Why don't you ask her today? Also, ask if anyone else may have seen him."

I thanked Dr. Stokes for not saying I was imagining that man. He said I could keep on taking my medicine same as before. Even if I was imagining him, I only seen him once. So there was no way to know yet unless I see him again. If I do, I'll let Dr. Stokes know straight away. He's good at helping people.

When I think about how scared me and Violet and Clara was for weeks after the fire, we could have probably used the help of a doctor or somebody like that. In fact, we did spend part of our earnings and go on the train to Chicago to see a fortune teller. It cost us fifty cents each to see Mrs. Harrison, but we was glad to pay her because we was afraid to go to a local fortune teller anywhere around Ottawa.

After we got off the train, we had to rush to get to the address on time for our one-o'clock appointment. We rode in a clanky bus to a unpaved street with horses and carts. A heavy woman wearing men's clothes yelled at us to watch our step. She was pouring some kind of messy liquid down the drain next to the sidewalk. She didn't want us to get it on our shoes.

Once we stepped up on the porch, we rang the little bell in the door by turning the teeny brass knob. The sign on the door read, "Private Residence. No Solicitation."

A woman opened the door. She didn't smile, but instead she frowned, with her dark hair pulled back in a bun, and she had her a patch of gray about the size of a lemon right on the side of her head. "You girls want me to tell your fortunes? It'll be four bits a piece. Just slide your money into the jar." She held up a old jar, far away from her face, like as if she was scared to touch it.

After we each dropped in our money, she took us into her parlor behind a fancy maroon colored velvet drape. The parlor was decorated nice, with pretty lamps and fuzzy wallpaper. I know it was fuzzy, because I touched it. When I did, Violet yanked my hand away from it.

"Okay, who would like to go first?" Mrs. Harrington asked.

Violet pushed me toward Mrs. Harrington. "Helen does."

I reckoned Violet was right. I don't much like waiting for my turn, especially if it's something I *want* to do. I sunk down into her low-slung wingback chair and after she lit a small candle, Mrs. Harrington reached for both my hands, squeezing them in hers across the top of the table. Her hands was dry and bony. She stared into my eyes, squinty like, and told me I didn't believe in her. Then she said I could get my money back if I wanted to fish it out of the jar. I told her yes I did too believe in her, and I didn't want to leave.

"Are you sure?" She let go of one hand, and kept the other. My right hand. She stared at my palm a minute, real hard, like as if she was studying a creature under a microscope. Then, she looked into my eyes, then to Clara's and then to Violet's, each one at a time. "How old are you girls?"

Violet told her our ages. Then, Mrs. Harrington sort of swallowed loud, and then she shifted her feet under the table. "Do you girls think you're mature enough to have your fortunes told?"

All three of us girls nodded and said yes. Then, Mrs. Harrington started to look again at my palm, and she chuckled. It was a sort of nervous chuckle, with a little tear drop. "I'm sorry, but sometimes my emotions get a little twisted. I laugh when I should be crying, and cry when I should be laughing."

At first, I reckoned maybe it wasn't such a good idea for me to go first. But then, I recollected how much we paid, and I decided we should get our money's worth. "Please go ahead whenever you're ready, Mrs. Harrington," I said. I almost felt like crying, myself.

She gazed at my palm a long while. "In your palm, I see something I almost never see in a young girl your age. That's why I asked your age. You see, this palm shows no lifeline. Like you've never been alive your whole life."

Clara sucked in a loud breath and clamped her hand on her mouth. I must have looked like a fool, just staring at Mrs. Harrington the way I did. I didn't know what to say, but I didn't have to say nothing, because Violet spoke up *for* me. "But what does that mean?"

"Well, I can't tell, really. I'm afraid I can't read much from her palm." While she said that, she was still staring into my palm, running her fingertips over the lines, and even flipping my hand to the back now and again. "Of course, you do have a long healthy *heart* line. I suspect you'll marry soon, and have lots of rambunctious children."

If I had no life line, and I wasn't even alive, I begin to wonder how I would ever manage to bear children. In fact, the whole time Mrs. Harrison was reading Violet and Clara's palms, I was thinking about my future. Mrs. Harrington didn't say nothing about us getting into trouble, or going to prison. She just said things about Violet and Clara that could be true for anybody, like they would someday live a life of luxury, or they would fall in love soon. I begin to think we was wasting our money.

Instead of worrying over what Mrs. Harrington said, I was busy thinking about the man I wanted for my future husband... Mr. Jesse Waterman.

Just as she was finishing up with Clara's palm, Mrs. Harrington said she wanted to look at her crystal ball, but we told her we had ran out of time. Then something peculiar happened. At first, I thought maybe the light was playing tricks on me, but it wasn't. A cloud formed around Mrs. Harrington's head. It started slow, like a teapot building up steam. Then, when she was showing us to the door, the cloud was all around her head. Violet asked me why I was staring at Mrs. Harrington.

"No...no reason in particular. I just thought I seen something."

"You'll have to forgive my sister, ma'am. Sometimes she doesn't know what she's doing."

Mrs. Harrington just helped us out to the front stoop and us girls left for the train station. All the way there, I was thinking about my future. I stared at my palms, wondering if I would even live long enough to make it back to Belmont at the end of the summer.

#

Just after I made my bed, Neely said she heard one of the nurses say I'd missed a telephone call from Pearl. I told Neely thank you. I knowed what Pearl wanted to talk about anyway. She had spoke to one of the folks at the laboratory, and they said to expect a delay of eighteen months to two years until they could have Violet's bones tested. "They said they had so many women ahead of my mother, they couldn't say exactly when they would get to her," Pearl had said.

I tried to console her, saying maybe they could work something out and test Violet sooner. Pearl said she already talked to Donald, reminding me he "knows people in Washington."

Later, Pearl called again. "Didn't the nurses tell you I wanted to talk to you?" I just shrugged, but I'm sure she didn't hear it over the telephone. "Benjamin is coming to see you today, so you better tell him what he wants to know."

Benjamin. What a sweet child he was. Clara was a good mama to him when he was a boy. She took him under her wing when the world was cruel. She give him books about birds and he was always studying them. One time, after Clara was married and already moved to Atlanta, she wrote me a letter about something that happened to Benjamin at school with one of the nuns. Clara wrote he had just finished coloring a picture of the mountains, with nice trees and flowers, but the teacher yelled at him. "Benjamin, you made the sky green and purple!" Sister Ruth tore up his artwork, saying he had to do it over, the *right* way. It turns out what Benjamin was drawing was just those Northern Lights up in Alaska.

Now and again I think about Pearl's twin brother and what sort of a child or man he might have become. But since he died when he was only a few days old, nobody will ever know. I recollect holding little William in my arms along with Pearl, but I knowed he wouldn't make it through that last night. He was just too weak, and Pearl was the stronger one, specially when she was hungry.

When the orderly come to get me for the waiting room, I was painting a new God's face. I was in the art room, working on God's nose and lips trying to match the one I scratched in Papa Noone's house. The nose was a good sturdy nose, long and wide, and the lips was straight but then curved at the ends, almost like a smile. That was the part I couldn't never get right.

I crumpled my picture and the orderly took me by the arm to the waiting room and then left. I just stood in the doorway for a minute until Benjamin invited me in. I wasn't nervous beforehand. I didn't get nervous until I recollected Pearl saying I better talk to Benjamin about the factory. Then, I made me a fist, squeezing it and letting it go. Next, I twisted the button on my sweater, and let out a breath, standing in front of Benjamin. I stared at him a minute. "You're left handed, aren't you?" I asked.

"Yes, I am. How did you know?"

"When you straightened your tie." I nodded toward his neck. "Did they try to get you to use your right hand?"

"They sure did. But after a while, they gave up."

"Hmm," I mumbled. I reckoned it was time we started talking about Violet. "They say my sister's body has arrived up north."

"Yes, by now, I'm sure of it."

Suddenly, a new resident named Juanita leaned into the doorway. She has her a shaved head. "Don't be late, Helen. We've got music appreciation later." I told her I'd be along soon.

"If you prefer, I can come back another day," Benjamin said.

"Oh, no, Mr. Reed. I know how long a drive it can be from Atlanta." I kept on chewing my lower lip. "What would you like to know?"

"First, may I say thank you for seeing me today."

"You're welcome."

"You know, it's funny, but I recall an incident during one of your visits years ago."

"What was it?"

"Well, I must have been maybe five years old at the time. Mother had brought a set of cups and saucers into the parlor for the two of you to have coffee. She was minus one saucer and asked me to retrieve it from the kitchen cabinet. I was not the most graceful child, and on the way from the kitchen, I tripped on the edge of the rug. The saucer took flight, landing inside the umbrella stand."

"Then what happened?"

"By the grace of God, it didn't break. Mother called me to hurry up with the saucer, so I scrambled to return as quickly as I could. When she asked me why I'd been delayed, I told her I had stopped to tie my shoe."

Benjamin was helping me to feel better. I told him so.

After a minute, I recollected the reason for Benjamin's trip to North Carolina. "I wish they would hurry up and put Violet's body back in the ground. She made me keep all her lies for her. Keep them from our daddy. Course, she told me what to do all the time, so I never had to think for myself."

I begin thinking about Violet's bones inside the casket. And the laboratory where they was testing the bones of so many other ladies. I imagined a sort of factory assembly line, where silent bones set waiting for their turn to speak.

Benjamin seemed like a nice man, just like when he was a boy. He was polite and dressed nice too. "May I call you Helen?"

"Certainly you may. I told you that before."

"Pearl mentioned you and Violet both worked together at a factory in Ottawa, Illinois. Do you remember much about it?"

"I remember real good. Clara visited us before the summer of 1923. I was just out of high school, because I quit. I was sixteen and I think Violet was eighteen or so."

"What was it like working there?"

Suddenly, I clamped my mouth tight, making my lips into thin lines. After a minute, I answered. "We worked hard, sometimes six days a week. We had to learn by practicing, but I was one of the best painters there. Clara too."

"What was my mother like at work? Was she just a typical teenager?"

"Well, she worked there longer than me and Violet did, but she was a hard worker. Did you know she could write her own name backwards? She was right-handed, but she could write her name backwards with her left hand."

"She could? No, I never knew that."

"Oh yes, she could do other things too, like cross all her fingers at the top, so her pinky touched the tip of her index finger, like this." I tried to force my fingers together, to show him. When it hurt, I had to stop and rub my hand and wrist.

"Actually, I do remember that one."

He paused a moment and his eyebrows curled into wiggly lines. "Helen, may I ask why you and my mother never mentioned this before? Why you kept the factory a secret?"

My lips parted, but I only stammered. "I... me and Violet..."

Just then, a orderly arrived to let me know it was time for music appreciation. I told Benjamin I had enjoyed his visit.

"One more thing, Helen," he added. I was standing in the doorway, arms folded. "Yes?"

"I just wanted you to know, I'm sorry you've had to go through all this. I'm sure the exhumation was difficult for you. You and your sister must have been very close."

I choked a little in my throat. He was right. Nobody likes to recollect the dreadful things in their lives. Specially not when your own sister gets so sick she can't take care of herself no more, and has sores all over and can't chew her own food. I don't like to recollect Violet unless it's how she was before she got sick. I try not to think of the other girls neither. They had festers on their jaws and fluids leaking from places on their bodies that wasn't meant to leak. We never knowed it wasn't healthy for us to lick the tips of our brushes and swallow radium paint. We was just doing our jobs.

"I loved my sister better than anybody else who ever lived, and that includes Neely."

"Neely?"

"Neely. I live here with her. We share a room together." I leaned forward and picked at a hole in my gown. Then, I guess my voice turned serious. "They say soon we'll be able to wear whatever we want. We can wear our own clothes. I still have some of my old dresses and things from before."

"Are you comfortable here at Mannington, Helen?"

At first, I shook my head in slow motion, my chin swinging wide from one shoulder to the other. Then, I stopped and held my palm against my forehead. When a place you live in is a comfort, it's like as if your life is filled with ever normal thing. Like honeysuckle covering a gate post, or morning glories sprouting up over night. Those are things I find a comfort. Of course, *I'm* a comfort to Neely.

"You know, I don't have to be here. I can walk out through that front door anytime I darn well please, but I won't. I could never leave Neely. She needs me."

#

My puzzle was almost done. For a day and a half I been working on it in the corner of the activities center. After staring at the puzzle pieces so long, I was starting to see puzzle shapes in the walls. Everwhere. Even in my breakfast oatmeal.

Sometimes I can see what people is thinking even before they speak to me, just like Benjamin Reed. I knowed he would be a gentleman. He was such a sweet boy. I liked the way he was dressed, and how he conducted hisself. Not like some of them reporters at the cemetery. They was ugly to me, staring at my suit and my wild hair. It wasn't their fault, really. They didn't know the routine. The only time I get my hair cut and styled is whenever the beautician shows up. She hasn't been here since April.

It didn't bother me none that Benjamin Reed come to visit, except his questions had stirred up those bad memories. Even so, I didn't tell him nothing I didn't want to. There's a lot I don't want nobody to know. And some things I just never like to talk about, like my husband. I get too choked up whenever I tell somebody how he died and so forth. So it's better I don't never talk about him.

I was glad Pearl didn't come along with Benjamin. If she had, I would've had to listen to her talk about Donald Schaeffer, and all about the election in November.

When Pearl signed the papers, she made me go to the gravesite to remove Violet's body from the ground. Pearl wouldn't allow me to wear one of my favorite dresses the way I wanted. Instead, she made me wear a cheap suit from the Ivey's bargain rack. She even made me wear some old shoes that hurt my feet.

If I was to tell anybody about the Radium Dial and what we done to Mr. Andrew Calder, I decided it would either be Benjamin Reed or Adrienne. Of all the people I know, for some reason, I trust them. It sure wouldn't be Pearl. Specially since the other day, when she reminded me how much she wanted to get me out of the hospital for good so's I could go and live with her at her new house in Charlotte once she marries Donald Schaeffer. I just wish I could stay right where I am.

At least at Mannington, folks leave me be most of the time. Like this morning when I painted a new face of God in the art room. Nobody else was there, so I didn't have to hide nothing. I took out the smooth cinnamon-colored paper they have there and slid a brush from the brush jar. I like to use the green one with the flat gray bristles on it. Next, I got me a jar of water and the paints with the white and blue in it, and mixed the two colors together so's I could have me a light blue to go with the white. God's face is always white with a fluffy white beard and bushy white eyebrows. Just like on that grandfather clock.

Papa Noone was always teasing me. He had him a hoarse sound to his laugh. Daddy would take me and Violet over to spend some time there, since our grandma worked nights and he didn't have nobody to talk to. Somehow, me and Papa Noone always ended up alone in his workshop. He said he enjoyed the company of a youngun from time to time while he worked, and Violet was always outside playing on the lawn.

One time, Papa Noone teased me because I couldn't reach to his work bench. He would hold up a penny between his finger and thumb and put it high on the bench just out of my reach, then laugh at me when I couldn't reach high enough to see it. One other time, he teased me because my hair was unruly and even with a ribbon, it was a mess of curls and tangles. Ever time he teased me, I would get to breathing fast and try not to let him see a tear drop to my cheek. I would turn away to wipe it with my hand.

The day I scratched that clock with God's face on it, I was barely old enough to know my letters and numbers. The clock face had Roman numerals on it, which to me looked like tiny black toothpicks, criss-crossed against each other. Papa Noone left the work bench for a minute. Left me alone. Before he left, he said he had to go see about a piece-a-property, which meant he had to use the privy. He said to don't touch nothing while he was gone, so I just looked at things. I walked over to the tools and touched the blade of a sharp knife. I spent some time gazing at a set of wrenches and a rusty awl. Leaning against the wall behind a wood box I seen a hay hook, like a farmer would use.

I pushed the wood stool over to the clock and climbed up to get me a closer look. God's face was smooth with no wrinkles, but his hair was bright white with robin egg blue and white paint, so's it would look pure. In a circle shape around God's face was the Roman numerals, one to twelve. I, II, X, V, and so forth. I tried to pick off one of the toothpicks, but I found out *they* was painted on too.

Just as I was climbing down from the stool, Papa Noone come back into the room and caught me. "Too short to reach God, are ya?" His hoarse sounding laugh got me to breathing fast again. He laughed at me until I was back standing on the floor. This time, I didn't shed a tear, but my fists curled up into a ball and I punched my own self in the stomach until I was bruised. Somebody knocked on his front door, so he had to tend to his customer. After he left again, that was when I took the hay hook from the floor and climbed back up the stool. The hay hook was heavy, but I held it tight in my grip and raised it to the clock face. Scritch scritch. I peered over my shoulder to be sure Papa Noone didn't see me. I stratched a line from God's high smooth forehead, down to his beard, like a deep scar.

Next thing I know, Violet is yelling at me to get down off the stool, but it was too late. Papa Noone seen what I done and he cursed. He give me a good spanking on my bare bottom. That night after me and Violet got home, I cried myself to sleep. I got no supper. My stomach was raw with pain from being empty on the inside, and the outside of my stomach was sore with swollen purple welts on it.

CHAPTER ELEVEN

Just as I was about to fit a new piece into the picture of the old covered bridge, the door to the activity center opened. Nurse Flora stood behind Mavis Payton, pushing her inside the room. I call Mavis a "rubber band resident," because she always snaps and comes back. Sometimes Mavis's husband drops her off after she stays drunk for three days and don't take care of her children. I wondered if this would be her final time coming, but it most likely won't be.

As soon as me and Mavis looked in each others' eyes, Mavis took a step forward. Flora nodded at me, and then turned to leave. Mavis smacked her chewing gum and blinked her squinty brown eyes, while shifting her boy-shaped hips around the pool table and the Monopoly game to get herself over to my table. When she reached me, Mavis stood still waiting for me to say something. I just kept on with my puzzle. Mavis picked up a piece and tried to force it. "That's not right. Give it here," I said, snatching it away.

"Sor-ry," she whined, sticking out her bony chin. "I remember you from before. You're Helen, aren't you?"

Why should I answer? I kept silent, pretending she wasn't there. That's what I always did with her, because she always tried to get on my bad side. If I ignored Mavis, maybe I could finish the puzzle before dinner.

Mavis leaned both hands on the table edge, with her face not inches from mine. "Look, I don't want to be here any more than you do, so why don't we just try to get along?" I didn't like Mavis's gum breath in my face, so I pushed her on the chin with my palm until she straightened back up. Folding her arms, Mavis snapped her chewing gum and stared at the puzzle.

I guess after a time, Mavis found some other way to amuse herself. She watched the men play pool for a while, then she hovered over a foursome playing hearts at the card table.

When it was time for dinner, I was first out of the activity center, but not the first in line for my food tray. I waited behind ten or twelve other ladies before I got mine.

No dessert again. Flora and the other nurses got so mad a couple of nights ago, they told everbody in Six-A they would have no dessert for the next two weeks, because of what that one dumb resident did at the end of the hall. Nurse Flora asked Lilly in room twelve to take her underdrawers and brassieres off the radiator in her room. They was hanging up to dry, and Flora didn't think it looked very nice, so she said, "If those garments aren't off that radiator by the next time I come down this hall, there will be no dessert for the next two weeks. For *any* of you."

Well, somebody was supposed to be "look-out" so the garments in question could be took down before Nurse Flora returned, but somehow, that failed. Now, I was on my second day with no dessert, and I'd ran out of tokens until the next time they pass them out, so I couldn't even afford a candy bar or nothing sweet.

Instead, I had me a extra banana from breakfast, and a small can of sugar hid in the chifforobe. Since Neely was gone on a day pass, I could break up the banana and sprinkle it with sugar without nobody getting a headache, because bananas always give Neely a headache. And I surely wouldn't want Flora to catch me enjoying my dessert, so I would have to wait until the afternoon shift was over.

I set alone at the big round table, waiting for somebody to come. Soon, Delores Winegarten set with me, then old Mrs. Rival, and then Mavis Payton took the last seat. Without asking, Mavis scooped her mashed potatoes right onto my plate. "I hate the mashed potatoes here," she said, licking her thumb. "You can have mine."

Something in the way Mavis said that—"You can have mine"—reminded me of Pearl. It wasn't no kind offer to share food. It was a command. There wasn't nothing polite or refined about Mavis.

When I think about what it will be like to live with Pearl, I can't exactly picture it in my mind. She's fussy about her house. If I'm visiting there and ever leave a coffee cup on the table, she says, "You know perfectly well, I don't allow that."

She was always that a-way, all worried about things being out of place. Even back when she was a young girl she kept her room tidy. Sometimes, she would have a girlfriend over, and they would get into some mighty big fights about how fussy Pearl was.

I have no idea what Donald Schaeffer's house looks like in Charlotte. Pearl tried to describe it, but all I recollect is it was in a old neighborhood lined with oak trees. Mannington has plenty of old oak trees. Plenty of other nice trees too. I just can't see no advantage to living in Charlotte, with all that traffic and noise. No advantage at all.

#

I seen that man again. The one with the overalls. This time, he wasn't wearing his jacket. He appeared to be a man of about 50 years or so. I was setting out on the back porch, when he walked from the outside of the infirmary building to the commissary. At the time, I was smoking alongside the Avery Building porch, just getting some sun.

Since the man stood at a distance, I couldn't call out to him to stop, or ask him who he was. A few yards away, I seen Mavis Payton walking to the porch from the sidewalk. I asked her if she could see the man.

"There, do you see him?"

Mavis made a shield over her forehead with her hand, to block out the sun. She squinted anyway, like as if the sun was in her eyes. Then, she took down her hand and got close to my face, like she always does, smacking her chewing gum. "I heard about you. You see people who aren't there."

I wondered how Mavis could of heard about it. I hadn't never told her. Then, I explained. "Dr. Stokes told me if somebody else can see him, then he's a real person."

Mavis made a little crooked smile with the corner of her mouth. "I don't see nobody."

Course, when I looked again, the man was gone.

"Helen, you probably need more medicine," she said, chuckling. "It ain't working."

As far as I knowed, my medicine was working just fine. I don't have no more bad dreams, and I feel good most of the time. All I needed was for one person to see the man, so's I would know he was real.

Then, if he *was* real, I wanted to know who he was.

#

Nurse Flora called me to the nurses' station again. Catty-corner from the station is a small room with a solid door they could lock you inside of, but this time, the room had a table and chairs. Pearl was in one of the chairs, Dr. Stokes was in the other, and a nurse I hadn't never seen before stood in the corner with her arms crossed over her waist. "Go on in, Helen. They're waiting for you."

I set at the table across from Dr. Stokes. It was too hot in that little room, so I fanned my face with my hand. Dr. Stokes had one of those patient folders. He opened it and stared at one of the papers inside. Then, he took off his dark rimmed glasses and pinched his upper nose with his eyes closed. After a second, he put his glasses back on. "Would you care for a cigarette, Helen?" he asked. I told him I would, and he lit one for me and shared his ashtray. "If you like, we have fresh coffee for you. Cream and sugar, just the way you like it."

I asked for a cup of coffee too. Dr. Stokes fixed it for me, while Pearl set still. He handed me a thin cloth napkin. "Pearl is here today so we can talk about your discharge."

I just smoked for a minute and didn't say nothing. They tricked me into this. Offering me a cigarette and asking if I would like coffee with sugar and cream. Nobody told me ahead of time. They expected me to just show up so I did. They always did things that a-way. It made me want to be cross with them, but I stayed quiet.

Pearl opened her handbag and took out her reading glasses. Dr. Stokes was handing her one sheet after the next to read and sign. "Helen, stop fidgeting," she said, signing a new paper.

Dr. Stokes talked to me all about how my new medication was helping me feel better. Then, he said I would need to see a different doctor from Gastonia a couple of times ever week. Name of Dr. Meyer. Then after Pearl and Donald got married and all of us moved to Charlotte, we would switch me to a new doctor there. I listened to it all. I set still while my coffee with sugar and cream got cold.

"How come everbody here wants me to leave? What's gonna happen to Neely? Have you asked her how she's gonna get along without me?"

I was cross now. Nothing much makes me more cross than people deciding things behind my back.

"Helen, we don't want you to leave us." Dr. Stokes explained. "It's just that this is a state run facility with more than 1700 residents, and the majority of them are much sicker than you are. Or, they don't have the family resources you do. They have no one to go live with, who'll care for them, the way Pearl will care for you. She'll even be handling your finances for you. As an out-patient, you'll begin receiving a social security check. So you see, Helen, you're really quite fortunate."

"But who will give me my medicine? Who will light my cigarettes for me? I won't have my puzzles. And what about my dresses? Can I bring my dresses?" I was starting to recollect that day at the dial factory when Glenda, the 14-year-old girl, punched Bess in the back. I wanted to do the same to Pearl.

Setting her pen on the table, Pearl snatched off her glasses. "Stop it, Helen. Dr. Stokes and I have already discussed this, so I'll tell you everything you need to know. Now let's get your things." She scooted away from the table, and asked the doctor to write her a script for a thirty-day supply of Haldol.

"Oh, and one more thing. Doctor Stokes, maybe you can talk some sense into Helen. I want her to go have that radium testing done at the laboratory. Didn't you say you've heard of the factory in Illinois?"

I hoped Pearl had forgot about my letter that come in the mail. Just like the one for Violet. Dr. Stokes leaned up in his chair. "I'm considered by some to be an expert on the subject. At my last position in Michigan, I treated a former dial painter." He took off his glasses and smiled, like as if he was proud. He said he had him a personal connection, because of relatives in Ottawa. He said a close friend of his mother's worked at the factory in the 1920s.

I didn't like the way him and Pearl was trying to force me to do so many things I didn't want to do, but I listened to what he had to say. A friend of his mother's, name of Mrs. Serena Redmon, told a disturbing tale before she died. She said in 1928 she recollected having her a test for radon. She was with a whole group of workers from the factory. He told Pearl Mrs. Redmon said nobody never informed them of the results, and she later found out it was because the dial company didn't want them to know. It would've started a riot.

"I'm sure it would have," Pearl said.

Dr. Stokes shuffled his shoes under the table. "In 1935, Mrs. Redmon died from necrosis of the hip and jaw."

"Lord have mercy." Now Pearl was shaking her head. "It seems this story is repeated time and again." Then, Pearl glared at me. "If you don't want to die of a horrible disease like that, you better agree to get tested too."

I snubbed out my cigarette and pushed the coffee cup toward Dr. Stokes. "I...I don't want to." Just the idea of it made my hands shake.

"You can stop this act now. We know you worked there, Helen. It's not a secret anymore. Doctor, she won't listen. I've got a notion to just go up to that factory in Illinois and see it for myself."

Dr. Stokes put his glasses back on, and twined his fingers together in front of him. "You could visit the city of Ottawa, but you wouldn't be able to see the old factory."

"Why is that?" Pearl asked.

"A few years back, the city demolished the building. The resulting rubble and debris was so radioactive they had to bury it in landfills."

After that, Pearl just shut up.

She reached behind her for a cardboard box with only one flap left. She held it up in front of me. I didn't think all my things would fit into just one box, specially my good dresses, but maybe we could carry them over one arm.

Dr. Stokes stood up and reached over to shake Pearl's hand. I chewed my lip again and tasted blood. I reckoned I would have to go with Pearl, even though it was truly the last thing I wanted to do.

CHAPTER TWELVE

I hate good-byes. I reckon most people do. Over the years, many folks have left Mannington. Some have left more than once, like Mavis Payton.

Five or six ladies was squeezed into our room. It was crowded enough, with Pearl and Neely there, and me trying to load my things into the box. Neely was crying again, and it made me want to cry, too.

One of the ladies, Mrs. Wilmont from down the hall, brought me a old greeting card. She did like we all have to from time to time—she crossed out the name that was on it first and then signed her own. "Thank you so much," I said. I hugged her, and the next resident come in to say good-bye to me too. I had to stop and hug Neely. She was in her bed facing the corner, sniffling like as if she had her a bad cold. "Neely, I'll be back to visit real soon. Don't worry." I tried to make my voice sound sweet and quiet, like as if I was talking to a butterfly that might flutter and be gone.

"I don't want you to leave, Helen," she sobbed. I pulled the edge of my blouse from my slacks, and wiped her cheeks and eyes. "I don't want to leave neither. You gotta get ahold of yourself, Neely. Even if I was to stay, you know as well as me, folks don't live forever. Sooner or later, you're gonna have to learn to take care of your own self."

Just after that, the head nurse come into the room. Nurse Dubois. She said to come to her office for a minute, so I followed her down the hall.

Me and Nurse Dubois walked past the drinking fountain and the nurse's bathroom to her private office. She handed me a little bag made of shiny paper. "You know, we don't normally do this, but the staff chipped in to get you a little something. For all those times you worked back here and helped us." I recollected stuffing all those envelopes.

I opened the bag quick, and inside was a pair of white gloves. I tried them on, and they was a little big, but I was happy to have them. I grinned and thanked Nurse Dubois. Then, some of the other nurses come over to say good-bye to me too.

When I got back to the room, Pearl had to spoil everthing, when she said we already had us enough to pack when we move to Charlotte, and I had to give the gloves back. She said my box was too overflowed. Quick as lightening, I stuck my hand inside my packed box, yanked out a couple of old scarves, and threw them on the bed. "Now there's room." I said, and put my new gloves in where the scarves was only moments before. Pearl just rolled her eyes.

#

Once we was at Pearl's house, she took me to my room, which used to be her extra bedroom. I hung my things up in the closet, then looked for a good place to hide my EXCELLENCE IN TRAINING plaque Mrs. Peltz had give me for being a good painter. I opened the bottom dresser drawer and put it in under some of my winter clothes. The last thing I needed was for Pearl to say we didn't have no room for it at the new house in Charlotte.

Next, I took my toothbrush to the sink across the hall. On the counter top, Pearl had her a old can of Colgate powder, just like Mrs. Yearsall used to have back at the boarding house.

Mrs. Yearsall wasn't too happy that night when the sheriff come to call. I recollect the look in her eyes, when she seen him come to the house asking for us girls. His automobile was parked out front. We could see from our upstairs window.

When he knocked on the door downstairs, I jumped out of my skin. "Good evening, ma'am. I'm looking for three young ladies here at your boarding house who work at the Radium Dial," he said.

Mrs. Yearsall said he was in the right place, and told him our names. "Clara Hart, Violet Meisner and her younger sister, Helen."

Since I knowed it was a sheriff at the door, my heart was flipping. "Violet." I tried to whisper, but it come out louder than I wanted. Violet was staring at her shoes, ready to tie the shoelaces. We both jumped when Mrs. Yearsall called to us from the parlor, saying we had us a visitor. As we passed her on the stairs, she said to Violet, "I don't want any trouble in my boarding house."

The sheriff was a young man, maybe only a few years older than Violet. He had him a nice smile, but with heavy eyebrows and a thin purple scar on his cheek. When he seen Violet, he set his sheriff's hat on the table and nodded to her. "Are you Violet Meisner?"

"Yes, I am. And may I introduce my sister, Helen."

Clara introduced herself too, but set down right away.

He nodded to all of us, saying he was happy to make our acquaintance. We asked him to set down, and he did. I was about to lose control of my bladder, and my mouth was clamped shut, so's my teeth wouldn't chatter.

"I'm sure you ladies have heard of the tragic fire last week at the home of Andrew Calder."

We said we had heard, saying what a sad thing it was for his family.

"I'm speaking to all the Radium Dial employees to see if anyone might have any information."

"Any information about what, Sheriff?" Violet asked, interlocking her fingers on her lap.

"We've got some evidence someone may have *set* the fire. We don't think it was merely an accident."

I couldn't make my knee stop bouncing, until Violet flung me a ugly look. I tried to hold still. I decided to just listen.

"Why on earth would anyone want to hurt a nice old man like Mr. Calder?" Violet asked, her voice dripping with honey. "We all loved him at the factory, didn't we Helen?"

"Ye-yes. We all did." I nodded extra to give the sheriff the right idea.

"Well, if you young ladies hear of anything that might assist in this investigation, you just telephone the sheriff's office. The family is prepared to prosecute to the fullest extent of the law."

He handed us a card, which Violet took from his grip, sliding it down the front of her dress and smiling, like as if she was smitten with him.

As the sheriff turned to leave, he reached for his hat from the table, but Clara got it for him first. We was standing right behind him, all but shooing him out the door, but he spun back around. "One more thing, for my records, do you mind if I ask where you were the night of the sixteenth?"

I didn't have to answer none, because Violet had practiced this for hours. "I remember that night very well, Sheriff. That was the night my sister and I went to the Ottawa Dairy Company with our friend Clara here, and we helped some of the old people. Helped them walk with their canes and so forth. Some of them were mighty hunched over."

"And after that?"

"After that, we were tired, so we went home."

After the sheriff left, all three of us girls done exactly the same thing. We all took deep breaths, and let our breaths out into the air. Then Violet pulled the sheriff's card from the top of her dress and tore it into pieces.

#

My first morning at her house, Pearl woke me up early. She said she wanted me to rise and shine ever morning before she went off to work, so's she could give me my first dose of Haldol. Since I'm already a early riser, I went along with it. I made my bed, just like at Mannington, and held my cigarette up to my lips so's she could light it.

"Oh come on, Helen, you're not in an institution anymore. You can light your own, just like when you're here on a day pass." Then she handed me a book of matches that was almost empty. I told her thank you.

After I had me a piece of toast, I drank the whole rest of the pot of coffee. I was jittery for a while, but I didn't care because Pearl told me I could add more sugar and cream in it whenever I wanted. Then, she said if I wanted to watch the television all day, I could, but I had to be out of my robe and dressed nice in case somebody was to come by. She said I could pick up two different stations from Charlotte, and maybe if the weather was good, I could get one from Spartanburg, South Carolina too, but it would probably be the same program. Then she left for work, and told me she would call me when she was able to.

For a while, I wandered around looking at things. I touched all her dishes and the trinkets on her shelves and over the fireplace. If she was home, she wouldn't never let me do it, so I knowed I had a few hours to touch whatever I pleased.

Then, I went in her closet. She had her a closet full of dresses and two nice coats in plastic wrappers, and ten or eleven pairs of shoes. On the top shelf was some magazines, and a round hat box with stripes on it. When I was done looking, I made sure I closed the closet and went back to the television.

Pearl's cat was setting way up on top of the hi fi, and there was a funny sound under my feet. It was a squish sound, and my slippers was wet on the bottom. I stared at Pearl's rug, and it was watery, like soaked ground after a steady rain. Water was running on the floor from beside her kitchen. I reckoned she forgot to turn off the water or maybe the commode had ran over. Maybe it was *me* who left the water on somewheres, but I couldn't find where it was from. I clutched my hand around my throat, because I was scared I would get into trouble and lose my tokens. Then I remembered I was at Pearl's and she didn't have no tokens anyhow.

The best thing for me I reckoned was to get outside, before the water overtook me, so I buttoned up my robe and went out into the yard. A man in a automobile drove by, and he just stared at me. I waved my arms, but he kept on. Then a lady in a station wagon seen me waving my arms, but her children stuck their noses against the back window and laughed. Then she drove on down the road.

Next, I tried to walk to the neighbor's house, but nobody was home, except for the dog. He wouldn't stop barking at me, so I just set on the curb to wait for Pearl. Even though it was early in the day, the sun was bright hot, and I just set there on the curb, trying to stay cool. That was all I could do, considering.

After a short while, a automobile slowed down and pulled up into Pearl's driveway. It was a sheriff's vehicle— that of Gaston County, with a black and gold star on the side of the door, and a red light on top, only the red light was turned off. When I got up from the curb, my heart was jarring me from the inside, and I couldn't barely swallow.

The sheriff got out of his car and asked me what was the trouble. He asked me my name and where did I live. Because I was on edge, I couldn't answer everthing just right. My thoughts was all in a tangle.

When he got near me, I seen a big angry boil on his neck and I screamed. Just like back at Mannington, only there wasn't no nurses this time. The sheriff made me get into the back seat of his car, and asked if I could calm down. First, I had to stop looking at his neck, because I wasn't expecting to see it, and it was making me more fretful. Finally I stopped screaming, and he asked me why I was out on the curb.

"The inside is all wet."

"Inside the house?" he stared at the front door. He asked me my name and I told him. I remined him it was all wet inside, but I didn't know why.

"Hmm. Let's go in and take a look."

"Oh no. Pearl told me don't let nobody inside. She's my niece. She said to keep the door locked."

The sheriff took off his cap and rubbed his short hair with his whole hand. "Maybe we can go in and telephone Pearl right now, so she can come home."

I had to think hard a minute. I started in chewing my lip. "Maybe we should."

I let the sheriff inside, and when he stepped on the rug, his eyes got big and I heard him mumble "Jesus," but I don't reckon he knowed I heard him. He asked me where was the telephone, and I had to stop and think a minute. I told him it was in the kitchen, on the wall. Then he opened the closet next to the Frigidaire, and he said the hot water heater was causing all the trouble. He reached around back of the pipes and turned it off.

"Do you have Pearl's phone number?" he asked.

I blinked my eyes and scratched a spot over my nose. "I can't recollect where she put it."

While the sheriff snooped around for a telephone number, I set at the kitchen table and took off my wet slippers. I didn't like the way my feet was wet, so I rested them on a chair.

"Where does she work?" he asked.

"In Gastonia. She's got her a personnel job at Belk's but I don't know the number."

He picked up the telephone and dialed zero. Then he asked for the operator to get him Belk's, and it was official police business.

In a little while, Pearl come home. She was madder than a nest of hornets, and cried when she saw her good shag rug ruined by all that water. The sheriff tipped his hat and left us alone. Then Pearl got on the telephone to Donald, and then she got on with Tony. When she hung up, she hollered at me to help her get towels, but there was too much water, and the towels didn't help much.

Then Pearl cried some more and swept some of the water out with a broom. She said Donald was having a insurance man come around to look at it. She told me to go to my room and stay there until she wanted me, so I did.

The whole time I was in my room, I was wishing I was back at Mannington, where I could have me some peace and quiet.

CHAPTER THIRTEEN

While me and Clara was washing dishes at the boarding house, we got to whispering about things. She nudged me with her elbow. She had a sour look on her face, which she had most of the time now. Since the fire.

"Have you been having any... bad dreams?"

I give a little shrug when she handed me the next plate to dry. "Well, I have always been one to have bad dreams anyway," I told her, setting the dry plate in the stack. "Ever since I was a little girl, remember?"

Clara said she recollected one time I woke up screaming from a bad dream when we was all sleeping outside on the screened-in porch back in Belmont. Our geography teacher at Belmont High used to say dreams was just your mind giving you its two cents worth.

Then Clara stopped washing her dish. Her arms turned limp, and the dish slid into the soapy water. She wiped her eyes by raising her shoulder and lowering her face to it. When she spoke, she stared straight ahead of herself. "I'm thinking of going to confession. I haven't been in a long time."

Just standing next to my friend, I could feel what she was feeling. I shared the same tightness in my belly. The same worry in my head. My ears burned.

"What's it like to go to confession, Clara?"

She stared over at me, tears still setting in her eyes. "It's like you send all your troubles up to God. The priest listens, then he tells God for you, and he gives you a penance. Like a little punishment."

Suddenly, I sucked in a breath. My whisper got loud. "But Clara. We promised not to never tell nobody."

"Shhh. It's okay, Helen. A priest never tells what he hears in confession. There's nothing to worry about."

I thought about it for a minute. "Okay then. If you do go to confession, can you choose which priest you tell it to? Can you go on the train to Chicago and tell one of them there?"

Clara dried her hands and sniffled through her nose. "I suppose I could. Somebody who doesn't even know me. Like that day we went to see the fortune teller."

"I think that would be better."

I begin to think about how it was ever Sunday when we took Mrs. Yearsall's children to church. We didn't never ask her, but I wondered why she didn't take them her own self. Back in Belmont, me and Violet went to church ever Sunday. But I knowed some people don't like to go to church, because then they have to be good all week, and that's hard to do.

I reckon I could at least tell God about Mr. Calder myself, even without a priest. Tell him straight away what we done. But then, I decided that would be silly because by this time, God already knowed.

#

Recollecting about God got me thinking again about the grandfather clock. One thing Violet never knowed was later that night after I scratched up the clock face, I started in scratching my stomach too. Only my nails was so short, I couldn't scratch very hard. Sometimes I wonder why I can't just forget a incident that happened to me so many years ago. It still comes to my mind, like ever time a new Monday comes around or when I feel like it's time for a cigarette.

Pearl was planning what to serve for supper the night Benjamin and Adrienne and Tony all come to eat. Benjamin was back in town visiting, and Pearl wanted to make a nice supper before he had to go back to Atlanta. "Helen, do you think I should make carrots or peas?"

I told her either one would suit me just fine.

Since Pearl's carpet is half torn up, Tony was at Pearl's house part of the day instead of at work. He has him a fixed-up and polished '57 Chevy, which is always blocking the driveway, specially when somebody comes over. Soon it was time for Benjamin to come. I heard him from the kitchen, where I was helping Pearl stir the gravy. "I'm Tony. Pearl's son. You must be Benjamin."

"It's nice to meet you, Tony."

After that, Tony left and went down the hall.

Benjamin come into the kitchen and hugged both me and Pearl, then asked if he could help with anything, but Pearl said for him to have a seat. "I'm so sorry about the carpet."

Benjamin said he didn't mind at all.

"Don't expect Adrienne to be on time," Pearl said. "She's always late." She opened the oven and leaned her tall body forward. Roast beef and seasoned potatoes was waiting in the oven.

While Pearl placed the last of the food on the table, one more car pulled up at the front of the house. Pearl said in a low voice, "Must be Adrienne. Didn't I tell you she would be late? She works a couple of jobs, so maybe one kept her," Pearl added.

Benjamin straightened his tie and stepped forward to shake Adrienne's hand. He was busy staring at her whole body, but I couldn't blame him with the way her clothing was so tight. Above the waist, she wore only a thin halter top, and below, those tight flare-leg jeans. Her youthful skin glowed, and her straight, light brown hair fell gently over her bosoms, like a veil. I knowed Benjamin was quite a few years older than Adrienne. She was in her late twenties, and Benjamin was near to Pearl's age, just in his forties.

Adrienne smiled and reached her hand to him, just as Tony interrupted, asking about supper.

Pearl had already decided who would set in what seats in the dining room. I set across from Tony and Adrienne, Pearl set at the head of the table, with Benjamin at the other end. I decided I would become as quiet as a mouse, just listening and watching while I ate. Across from me Tony and Adrienne hardly never looked at each other, but sometimes, Tony poked his tongue just out of his lips at her, which made him grin. Then Adrienne just looked disgusted.

Once everbody had them a plate of food, Pearl spread butter on a small piece of dinner roll. "Adrienne, Benjamin is staying at the motor court. Maybe you'll see him there."

Adrienne smiled. "I clean rooms," she said, smiling a little smile.

"She also works at the clinic," Pearl added.

"You're a nurse?" he asked.

"Yes. I'm a practical nurse. I graduated last spring." Adrienne glanced over at Tony, then tilted her head toward him. "Tonight's the first night this week we've spent more than a few minutes together."

If I hadn't looked just then, I would of missed it, but when Benjamin looked at Adrienne, he blushed. I think he was taking a glance at her bosoms again.

After a time, they got to talking about the radium. Pearl wondered why some of the women got sick and others didn't. Benjamin answered. He said it depended on a person's individual body chemistry and how much radium paint they'd ingested.

Tony asked about how come the managers and supervisors allowed the girls to do something so dangerous to their bodies, and I answered it was because we was just working at a job and following directions.

Tony got a evil look to his eyes again. "I wouldn't want my shit to glow in the dark just so some big shot in an office could line his pockets with spun gold."

I know it was wrong for our supervisors, but I reckon no matter how much folks would like to, they can't go back and change things they done wrong. Besides, when I recollect Mrs. Peltz kissing that brush with her toothless mouth, I don't know if supervisors like her really got away with much. Maybe she was just doing *her* job just like all us girls.

With the meal half over, Pearl asked Benjamin if he wanted any seconds. "You don't like vegetables much, do you?" she asked, pouring him a second glass of sweet ice tea.

He smiled. "I'm afraid not. Just never acquired a taste for them. I'm more of the meat and potatoes type."

Tony scooted back from the table, taking Adrienne by the hand. But she slid her hand out from his, reaching for her soda. "Tony, I'm not finished yet. Please wait for me on the porch."

Even though she spoke to Tony, Adrienne's eyes was on Benjamin, like as if she wanted to get to know him better. For a second or two, Tony and Benjamin locked eyes. Then Tony shrugged and grabbed his lighter off the window sill and went out to the porch.

Pearl stood at the sink, scraping her plate with a knife. "Adrienne, would you like any more roast? Benjamin, would you care for any?"

Benjamin answered that he honestly couldn't eat one more bite.

Adrienne brushed her long hair from her shoulders. "I think I'll quit while I'm ahead." She winked at me, then sipped her drink. Both her hands gripped her glass, like as if she couldn't find no place else to put them. I reckoned she had took one of her pills just before supper. "Helen, I understand Benjamin came to see you at Mannington," she asked.

"Yes, he did. I enjoyed meeting with him."

Benjamin said he was glad I was out of there and living with Pearl now.

After a minute, Pearl had her a telephone call from Donald, which she took in her bedroom. So Adrienne and Benjamin just talked between theirselves.

Adrienne started fidgeting with the salt shaker, twirling it in circles, while Benjamin got a excited look to his eyes. They continued talking together for a good while, like as if they had a great deal in common.

For some reason, it just seemed more natural for Adrienne to get along with Benjamin instead of with Tony. I recollected how Jesse and I got along the first few years. Once, me and Jesse saved up and took us a trip to the Smoky Mountains. We stayed in a one-room cabin, with lace curtains and a stone fireplace. One other time, for our 10th anniversary, we took us a train down to Florida and stayed in the Palms Away Motor Inn for three days and two nights. On that trip, Jesse give me a fancy hat with rabbit fur on the edges.

Adrienne leaned toward the table, with her arms crossed. "Benjamin, do you mind if I make an observation?"

"It's not about my disinterest in vegetables, is it?"

We both snickered at that one. Then Adrienne said she changed her mind. She didn't want to give her observation after all, but Benjamin said he insisted.

After Adrienne set still for a moment, she finally got the nerve to say what she wanted to. "Do you know you're a very attractive man? Helen, don't you think Benjamin's attractive?"

He answered her, but his face took on a blush when he did. "You're only the fifth or sixth person today who's mentioned it."

She giggled again.

For a minute or two, they chatted some more. Adrienne told Benjamin about her brother Ron. "I'm hopeful he'll be able to come back to the states in time for my birthday. That would be the best birthday present ever."

She told Benjamin how her brother got shot up in the leg pretty bad in Vietnam, and the doctors said he might get disability if he couldn't learn to walk better. He was going to need more operations on his leg. "You know, I'd take him in if he needed me to," Adrienne said. "I'd be happy to take care of him." Adrienne is a good nurse. And a good sister.

After that, Tony come back in again from the porch, with a cigarette pinched between his finger and thumb. He stomped through the room, reached for a ashtray, and stomped back to the door. He held it open a few inches. "Adrienne, you coming?"

Tony held the door, glaring at Benjamin, like as if he was starting a fight. After excusing herself and setting her silverware and plate in the sink, Adrienne tiptoed behind Tony to the porch. He allowed the door to slam, and me and Benjamin blinked.

Pearl come back from her phone call, and Benjamin asked her if he could help clear the plates.

"No thank you. You're my guest."

I stayed in my seat, finishing my iced tea. Then I excused myself to go lie down. While I was in my room again, I heard Pearl and Benjamin talking, just like before.

"Tony doesn't think much of Helen," Pearl said. "When he was nine years old, I told him the story of how she first ended up in Mannington, and ever since that time, he's acted strange around her."

"Strange in what way?"

"Like he was scared of her. Before I told him, she was just like a grandmother to him. Whenever we visited her at Mannington, he would sit on her lap and she would kiss him on his cheek. He'd never known her any other way than as a mental patient. Of course, I knew everything because I was thirteen years old when Justice, her husband, was killed in the war. That was when we put Helen away."

Benjamin was quiet for a moment before he answered. "I can't imagine how difficult it must have been for her." He paused a minute, then continued. "But was it something more than just losing her husband in the war?"

"Helen was always a little unstable. Always convinced she was dying of cancer. But I suppose it was the way Uncle Jesse died that caused her eventual breakdown, and the idea of it was too shocking for Tony, too."

"How did he die?"

"My uncle died in a battle near the end of the war. He died instantly from decapitation. Oh, and Benjamin...his head was never found."

When Pearl said that, I squinted my eyes and covered my ears. Then I pretended I never heard it at all.

Chapter Fourteen

One afternoon, me and Violet was hanging out clothes to dry on Mrs. Yearsall's clothes line. I held up a pair of little Frank's underdrawers and clipped a clothes pin to the waist. "Violet, do you believe in the afterlife?"

She stared at me, shaking out a dish cloth from the basket of wet clothes. She snapped the wet cloth in the air. "Of course I do. Don't you?"

"I think so." I told her I hadn't never seen a ghost or had any sign that the soul went right on after somebody was dead, but I still wanted to believe. "It's just like faith in anything you can't see," I said. "Like believing that our mama is up in heaven, and maybe she's smiling down on us right now."

"How can you be so dumb and still be my sister?"

"I'm not dumb. Don't you think Mama is up in heaven?"

"Of course not. If you take your own life, you go straight to hell."

I stopped hanging clothes for a minute and tried to recollect that picture of our mama when she was young, and now, what it would be like for her to be in eternal damnation. It give me a itchy feel to my skin.

Me and Violet didn't talk for a few minutes. I reckon we was both thinking about things, and about hell. It made me think about God's face on that clock. About time and how God is always with us. "Maybe she didn't know she would die if she swallowed the poison. Maybe she was out in the shed that day, and just wanted to take a little taste, to see if she could tolerate it or not."

Violet got a mean look to her eyes. "Oh, she knew all right. Daddy said she'd been talking about it for a long time. She kept on saying she couldn't live like this, and she didn't care what happened."

I hung up a pair of socks and reached for a blouse. "Violet, do you care what happens? I mean, when you die, won't you go to hell for what you done?"

She froze in place for a minute, then continued. "Helen, I won't mind so much going to hell when I die. At least I'll finally get to see Mama."

#

Me and Adrienne was under the big tree in Pearl's front yard setting in folding chairs. It was a cool summer day, just after a rain. I pushed my sweater sleeves up my arms, and asked her to tell me how her brother was.

"I'm supposed to find out tomorrow. He may be coming home soon."

For a minute or two, Adrienne told me some things I never knowed about Ron. "In high school everyone thought he was a genius. He was really good in science, but you'd never know it from his grades. He was such a hard worker, but he was always running into bad luck. Plus, he has a problem with authority figures." Adrienne rolled her eyes when she said that. "Although since being in the Army, he's had to work through *that*."

"Sounds like you were very proud of him as a youngun."

She paused a moment before she answered. "I wasn't there with him during his last years in high school, but we kept in touch by mail."

"You left home right soon after you graduated?"

"Before, actually." She give a shrug of her shoulders. Then I recollected about her going to her first birth. "Adrienne, tell me about the baby."

"Oh, Helen, it was so emotional and exhausting. So exciting. So…" She had to stop and decide what to say next.

"For one thing, I felt guilty about being there."

"Why?"

She stared down at her fingernails. "Because I hated to disappoint Tony and cancel our date to the Grateful Dead concert. He'd been looking forward to it for months, and he'd already bought the tickets."

"It's just like I told you at the hospital that day. You can't always plan when a youngun comes into the world."

"You are so right."

"Did you have a idea the mama was about to be ready that night?"

"Oh, I knew. She'd phoned three times in three days about the pain in her lower back."

Then, I got sad because I was recollecting how years earlier, girls would lose their babies, like Violet's little boy William, or like me who couldn't have no children at all. When the doctor told Violet William wouldn't live more than a few days, her and Grady cried together. In fact, Grady didn't know how to hold little William, so he asked me to hold him instead.

I set in a rocker with the baby, with his little nose and his chest breathing so hard and I cried, thinking how Violet had two, and I couldn't even have one.

But I really don't know which was worse. A lifetime missing a child you almost had, or a lifetime of wishing you could have younguns, but they never come.

"In the old days, they didn't know the things you know now about giving birth to babies. They didn't have all them tests and things. No machines, except for x-rays and special kinds of sun lamps." Pearl and her twin brother little William had to be set under one of them lamps. But it only helped Pearl.

"I can't imagine what that must've been like." Adrienne cocked her head to one side. "You know Helen? I envy you. You're from a... simpler time."

"I reckon so."

"I don't know why I've spent all this money on an education, when I see someone like you. I'm amazed at how you've been schooled by life, instead of earning diplomas."

I reckon I've learned plenty over the years. I coaxed Adrienne to continue. She lifted her long hair up into a pony tail, then allowed it to fall over her shoulders. Her green eyes sparkled when she told the next part.

"When the baby was just about to be born, the midwife reached for my hand, and she held it against the mother's belly. I gasped when I felt the baby moving inside. I felt his tiny shoulder beginning to dip forward."

"How exciting."

"You know of course, my eyes filled with tears, and I blinked them onto my T-shirt. Then I smiled, realizing I was about to witness a textbook delivery."

Adrienne seemed like as if birthing babies was the most important thing in the world to her.

"She turned the infant so its feet were in the air, and I saw it was a girl."

I couldn't help it. I clapped my hands together, and my eyes got wide. "A little girl? How precious."

"She was precious." Adrienne smiled with her memory. "The whole thing was such a miracle. For a moment, I felt an urge to hold the baby and cuddle with her, right along with the mother."

"That's just wonderful. I'm so proud of you for helping with your first baby."

"Thank you, Helen. That means a lot to me."

"What did Tony say when you told him all about it?"

The smile on Adrienne's face fell away. She got pretty quiet after that. "He was okay, except later he criticized me."

"What for?"

"He called me weak, because when I held that baby in my arms, I cried."

#

Stretching and yawning a little, I reached to my night stand, but my cigarettes was gone. When I got out of bed and finally come out to the kitchen, I asked Pearl where was my cigarettes. "I looked everwhere, including my night stand where I left them last night, but they wasn't there."

Pearl was fixing to leave for work, wrapping her sandwich with plastic wrap. "I don't know, Helen. Maybe you didn't leave them on your night stand."

I knowed I did leave them there, because at Mannington I couldn't leave them setting out anywheres. Somebody would of come along and took them. At Pearl's house, I could leave them right out on the table top.

Out of the blue, a idea come to me. About my picture. "What ever happened to my water color?"

Pearl wasn't listening, so I asked her a second time.

"Hmm? What water color?"

"The one I done when I was a young girl. It used to be on the wall at the old house, before you moved into this one."

Pearl gazed across the wall, thinking for a minute. "You mean the painting of the park? With the blue ribbon on it?"

"Yes, that's the one."

"I imagine it's in the attic, with your other old things."

"Could you bring my things down for me?"

Then, Pearl threw both her hands in the air, over her head. "I haven't got the time right now, Helen. We still have so much down *here* to get packed, I don't know when I'll get the chance to search up in the attic." Pearl's eyes got big. "And I do *not* want you going up there by yourself. You could fall on the stairs. It isn't safe."

Of course, I was already planning to go up in the attic while Pearl wasn't home. That a-way, if I did, I could see my water color picture sooner. Maybe she could buy me a little set of paints, and I could begin painting again here at the house.

I begin to think of what else might be up in her attic too, like some of my favorite old things. My best china and a special needlework pillow that was passed down from me and Violet's mama. If Pearl was at work, how would she know what I was up to? If I was careful, like that day I snuck into her closet, she would never know.

"Remember, Helen, the work men might call today about the new carpet. If they do, just give them my number at the office."

She picked up her key ring and her handbag, then headed out the door.

"What about my cigarettes?" I asked, peeking around the living room. I looked under magazines and behind the pillows on the sofa. Pearl just snickered. "I took them last night. I have them hidden in a safe place, until you agree to go have that testing done at the laboratory."

Pearl had did it again. She got me riled up over that testing. "I...I'm not ready yet. I don't want to go up to Illinois. You can't make me go."

In a instant, she got a mean look to her eyes, all squinty. "Don't argue with me. You *will* have that testing done. As soon as you agree, I'll give you your cigarettes back."

Recollecting how I used to keep Pearl in line when she was a girl, I snapped back at her. "If you don't give me my cigarettes, I'll tell those carpet men we changed our minds, and we don't want no new carpet."

Pearl stood with one foot inside the house, and the other foot on the porch step. She let out her breath all in a big huff. "Your cigarettes are in the bread box, way in the back. But we *will* talk about this tonight, Helen."

When she left, she slammed the front door. But I wasn't really paying it no never mind, because I had already darted to the bread box to get me a smoke.

#

All day Saturday, it rained. Rain can get some folks to weeping and feeling low. Just like the day Jesse come over to the boarding house and set with me on the back porch. We was both in a depressed mood. He didn't want me to leave with Violet and go back home to Belmont. "Why don't you stay? You're not still worried about the sheriff are you? I think he's forgotten all about the investigation."

I didn't think the sheriff would ever forget.

"Ottawa's a nice town," he said in his deep voice. "You wouldn't have to keep working, either. We could get married, and we could live with my parents until we saved enough to go out on our own." His long arms was wound around my waist, as I set scooted up next to him.

Too many ideas come barreling toward me too fast. I didn't know if I could manage being a wife. I loved Jesse a lot, but I didn't want to be in Illinois no more. It reminded me too much of what we done at Mr. Calder's house.

"Violet says we have to go home. Our daddy would skin us alive if he knowed what we done here. Then if Violet don't bring me home with her, she might get in worse trouble." I held onto Jesse's hand. Then he put his arms around me again and we squeezed each other. A light from inside the boarding house startled me, and I heard the children's voices and footsteps. Then they went away. "I wish you could come with us, Jesse."

He pulled hisself away and stood up. "They're talking about making me the boss now that Mr. Calder is..."

"Dead, Jesse. Mr. Calder is dead."

When I said that word, Jesse got his eyebrows twisted and a funny look in his eyes. "We both know whose fault that was, don't we?"

I stared down at my shoes a minute. I knowed it was Violet who done most of the mischief, but what happened after that was a accident. "She didn't mean for him to die."

He stared out into the rainy yard. "There's something I never told you," he said. "That very next morning the sheriff came to my house. He told me Mr. Calder was dead. Burned

114

to death in a fire. I never mentioned it to you, because after the sheriff left, I sat down and cried. I was too embarrassed to tell you."

I patted him on his back. "You think you cried because you was sad he was dead?"

"No, I cried because I was sorry for what we did. I mean, even *I* wanted to hurt him. But not like that. God almighty, Helen, that smell. That smell of him... burning."

Then he whipped back around and faced me. "Maybe you're right. I should try to get away from here. They can find somebody else to be the maintenance manager." Slowly, he was beginning to calm down. He rested his hands by his sides.

"If you was to come with us to Belmont, what would you do to earn a living? Where would you stay?"

He rubbed his jaw a second or two, then he licked his lips. "I could maybe...I could hold my hand out on Main Street." I laughed at him, and he laughed too.

"Or, you could come down to Belmont after I ask around to find you a job. I'll send you a letter in the mail. How would that be?"

Jesse kissed me and said he couldn't wait to be with me again. We held each other for a long time, until time for him to leave. Now, all me and Violet would have to do is try to remember what we agreed we would say to Daddy when we got back home.

#

While I was trying to watch a television program, I had trouble hearing the sound, because Tony and Adrienne was at the house to help Pearl pack some boxes, and they was having them a argument.

I knowed there was some trouble between Adrienne and Tony, because I heard Pearl talking about it on the telephone last night with Lorna, one of her girlfriends. Something about before Benjamin went back to Atlanta, him and Adrienne went out together to eat, and Tony saw them. He wasn't happy about that at all.

Now, Pearl was going to miss the next part of the argument, because she left for her friend Lorna's house for a visit.

Tony and Adrienne was on the back porch, and I reckon besides *me* hearing all their problems, the neighbors most likely did too. First, even though Adrienne had lunch with Benjamin, she wasn't the only one who done something wrong. She said she was angry with Tony about what *he* done, and Tony yelled back. "Will you *please* let me explain?"

"Explain that you were with another woman, and explain what the two of you were doing? I'm not an idiot, Tony. I know what I saw."

Tony's voice got quiet and soft, so I turned down the sound on the television. "Do you hate me? I'm human. I make mistakes."

Adrienne didn't answer, but they come inside and somebody opened the Frigidaire.

"Besides, I heard you weren't alone all that afternoon, either," Tony added.

This time, she spoke right up. "I don't know what you think you heard, Tony, but whatever I was doing that afternoon wasn't half as bad as..."

Then I heard a scuffle of shoes and a kitchen chair.

"Let me go."

"You need me, bitch. Admit it. You won't last another week without me. And I don't mean the pills either. You know exactly what I'm talking about, don't you? Don't you?"

"Leave me alone!" She hollered at Tony, and the next thing I knowed, he left Pearl's house.

I was setting on the living room sofa. As he marched past me, he didn't even say good-bye. He just slammed the door.

I turned my head back around to see if Adrienne would come talk to me. Sure enough, she stuck her head around the living room corner. She had tears in her eyes, and one dripped down her cheek. She reached up to dry it.

"Tony's wrong. I do *not* need him."

I just nodded my head, and waited for her to continue.

"How much did you hear?"

"I reckon I heard everthing."

Then Adrienne plopped down on the sofa and bent her knees up to her chin. "I guess I should have realized it months ago, but I don't think I love Tony any longer."

"You don't?" Even though he was my nephew, I found it hard to love him, myself.

"You know what else I should've realized? Each one, each man in my life, from the first up until Tony, fulfilled some sort of need." She was staring ahead, not looking me in the eye. "I've been attracted to men who were strict with me. Men who were like my father in many ways."

I wondered if she was fixing to take her a pill.

"I don't know. Maybe Benjamin's different."

Then, Adrienne turned her head to face me. "How will I know, unless I have the chance to get to know him better?"

When I really thought about it, I didn't think I was the right one to give her any advice. I wanted to help, but the only advice I knowed I could give her was to be sure to not be Tony's girlfriend anymore.

#

A couple of days later, after Pearl left for work, I set in one of her reclining chairs with my feet up, waiting for the carpet men to call. Instead, a automobile pulled up to the front, and Adrienne come to the door. I got out of the chair and let her in. "Hello Adrienne," I said. She was dressed for work, with her white shoes and a sweater over her uniform dress.

"I'm glad to see you again, Helen." She hugged me. "Aren't you still glad to be out of that horrible Mannington?"

I told her I reckoned I was. But with the carpet tore up, I have to spend most days in my room, or on the back porch.

Then, she started wandering around, snooping at things in the kitchen and dining room. She reached to the top of the hutch. After she stared at the floor a moment more, she narrowed her eyes. "I need a favor, Helen."

Any other time, I would be glad to oblige, specially for Adrienne. But I decided I better listen first.

I asked Adrienne what was it she wanted me for, and she wanted me to help her find that envelope Pearl had with Benjamin Reed's address on it. I knowed exactly where it was, and I went right for it. It was stuck behind the cookbooks on the kitchen counter, with some other mail. "Here you go," I said, when I handed it to her. "I bet you're gonna write him a letter."

"I am. I'm going to write to him."

I told her that was a good idea. I even told her Benjamin and her would make a nice couple, but she was in a hurry to get to work on time.

She asked if I had any scrap paper to copy the address.

I knowed exactly where the scrap paper was too, so I give her a piece of it and a pencil. "If you do write him a letter, would you tell him hello for me?"

Adrienne smiled, and said of course she would say hello for me.

"I think his telephone number's on it too," I said, waiting for her to write it.

"Thanks so much. I've got it all written down now." She stuck the scrap paper in her handbag, and handed me back the envelope and letter.

"Oh, I almost forgot," I said. "I got me a letter from my old roommate at Mannington. Remember Neely? One of the nurses there wrote it for her."

"Oh. What did her letter say?"

"I'll read it to you."

I went to my room and got the letter, and read it aloud.

"Dear Helen,

We miss you so much. When are you coming to visit? They still don't have anyone for me to live with, but they say a new lady might be coming next week. I just hope she's as nice as you. I hope we can get along.

My mother came to see me and gave me a package of new underwear. The new ones are soft and don't rub my skin like the old ones did. Also, they gave me a new kind of medicine and now I don't cry so much.

Yours very sincerely,

Neely."

Then, underneath, it said, *"Transcribed by Nurse Dubois."*

Adrienne said it was a nice letter. Then, she said she had to rush off or she'd be late to the clinic.

"Take good care of yourself Helen. Thanks for the address. I'll come by and see you again soon, okay?"

I told her that would be nice, that maybe we could just have us a chat. After she left out the door, she turned around once and waved good-bye. Adrienne sure has her a lovely smile.

Chapter Fifteen

With Pearl gone to work, I decided I would sneak up to the attic and look for my water color picture. She had no business putting it up there in the first place. She should of hanged it back on the wall, like where it was in the old house.

After I had my coffee with sugar and cream, I recollected how hot it was in the attic, so I took off my robe. Then, I opened the door to the attic stairs. I stared up at them, thinking how steep they was, and wondering if I shouldn't go up there. But I wanted my water color picture, so I took me a breath, stepped on the first step, and climbed up to the top. My heart went pitty pat for a minute.

It was still dusty up there, but the last time me and Pearl was up, we swiped away most of the old cobwebs. There was still a smell of old leather and wood. I didn't reckon where to start in looking. Some more memories come flooding into my head. I seemed to feel Violet's presence just then, like a little breeze, even though I know in a attic, there shouldn't be a breeze. But I felt it anyway. I recollected when we left Illinois at the end of the summer.

Me and Violet was back home in Belmont. The whole way home on the train, we practiced what we would tell Daddy about what we done in Ottawa. We was setting at the dinner table when he started in asking us about our summer. "What was most of your music store customers like? Was they younguns? Grown folks?"

I let Violet do all the talking. "We had all kinds of people for our customers. Farmers, businessmen. Little old ladies with lace gloves. Even musicians from Chicago and St. Louis."

That last part Violet made up on the Q-T. We hadn't never talked about having no visitors from Chicago, but she had her a good imagination.

Daddy rubbed the tip of his round nose with his index finger. "I reckon Mrs. Yearsall was mighty glad to have you girls there to help with her younguns. Was they well-behaved?"

This was the part I practiced the most. "We spent nearly all our spare time with them. They was sweet children. Like we told you in our letters."

Then, Violet did what she always done best. She changed the subject to something else. "I met a boy at the train station, Daddy."

"Oh?" He pushed his plate away and lit his cigar.

"He was working behind the ticket counter. He told me he would like to take me out on the town one night."

"You mean all the way to Charlotte?"

Me and Violet giggled. Then she answered him. "No, Daddy. He means Gastonia. Wants to take me to eat at the fish camp, then to a picture show."

"What's this boy's name?"

"Grady. Grady Rodgers. He's handsome as all get out. Slick black hair, deep set blue eyes that just get me all breathless."

"Violet!" I hollered. Daddy was silent, but he was staring right at Violet and blinked a few times, like as if he was shocked. He should of knowed she was prone to say just about anything. I was surprised Grady had asked Violet to the fish camp and a picture show. She hadn't never told me that part. She always seemed to have secrets she kept from me.

Daddy puffed again on his cigar. "I reckon you girls is old enough now to make your own decisions about boys. If you can manage a train ride by yourselves to Illinois and spend the summer there, I reckon you can choose who you spend time with here in Belmont."

Violet closed her eyes and said, "Praise God in Heaven."

After dinner was over, Violet called me into our room. "I forgot to show you what I did before we left Ottawa."

She opened her suitcase, and under her clothes was a couple of brown folders with papers inside. "When Mrs. Peltz wasn't looking, I took these from her file cabinet. It's our work records and all our papers. That a-way, nobody will have our names and address if they was to try to find us."

"You mean somebody like that sheriff, or a investigator?"

"Mm-hm. It would be as if we never worked at the Radium Dial. We were just a couple of girls there, out of many."

When she showed me those folders, I felt weak in the knees and I set on the side of my bed. I asked her if we couldn't even tell Daddy where we worked, not tell him about the fire and Mr. Calder, but just so's we could be honest about *some* part of it. Violet said we couldn't never say where we worked.

Even with all the extra money we made, I still felt like it wasn't worth all the trouble we gone through over the summer. I worried about that sheriff, whether he might find me and Violet. I worried if Clara might slip and tell somebody where we lived in North Carolina.

I tried to think of the nice parts of Ottawa. I recollected the public park, and how the pretty greens and blue of the trees and flowers made everthing look so nice. I decided one day me and Violet should go to Charlotte on the bus, and maybe I could get me some supplies. That a-way, I could paint me a picture of it.

Next thing I would need to do was try to figure out where I could find a job for Jesse.

#

At my new doctor's clinic in Gastonia, Pearl pulled us into a parking space. As we was stepping into the building, she started in fussing with me and my dress. She said I would need to get over to Hannah's Beauty Shop soon and get my hair done, because it was starting to look like a horse's mane. "But right now, you're going inside and meet your new doctor," she said, holding the door for me.

"I hope it's a nice doctor."

I hoped he would be as nice as Dr. Stokes. I knowed I needed a doctor I could talk to about my feelings and all, and it was important that it was somebody I could feel at ease with. That a-way, coming to the clinic so many times ever week wouldn't be so bad.

When we got inside the waiting room, there was only a couple of other people there ahead of us. Pearl filled out some forms and I started in chewing my lip. The air in the office smelled like coffee after it sets all day in a percolator. Behind me was a window air conditioner blowing on the back of my neck. After we filled out some more papers, the nurse told me it was time to go see the doctor. I followed her back to a room with two soft chairs with armrests and footrests. I set in one of the chairs, and put my feet up. Shoes and all.

"Dr. Meyer will be right in. She's just finishing up with another patient." I never knowed it would be a woman doctor.

The walls was painted all white, and on the window there was curtains made of striped material. Next to the window, Dr. Meyer had her a picture of a railroad station in a foreign country.

To pass the time, I recollected about how worried Adrienne was when she called me and told me her brother Ron was going to have his other operation soon on his leg. She cried a little thinking what it would be like if he had to get one of those jobs for handicapped people who can't walk by theirselves.

After a little minute, Dr. Meyer come into the room. She nodded her head at me. Right away, I didn't think I would like her. She was about Pearl's age, which I could tell by her face, but she had straight white hair like a old lady, which was one of the new styles, but that wasn't why I didn't like her. It was because of the way she looked at me, like as if I was a stupid person. It was in her eyes, just a quick second in the way she formed her eyebrows. Then she looked away. "Helen Waterman?" she asked, while reading a thick folder of papers.

"Yes. I'm Helen."

After she put the papers away, she set them back on her desk and patted the top of the folder with her hand, like as if she was tucking a baby in for the night. Then, she come over and set across from me in the chair, stuffing a wadded tissue into the pocket of her white doctor's coat. Under her dark red skirt, she had on those white nylons, and I could see right through them to the freckles on her legs. "For my former Mannington patients, I like to just try to get to know them a little first."

I tried to think of something to say, but nothing come to mind.

"Tell me about yourself, Helen."

I started in chewing the inside of my lip, and Dr. Meyer stared at me again, like as if I was stupid. I wasn't sure how to answer her. How do you tell about your own self? You can tell about other people, like people you love, or people you used to know, or people who make you mad, but I reckon that don't mean nothing to a doctor.

"Can you tell me how you first entered the hospital, in the 1940's, I believe it was?"

"The itching. I had itching all the time. Under my skin."

"I see. And since that time?"

Dr. Stokes and Dr. Winslow already knowed all about me. But, I reckon they forgot to tell this new doctor, so I would have to explain everthing. Since I seen other patients waiting for their appointment, I just told her quick.

"My husband died and after that, I wanted to know where the cancer was, so I took a knife from the kitchen drawer and cut my arms and my stomach."

Then, I held out my wrists so's Dr. Meyer could see the thin silver lines. "I made a mess with the blood, but Pearl telephoned the operator and said to send somebody right away. Next, I was at Mannington in a room with some other sick people in beds, and they stitched up my cuts and put bandages on me, and I couldn't set up in bed or cough without it stinging and burning to do so."

The doctor pressed the tips of her fingers together in the middle of her lap. "I see. What made you think you had cancer, Helen?"

"I could feel it. It would crawl around in there, making me itch and sometimes it tickled me and I would rub my palm against it."

"Are you taking your Haldol every four hours?"

"Yes."

"And is it helping you?"

Before I could give her a answer, I had to stop and think a minute. The only way I reckoned I could answer that question was to tell her how my life was with Pearl. "I was happier back at Mannington. I had me some friends there, and now I don't have nobody, and I don't have my puzzles or my paints, or nobody to take care of."

Dr. Meyer took a peek at her watch, then she started in winding it. "I'd like you to start coming three days a week. Do you have reliable transportation?"

"You mean can Pearl bring me? She can. Course, she has to miss some work at her job, but after she gets married to

Donald, she can quit work and then we're moving to
Charlotte."

"I'll need to meet with Pearl too." Dr. Meyer stood up
and reached for my elbow to help me scoot out of my chair.
"I'll see you in a couple of days. Just stop at the receptionist's
desk and she'll set up your next appointment. Pearl's too."

"That'll be fine," I said, heading for the door.

"Other door, Helen. That's my private washroom."

Pearl was waiting for me in the waiting room. We made
the next appointment. On the way home, she mumbled and
grumbled. She was complaining about quitting her job early
to make time for "all these trips back and forth to the clinic."

#

Soon, Benjamin come to the house again from Atlanta,
wanting to talk to Pearl. When I let him in the door, he give
me a little hug, and I liked the way his aftershave smelled.
Benjamin said Pearl was supposed to meet him at 3:30, but
we figured maybe she was delayed at work.

I got to wondering if Adrienne ever wrote a letter to
Benjamin. He's such a nice man, just like I knowed he would
turn out to be. Clara did a fine job with raising him. I was sad
that me and Clara lost touch with each other. But I guess
sometimes that happens to folks. Even the best of friends.

I recollected the last time me and Clara was together, and
that was when Violet died, and we had us a little argument. I
reckon when folks go to funerals, they can get a little cranky
with each other. By the time Daddy died in 1953, I was
already at Mannington. Me and Pearl argued a lot about it,
but they allowed me to go to the funeral. At the time, she
had her a new boyfriend named Cliff, and he didn't want me
to come out of the hospital. He didn't think it was safe. Since
I was already dressed and ready to go, they helped me into
the car, but Cliff didn't speak to me the whole way there or
the whole way back.

Cliff had him a head of greased-back hair and long,
bushy sideburns. Pearl was always hanging onto his arm, like
as if she was afraid he would get away. I recollect Tony was
just in grade school at the time, and he didn't like Cliff one
bit. In fact, he once bit Cliff on the arm.

I got to thinking about Clara, and how after we lost
touch, I never knowed she was even sick or had already died.

Then, I begin to feel sorry for Benjamin, because he had to bury his mama.

I asked Benjamin what it was he did at his job. He said he worked for the Atlanta Field office for the GAO, which is a government job. He said his work is "routine to the point of absurdity," but at least his supervisors have been good about him being gone to settle his mama's affairs and so forth.

For a while, we set on the back porch to wait, but then he wanted to walk around in Pearl's back yard. Benjamin still likes birds, and he said he thought he seen one he recollected. "There," he whispered. "Half way up the maple. See him?" Both of us gazed up at the tops of the trees, but the bird flew off.

"I recollect you always liked looking at birds, didn't you?"

"I've always had an interest, but…I don't think of myself as a typical bird watcher."

"Why not?"

"I don't know," he said, staring again at the tree tops. "Perhaps it's because I don't think of myself as typical in *any* respect."

Just then, we both decided to go back on the porch. "I'm sorry about Clara. I didn't know she was sick."

"Thank you."

"Was it a nice funeral?"

Benjamin didn't answer me right out. He hemmed and hawed a few seconds, like as if he was thinking about how to answer. "We had a simple memorial service. My mother's will specifically requested no funeral. Cremation and memorial service only."

"I'm sorry."

"No, that's all right," he said, folding his hands across his lap. His suit was tight around the middle and he had the beginnings of gray in his temples.

"How old are you now, Benjamin?"

He stared at me before he answered, but he said he was forty-five. Then he told me he wished he was back in his twenties. Before his heart murmur got so bad. "Time marches on," he said. "According to the government height and weight charts I'm average. Although perhaps at the upper range for weight, because I'm stocky." He took in a breath when he said it.

"Wasn't your daddy the same way?"

"He was taller, but yes, he had big bones, like mine."

Benjamin told me something sad after that. He said he is now the exact age his daddy was when *he* died.

"What did he die of?"

"Natural causes."

For a minute, he stared back out into the yard. He begin talking about when he left home the first time. He was just out of high school, and he had decided he would learn to be a priest. He recollected how the other boys in his neighborhood thought he was just a coward and he didn't want to be a soldier. But that wasn't it at all. Even if he did want to be a soldier, he said he couldn't be one because of his heart murmur.

"Something kept you from being a priest. What was it?" I asked.

"I got married instead."

"Oh."

After a little while, he told me more about Clara. He said even with a private nurse coming in ever day to care for her, he knew she'd lost her will. After she had her last surgery and a stroke, she couldn't speak no more. "But she could express fear or worry...any emotion, using only the muscles around her eyes," he said.

Then, Benjamin stared into his palms. "I told her I'd never put her in a home." Then he said, "But when I later suggested it to her, I could tell from the way her face relaxed she'd finally resigned to the inevitable."

Also, I asked Benjamin more about his wife and did he have a family. He said he didn't care to talk about it much, but he lost his wife and baby daughter in childbirth. Then he never got married again after that. I told him I was sorry to hear it.

For a few minutes after that, we just set and didn't talk, just listening again to the birds. I got us both a drink from the kitchen, and then Benjamin smiled at me. "Maybe sometime, you can tell me more about my mother and the factory job." When he said it, he had just took him a drink of his water, and pointed his finger at me from the glass. Course, I wanted to tell him about his mama, but then he would want to know too much, and I didn't never want to tell about the fire. Instead, I asked him some questions. "Did some of Clara's family come to the memorial?"

He said Clara's cousin Jean come to it. She was a rich lady and she invited Benjamin to come to her home some time, but he hasn't gone yet. Jean told him she had her some old photographs of Clara from when she was a teenager. Then he said after he got the letter from the laboratory, he called Jean, but she didn't know nothing about the Radium Dial either.

Then Benjamin said something I've knowed almost my whole life. Something that was true for Violet, and maybe for Clara too. He said that people go to their graves with secrets the rest of us will never know.

Chapter Sixteen

As soon as the postman left our mailbox, I run to the road to see if there was a new letter from Jesse. He had been writing to me for three months now, and we was falling more and more in love. He said they hired a new maintenance manager at the factory, and Jesse was allowed to take care of some of the paperwork now. Sometimes in our letters, we talked about ways to be together, but Violet was still mad at me for keeping in touch with Jesse. "If you'd just forgot about him like I told you, we wouldn't have to worry." I think me and Violet was alike... she just wanted to forget that summer as soon as she could. But it kept on haunting both of us, nearly ever day. No matter what, I still couldn't forget Jesse. Not in a million years.

One of his letters said he had saved up enough money to send for me. He wanted me to come back to Ottawa. "You're not guilty of anything. It was your sister who was mostly to blame."

I wrote him back the very same day and said I couldn't leave home. Then, in his next letter, he said, "Then I'll just come to you." I giggled when I read it, but then one evening a while after that, he knocked on our front door.

"Jesse!" I screamed, hugging him tight. He was holding me up in his long arms, and they was wrapped all the way around me. He told me he'd been on a train for a day and a half, and never got a wink of sleep the whole time. We told him he would have to find a place to stay, because Daddy said it wouldn't be proper for him to spend the night under our roof with his two young daughters. He asked, "What would the neighbors say?"

Since it was cold and rainy outside, Daddy changed his mind and let Jesse sleep on our covered porch until he could find hisself a place.

After dinner, Violet and her new beau Grady returned from a outing, and when Violet seen Jesse, she frowned. Daddy asked her what was wrong, and she zipped her lip about why she was sorry to see Jesse in Belmont.

By the time we all finally got to bed, I told Violet not to worry so much. "Jesse told me he wants to stay in North Carolina. He don't even want to go back up north, so he won't be telling nobody where we are. His best friend is a very honest and proper fella, named Ray Peeler, and he's the only one he told."

She lay on her back in her bed, then turned off her light. "I guess I'm worried somebody will find me. Worried I'll have to go to jail."

I asked her if she had told Grady.

"No, and I don't ever want him to find out, either. Don't you ever tell him, Helen."

I promised her again.

Then, out of the blue, a idea come into Violet's head. "You don't think Clara will tell, do you? I mean, she still works at the Radium Dial. What if that sheriff comes back to the boarding house, asking for us?"

I reminded Violet how Clara had promised too, and she said she was going to go back to secretarial school in the fall, all the way up in Waukegan, so nobody should worry about nothing.

#

For twenty minutes or so I waited for Tony to pick me up and take me to my appointment with Dr. Meyer. Pearl said she couldn't get off work, and would send Tony instead, and he was late getting me. I reckoned he got tied up with one of those automobiles he works on. Sometimes he gets right angry when things don't go the way he wants.

Soon, Tony pulled into the driveway. He had a angry look on his face, and motioned to me with his hand that I should hurry to the automobile. Then, I recollected I forgot my nice gloves from Nurse Dubois at Mannington, so I hollered out the door to wait a minute. I pulled them onto my hands while he waited out front.

Then, I went to the door and he was backing his old Chevy out of the driveway without me. "Wait!" I hollered at him. I did my best to run to the driveway, and I stood in the middle. Then, he was turned the other way, backing his car again into the driveway, fast, like he was a angry driver. I reckon he didn't see me there, and he kept on coming. I can't move as fast as I used to, and when I tried to get out of his way, I tripped and fell. Tony's car bumped into me and I heard a funny sound. It was my leg snapping like a branch.

The pain made me taste blood and I felt my head swell up. Then my leg got to hurting so bad, I screamed and begin to cry. In a instant, Tony was next to me, trying to get me to calm down. He smelled bad, like he does after he works all day. Like salt and grease. Then he got angry with me, and his face begin twitching. "Didn't you see me coming? I was backing in so we could pull right out."

"I thought you was leaving without me!" I hollered, while holding my sore leg. When I looked at it, it was bent wrong, below the knee. It was my right leg, and it was starting to turn a funny color, like the color of a old bruise.

"There's no way I would leave until after I dropped you off at the clinic. Now, I'm gonna miss even *more* work."

Tony helped me get up from the grass, and lifted me with his strong arms to the automobile. He held me up by one knee so's he could get the back seat open. Then, he set me down with my legs as straight as he could out on the seat, and tossed my handbag next to me. After that, he run to the front seat. He turned on the engine, and there was a loud pounding noise, like some sort of music. He turned it off right away, and I'm glad he did, because it was hurting my ears.

"I'm taking you to the hospital, okay?" he said, while turning his head, looking both ways for the traffic.

"I never broke a bone before. I got to be sixty-five years old before I broke a bone."

Tony was driving too fast around the corners, and it was making my leg hurt all the way up to my hip. After a few minutes, there was sirens, and out the window there was trees and pretty lawns and such, and I knowed we was at Gaston Memorial. He parked in front of the big sign that said EMERGENCY, and run inside. Next, he come out with a wheelchair and a couple of nurses. A old one and a young one. He opened the back door for me, and then the old nurse said to Tony, "Can you get her out of there?"

They worked on me together to get me out of the seat and into the wheelchair. I screamed a couple of times, but soon, they had me inside and moved me to a gurney so's they could check my blood pressure and see if I had any insurance and so forth. Tony was gone, but when he come back, he said he just called Pearl, and she would be right over.

The nurse said she was going to stick me with a needle to ease the pain, so she did. I was still awake, but when the nurse asked me a bunch of questions about my doctors, about my pills, and my address, I just told her to wait for Pearl, and she would tell her everthing. She took my handbag and told me it would be in a safe place, and Tony was running his hands through his hair and his beard and so forth, like as if he was worried.

Next thing I know, Pearl was there, and she was hollering at Tony. "What did you *do* to her?"

He explained what happened, but he didn't tell her the part about being late. The nurses told them to shush, since they was having them a argument out in the middle of the waiting room, and there was other sick patients out there too. A man in a green shirt rolled me on the gurney, down a long hall. "Wait here." A sign said, "X-ray." I reckoned they was going to x-ray my leg. I already knowed it was broke without no x-ray.

Out of the blue, Pearl was by my side. "Helen, let me see." She lifted the sheet off my leg and looked at it. "It's not so bad, is it? You'll probably still be able to walk with crutches. Donald's mother wants us to come for dinner on Sunday, so hopefully..."

I scrunched up my eyes. "It hurts something awful."

"Helen, why didn't you move out of the way? Didn't you see Tony coming?"

"I seen him coming, but I just couldn't move as fast as I needed to."

After a minute, the pain begin to depart. I felt my shoulders loosen up some.

While we waited for the x-ray, I recollected that story about Jesse, when he was a little boy and his thumb was broke.

Now I knowed exactly why Jesse hated Mr. Calder all those years.

#

The doctor said I had to stay the night in the hospital with my broke leg in a cast. The cast reached only to the top of my calf, but now I had crutches, which was making my underarms sore. They wanted to make sure all my medicines worked okay together. I lay there in my room, wishing Jesse was with me. I begin recollecting the night Violet's beau, Grady Rodgers found out he had a weak stomach. Grady was a funny one, all the time nervous and worried about things.

Him and Violet was already engaged and he was over at our house. We set together outside on the porch. Violet was setting across his lap in the big rocker, and we was talking about our daddy's business. I set with my knees under me, making sure I slid the hem of my dress down to be proper. "Maybe you and Violet could live here at first, and you could help Daddy with the chickens."

Grady glanced at Violet, sort of smiling sideways. "The chickens?"

He wasn't really the type for chickens. He was too tall and handsome to waste his good looks in a coop. But to be sure, we took him to see the little critters.

"This way, Grady," Violet said, while tugging his shirt sleeve. We directed him past the pecan tree, under the vines and to the old wooden chicken house.

We took him to the incubator so's he could see the baby chicks. Their little peep sounds was like music to my ears. Grady peered down at them, reaching his hand to one of them.

"Go ahead," Violet said. "You can play with one."

Just then, Grady drew his hand back. "I don't want to hurt it."

Violet snickered. "Just watch me. You have to be firm but gentle."

Finally, Grady held one in his hand, and made his own peep sound, right back to it. He smiled at that baby chick like it was a real youngun. Violet snatched it away and put it back in the drawer. "Maybe you should work with Daddy, after all."

Next, Violet closed the drawer with the little chicks. "Wait. Look at what Helen found last night," she said, pulling out the bottom drawer. One of the eggs had hatched with a sad looking little creature inside. A baby chick with four wings and a crinkled up little pair of legs. We reckoned he would be dead in a few days, but he was still breathing. His body was fairly gasping for air.

When Grady leaned over and looked at it, his hand covered his mouth and his skin turned pale. Then, he backed away from that incubator like as if it was going to suck him up in it. Me and Violet just looked at each other, wondering what was the trouble.

Finally, Violet asked him. They was over by the vines together, but I heard ever word. "I'm sorry. Are you all right?" She cuddled up to him, as way of apology, whispering to him, and staring up into Grady's eyes. "You mad at me?"

He answered he had not been expecting to see a thing like a deformed chick. By now, she had slid her hands around his waist, and was clutched up against him. How could he say he was mad at her now? He was going to marry her soon. I was happy for my sister, but at the same time, I wanted a life like hers too. What I wanted more than anything else was for Jesse Waterman to marry me. Jesse wouldn't never be scared of a deformed baby chick.

#

Finally, the day come when me and Violet could take the bus to Charlotte to get me my water color paper and brushes. I still had plenty of money left over from the Radium Dial. We hadn't quite saved up enough to get Daddy his new ice box, but he said that was all right.

We got on the bus in Gastonia, and rode across the Catawba River on the Highway 74 Bridge. As we was going over the river, the side of the bus was right up against the wood bridge, and I closed my eyes worried the driver would bump against it. Violet didn't want to talk. She had her a detective magazine, and she was busy reading a story about a bank robber who didn't think he would never get caught. I tried to read some of it over her shoulder. He thought he was smarter than everbody else.

Once we was at the bus station in Charlotte, we had us a long walk to the department store. The tall buildings blocked out the sun. I gazed to the tops, but Violet stopped walking and asked me a question. "After you paint the Ottawa Park, what else do you think you'd like to paint?"

I chewed my lip a little, thinking of a answer. So far, the park was the only thing I could think of. But I knowed I wanted it to be a big picture, so's we could hang it up at the house. I also knowed I wanted it to be water color, because I knowed I liked water color pictures.

At the department store, they had paper and canvases of all sizes, and dozens of different colors of paints. As we was standing in front of all the paint colors, I recollected how the radium paint was always the same exact pale color. I was happy to be choosing a set of many colors. I decided on a set of 12, all bright and cheery.

"That is one of our nicest sets of pastels," the sales lady said when we went to pay. She took the paper I picked out and rolled it up before she wrapped it in brown paper. "Do you need anything else?"

Me and Violet told her we didn't, but Violet seen a flier hanging on the side of the counter. It said there was a art contest, and anybody in North Carolina could enter it. I got to thinking maybe I should try to paint a few different pictures. Just to see what looked best. "May I please have a few more sheets of water color paper?"

The sales lady said of course I could, and she give me three more sheets. "Will this be enough?" she asked.

I told her I reckoned it would.

When we got home, me and Violet took everthing into our bedroom. I wanted to start painting right away, but first, we had to make supper and eat. After we did the dishes, I started my picture. I recollected a water color picture I seen once with a sunset at a seashore, with sea gulls and way off in the ocean was a fishing boat. I tried to do the same picture, but it didn't come out the way I wanted. I tried and tried, but after a while, I just started to cry. Instead, I tried to paint God's face. I got the beard right, but the forehead was wrong. I felt a little twinge of shame for ruining the face on that grandfather clock. I gripped the edges of the God painting in my two hands, staring at it, all the while wishing I hadn't never picked up that hay hook back so many years before. That was when Daddy come in and seen me. I wadded up my picture.

As he stood in the doorway of the bedroom, he just frowned at me. Then his face turned to like he was in a sour mood. I wiped away my tears and put my brush down, waiting for him to speak. If I could of chose what I wanted him to say, it would be for him to ask where did me and Violet *really* work all summer. To ask how come we didn't come back to Belmont all chattering about sheet music and songs we learned and how do you tune a piano. Because then, I would of told him the truth. That we never set foot into a music store all summer. We worked in a factory, and we lied about it. We took oil and poured it on a man's porch and he come out with a lantern and burned to death.

Instead, Daddy asked me if I ever seen the pictures my mama did.

"I...I never knowed she did any pictures."

"She did some of them little flowers in a frame. About this big." Then he showed me with his hands, holding his fingers about four inches apart in the shape of a square. "Do you still have them, Daddy?"

"In the back closet. In a box." Now Daddy's nose was turning red, like as if he was getting weepy. He was looking more and more depressed, but he took me and showed me the teeny flower pictures. They was darling, and I asked him to let me keep one of them.

Then, he set on the floor in the corner, with one leg bent up and the other out straight. For a minute or two, he just set still, not saying nothing. I reckon he just needed a minute to think about things. "She went to the shed that day. Then, when she come out, she went straight to bed." Daddy's voice got choked, and it turned to a high pitch. "When one of you girls started to cry about your milk or you needed your diaper tended to, she didn't get up. I opened the bedroom door and hollered at her. Get up, you lazy bird. I hollered, but she didn't budge. I tried to shake her, but...the poison... she just lied there, deader than..."

"Daddy, I'm sorry you have to have such a sad memory of Mama." I stooped down to put my arm around him, but he pushed me away and got up. Then he stomped into his room and shut the door. Just like so many times before, I knowed not to try to talk to Daddy when he got into one of his moods. And also, just like so many times before, when Daddy got into one of *his* moods, I did the same. I left for my room.

Staring at me was my water color of the seashore with the fishing boat. I snatched it and tore it into teeny pieces. Then I set on the bed and stared at the rug.

In a minute, Violet come into the room. "Some day, he'll stop fretting over Mama. Don't let it bother you so much,

Helen. Do your park picture like you wanted. Don't let him get you so mad that you can't paint whatever you want."

My hands was together like when you say grace at the table, and I didn't even know they was. Without speaking, I got up from the bed and picked up the brush to start the picture of the park. She was right. Nobody could stop me from painting whatever I wanted to.

Then Violet said for me to wait a minute. She opened the top drawer on our dresser and took out a little jar. It was a jar of radium paint.

"You brought some of that with you?"

"Sure, why not? Why don't you use some of this in your picture? Then, when we turn off the lights, we can still see it."

I told Violet that was one of the best ideas she ever had. I only used a little in the picture though, because I had me a better idea for the rest of the paint. I thought of something *else* I wanted to paint, so it would glow in the dark too... my *Excellence in Training* plaque.

#

At the hospital, Pearl tried to make me do things I didn't want to do. When the nurse asked me if I wanted a few more minutes with my dinner tray, Pearl spoke up for me, and told the nurse to take it away. I wasn't done with my pineapple Jell-O yet, but Pearl wouldn't listen. Later on, Pearl made me put down the magazine I was reading so's she could tell me about something Donald said, and that made me cross.

I recollected one other time somebody made me do something I didn't want to do. It was in May 1929, when me and Violet went to Illinois to spend some time with Clara. While we was there, we had to visit Bess who we used to know from the Radium Dial. She was very sick.

"Why can't I just stay here at Clara's?" I asked Violet. She was trying to get me to leave Clara and Jim's house to go visit Bess. All I wanted to do was visit with Clara, since we hadn't seen her in so long.

"I'm surprised at you, Violet," I said. "I thought you wanted to stay away from all the Radium Dial people. Why do you want to see Bess?"

"We have to go to pay our respects."

"Pay our respects? She's not dead, is she?"

"No, but I heard she was in poor health."

I told Violet I didn't want to see Bess, because she wasn't never nice to me when we worked with her. She was all the time teasing me and Jesse, but Violet said to let bygones be bygones and go along with her and Clara. They *worried* me into going.

On the way, we stopped and got Bess some flowers. Then we drove to a old shack out on a dirt highway, and walked up to the door together, all three of us. Clara knocked on the door. A old woman opened it and asked us who we was and what did we want. Violet told her we was there to see Bess. Then Violet said we used to work with Bess at the Radium Dial, and we wanted to set with her a while.

The old woman allowed us in, and we walked to a section of the shack that had a rope strung across with a blanket draped over it to make a private room, like in a hospital ward. Even though we was there in the spring, the old woman didn't have the windows open to give the room some fresh air, so the shack had a sick smell, like old cheese or dried vegetable peels.

She pulled back the blanket curtain and told Bess she had some visitors, and would she like to see them. Bess's weak voice was so quiet, we almost didn't hear it. But she said to allow us in.

As we reached our heads behind the curtain, we seen a skinny girl laying on a narrow bed, with her arms outside of the blanket. She didn't look at all like the Bess we knowed from the Radium Dial. Bess used to have plump cheeks and a round stomach. This girl's jaw was covered with sores, and some of them was leaking into a fluffy scarf that was around her neck. My breath sucked in at what I seen next. She bit down, like when you clamp your teeth together, only her bottom jaw folded into the top, like a old toothless grandma. I asked where was Bess, and the skinny girl said "it's me." I covered my mouth with my hand, and I felt like I wanted to be sick to my stomach.

I turned to the side, and Violet and Clara was also sick. Their faces was white, and when Bess reached her hand out to us, nobody reached back. We just stood there, froze like as if we was nailed to the spot. Finally, Violet said a few words. "Bess, how long have you been sick like this?" Then, she give her the flowers and Bess said thank you.

Her voice was more like a croak, and she couldn't say all her words right, but she was cheerful enough. "For a few months now. The doctor said to go home until I passed on, so that's what I'm doing. My grandma was the only one who would take care of me. Nobody else could tolerate being around me for long."

"That's a shame," Clara said, tilting her head to one side. "Not even your own mother?"

"No, she's got enough to take care of right now, with the younger children." Bess stopped to cough into a small towel next to her bed. "But my mama and daddy come to see me whenever they can."

Finally, I got up the courage to ask a question. "Didn't the doctors say there was something they could give you?"

Bess took her a deep breath, and tried to answer. "Only for the pain. He said he couldn't treat me anymore for the wasting. Just a matter of time."

Bess's eyes appeared to be clouded over. She was tuckered out just talking to us for a few minutes.

Violet asked the next question. "Is there anything we can do?"

"No. Just having you visit means the world to me."

While we was visiting Bess, a strange thing happened. She spoke real nice to me. She told me she was sorry for all those times she teased me, and she hoped I would one day forgive her. I said of course I forgive her.

We only stayed a short while, since we had run out of things to talk about. As we was leaving, Violet said we would pray for her. Mostly, I just knew we would be more scared then anything, since any of us could come down with the same thing. A cancer that takes away your jaw, your teeth, and your very breath and soul.

CHAPTER SEVENTEEN

Pearl took me home and set me up in bed with my medicine for pain. "The emergency room doctor said these make you sleepy, Helen. Do they?" she asked, while pushing a pillow under my cast. I told her they did. She give me some magazines too—a few of her Ladies Home Journals, and a National Geographic, with a picture of a Eskimo fisherman holding up a baby seal. He was smiling so hard, his eyes disappeared up into his cheeks.

I was glad to rest. It give me more time to think about things. I was still surprised I got to be this old, and I hadn't never broke a bone before. I almost did once—my wrist, when I fell off a wood box. I was only nine at the time. Violet was the one who had problems with her bones and her joints.

I recollected a particular night in 1933 during the Depression. Violet's teeth started to come loose. Me and Jesse was in the middle of decorating the house for Violet's birthday. I asked him to hand me a little nail. He was in the kitchen, and I was in the parlor, standing on a chair. Depression or not, we wanted to have us a good party.

Me and Violet was even closer to each other now, since me and Jesse shared a place with her and Grady. Lots of folks had to double up when they couldn't find work or afford no place of their own. Now, it was like we was back to being young sisters again. Just like when we was girls and we shared a room.

Grady had took Violet for a long walk. He was supposed to keep Violet away, so's we could surprise her with food and a banner hung across the doorway to the parlor. It said, "Happy Twenty-eighth Birthday, Violet." I had wrote the words in blue and red paint.

Little Pearl was in the back yard playing with her friends, but she wasn't supposed to be because she was in her only good dress. I hollered to her to get inside before she got it dirty.

Me and Jesse tended to the last minute details. We made sure everbody was hid before Violet walked into the house. We made sure the presents was hid too. Since nobody had no money, the presents was all home-made items, like a cloth hat, or a decorated vase. Some was hid in the hall closet, and some was under the old wing back chair. Folks who drove had to park their automobiles down the block, so's Violet wouldn't know we was planning to jump out and yell surprise the moment she walked into the house.

"Now, everbody be quiet. Shh sh." I said, with my finger over my lips. Me and Jesse was hiding behind a chair, and he nuzzled his nose into my ear making me giggle. He was always doing that to me, and it always give me the shivers.

We had all the lights off, and Grady opened the door first. Then Violet stepped into the parlor and said, "Let's get some lights on in here." As soon as she said that, we hopped out from behind furniture and from the kitchen, and Violet squealed and laughed at the same time. Then, when she seen all the friends we invited over, she cried with tears of happiness.

After Violet opened her presents, the ladies all set together in a circle in the living room, while the men all went out back in the yard. I told Jesse he should wear his coat and hat, but he said it wasn't cold outside. He said cold was when the pond froze over back home in Ottawa. We lived in the south now, in Belmont, and Jesse was hot all the time, even in February.

Our neighbor, Mrs. Nora Zerkle, set across from Violet, and asked if she wanted any more three-bean salad. Violet said she was full, but there was still half the dish left. We had growed plenty of vegetables and beans in our summer garden that year.

"I'll take a bite," I said, reaching for the dented metal bowl. I couldn't help noticing how worn through my skirt was. "I hate this old Depression. I miss sugar, and I miss real birthday cake, but at least we're all still breathing."

Then, Mrs. Zerkle leaned forward and lowered her voice. "I saw the most dreadful article in the paper this morning. They say there's been another case of those poor girls who died. Died from the radium poison in Illinois."

Some of the other ladies hadn't never heard before, so Mrs. Zerkle explained about the radium. "They say it settles in your bones. The girls used to lick the tips of their brushes but they told them to stop when so many of them began to get sick."

Me and Violet just stared at each other from across the room. Only we knowed we was likely to become one of them girls, but so far, neither one of us was sick. Just thinking about it, my skin got that itchy feel in it, like as if something was crawling around under there. I got fidgety, and Violet frowned and made a scowl on her face.

Then, Violet's girlfriend, Ursie stood from the sofa. "I think it's just shameful the way that company wouldn't pay for those girls to see a proper doctor. Their lives could have been saved."

Everbody in the group nodded their heads and agreed. Even me and Violet. We already seen a newspaper article all about it. There was another factory in New Jersey. Like the one in Illinois. Some of those girls was getting sick too, and the doctors said they had other diseases and not cancer. They said the girls was sick from something else, instead of because they worked with radium paint.

After all our friends went home, Violet was standing in front of the wash basin in her room. Setting next to her hand towel, the Sloan's Liniment tube was squeezed flat.

She knowed I was standing next to her, but she didn't say a word. She just reached to her table and picked something up with her finger and thumb. "I lost this just now, and I've got another one loose too."

She dropped her tooth into my palm. It wasn't a healthy tooth. It was dark gray, like it was rotted. "I didn't want to tell you this, but there's another problem." She went over to a pile of clothes on the floor, and reached down for a pillowcase. Right on the middle, where you rest your head was a ugly brown stain, like as if she spilled something on it. "What happened to your good pillowcase, Violet?"

"When I woke up this morning, something had leaked out of my ear. I guess it was sort of... watery blood."

"Why didn't you tell me?" I screamed, hugging Violet around her neck. "I don't want you to end up like Bess." Out of the blue, I felt as scared as I ever had in my life, worried about my sister. "Violet, do you think you want to go see the doctor?"

She stared at me, then turned to the side. Her voice was real quiet. "You know, Clara and Jesse aren't the only ones who know we once worked at the Radium Dial. There was Mrs. Yearsall and her children. That sheriff. By now, most of the girls who worked there have likely scattered across the country, and we can only hope they don't remember us." She looked toward the door. "I know we was only there for one summer, and that was ten years ago. But we still have to be careful. If I was to go to the doctor, and if he was to discover I had the radium cancer, they might put me on a newsreel, or in a newspaper article, and that could be dangerous. What if the authorities were to see my picture in the paper?"

She was right. I crossed the room and folded my arms. "Somebody from that summer might recollect you."

"That's why I don't want to go to the doctor."

Then, I crossed back over to her and touched the side of her arm. "I don't want you to get sick, Violet."

For a minute, she just looked at herself in the mirror, but didn't say nothing. Then, little Pearl skipped into the room. "Mama, come now and tuck me in."

I knowed Violet was sad, so I told Pearl I would tuck her in for her mama. She stuck her hands on her little hips. "You're not my mama. I wouldn't *never* want you for my mama. You're not the same."

Instead, Violet took her little girl herself, and walked her to her bed to tuck her in for the night. I just swallowed and set on the bed, sniffling my tears.

#

The other day, I had me a nice visit from Adrienne. She set next to me while my leg was resting on a pillow in my bed.

"I'm so sorry I haven't been by to see you before now," she said, gazing at the rose in a vase she just give me.

"How pretty. Thank you. Don't you worry about not coming before now. I know you can't never come unless Pearl's gone to work or gone out with Donald."

Adrienne's head was down, and she was picking at her fingernails, with a little grin.

"Did you ever get in touch with Benjamin?" I asked.

"Yes, I did. Benjamin and I are sort of...dating now."

"You are? That's wonderful."

"He is the sweetest, most attentive, caring man I've ever met. So different from other men I've dated."

I didn't know none of the other men, but I reckoned *anybody* was nicer than Tony.

Adrienne spent some time making me all fancy. She asked me to hand her the last curler. "I can't reach it," she said, stretching across the bed. We had one side of my hair done, and only one curler to go on the other side. I leaned over to reach it, but she stopped me. "Wait. I don't think your nails are dry yet."

She had just finished putting on the color—pink raspberry foam—to my fingernails. My toenails was still waiting. I told Adrienne the last time I had my toenails done was in 1949.

"I sure did enjoy getting my shampoo," I said, smiling and peeking at myself in the hand mirror. She finished up the last curler, sliding in the hair pin. "There you go. All done. Now, after it's dry, I'll style it for you. You'll look just like a movie star."

"Which one?"

She had to think a minute. I don't know if Adrienne goes to the movies much. "You'll look exactly like Faye Dunaway," she finally said.

Checking my face in the mirror, I scowled at myself when I looked at my teeth.

"What's wrong?"

"My sister lost all her teeth before she died. They fell out, one by one, like corn from a cob."

"Oh, how awful. I can't imagine losing my teeth."

Opening the bottle of nail polish, Adrienne scooted the chair up to the side of my bed. "Comfortable?"

"You mean, for my toenails?"

"Yes, your pedicure." I said I was right as rain, and ready to go.

First, she had to clip the longer nails. "Would you like a foot massage also?"

"I wouldn't have it no other way," I answered, smiling at her. Then she rubbed and massaged both my feet.

"Are you and Benjamin starting to get serious?"

A sudden smile caught hold of Adrienne's lips. "Yes, I think so." She was clipping my big toenail now on my right foot.

"Are you two going to visit again soon?"

Trying to hide her smile, she barely answered. "Yes, very soon."

"I'm glad you and Tony..."

"Why do you think I came over here in the middle of the day? So I wouldn't accidentally run into him. Or have to deal with Pearl. She's such a depressing person, don't you think?"

"She sure is. She told me she was so tired of all the brouhaha over the wedding. She was about to just say forget it and go to the Gaston County justice of the peace."

Adrienne asked me how did Pearl get to be so negative.

"I reckon it was because she was a teenager when I went to Mannington and she was embarrassed to have me in there. After they got me on the right dose of medicine, I remember her visits and she told me the social work people put her with a family we knowed, since she was underage. Our neighbors, the Doyen's. She fell in love with a Puerto Rican boy she met at school, Enrique Velasquez. Pearl got herself in a family way and they got married."

"How old was Pearl?"

"She was thirteen when she went to live with the Doyen family, and when Tony was born, she was about to turn seventeen. Then a year later, Enrique run off, and he divorced her by mail. His family moved somewhere and we don't know where they are now."

Adrienne laid down the clippers, stuck the teeny brush back inside the top of the bottle, and slid off the extra polish. "Tony never wanted to talk about his father. Now I understand why."

Soon, Adrienne was having some trouble with my smallest toenail. "This one's so petite. I can see why they wanted all of you to lick the tips of your brushes."

Out of the blue, I leaped forward in bed, grabbing the teeny brush out of her hand. "Don't you dare!" I yelled. My heart was pounding, and I held the brush in the air. Adrienne set still with her hands folded in her lap. "I promise, Helen. I won't put it in my mouth. I'm sorry I upset you."

"It's just that I wouldn't want you to lose your teeth too. I didn't like the taste none, so I stopped putting the brush in my mouth. I was one of the best painters there."

"I can't imagine swallowing paint, either."

I told Adrienne to open my bottom drawer, and pull out the plaque. She found it and read what it said. "Excellence in Training." Then, she put it on my nightstand.

"I earned it for working so hard. You know, some of those supervisors showed us it was safe. One had her a little spatula, like you would use in the kitchen. She stuck it in the jar of paint, and ate some of it off the end of the spatula. Then she said, 'See? Nothing to it.' Course, at the beginning, me and Violet was only there on a trial basis. They had to see how we done for a few weeks, before we was considered good painters. It was a good place to work though. We each had us a desk, like a old school desk, with two little trays on the side with the watch dials. The auditorium had plenty of light. It was a cheerful room. And the ceilings was very high." I held my arm straight up to show her.

"Why did you keep it a secret all these years? That you ever worked there?"

"We had our reasons."

I started in chewing the inside of my lower lip. Then I reached to my nightstand and showed Adrienne my letter from the Argonne Laboratory. "Remember when you and Tony brought me this letter to Mannington? It says I should go to Illinois and let the doctors there take a look at me too. Pearl has been trying to make me go."

"Don't you want to?"

She stared at the cast on my leg. "Well, maybe later." Then, I took the letter back and returned it to the nightstand, but I didn't want to say no more about the subject. Soon, my last toenail was done.

Closing up the bottle with the brush inside, Adrienne leaned forward and blew a little air on my toes. "Dries fast, doesn't it?"

I wiggled my toes and nodded, staring at my new pink raspberry foam polish. "Yes, it does. Just like the radium paint."

CHAPTER EIGHTEEN

One night when Pearl was out with Donald, Adrienne come over and took me to her apartment. She had her a box of things from when she was a girl. We was having us some fun, with my broke leg propped up on her sofa pillows, and Adrienne showing me her childhood memories box.

First, she held up a old book. It was torn and the cardboard was shredding on the corners. It was a child's book about *The Little Match Girl*. She had it from when she was only five years old. "I must have read this a million times, Helen." Then, her telephone was ringing, but she wouldn't answer it. "I'd rather talk to you," she said. "In fact, I wanted to tell you what happened last weekend when I went to see Benjamin. We had our first real...disagreement."

"I'm sorry. Tell me what happened." I had to shift my leg and suddenly, I felt a twinge of pain. "Could you kindly hand me one of my little pills, Adrienne?" I asked. She helped me, and got me a sip of water. Then she continued. "It was my fault. I brought up the subject of Benjamin's wife."

I recollected about Benjamin losing his wife and baby daughter, and I got tears in my eyes when Adrienne reminded me.

"I was in his apartment, and I asked him about a picture hanging on his wall."

"You mean, like a old photograph?"

"Mm hmm."

"He said her name was Gwen."

I took me one more sip of water, and waited.

"From the look on his face, I could tell Gwen was someone he had difficulty discussing. Then he said Gwen was his wife. Benjamin tried to smile, but it was the most painful smile I'd ever seen. His eyes were swimming in liquid, and I told him I was sorry for having brought up the subject.

But then, he assured me he wanted to tell me about Gwen. He wanted me to know. He said they'd been married about a year and a half when it had happened."

The next part made me sad too. Adrienne said she cuddled up to Benjamin's muscular arm, hugging it, and he didn't move. "The baby had died in the womb, and they weren't able to save Gwen."

I was still listening, but I couldn't seem to speak. Adrienne kept on with her story. "I cried, Helen. I cuddled right there in bed with him and cried. I thought of the most unbearable pain I'd ever experienced, and it couldn't come close to what Benjamin must have felt. I wiped my tears on his arm. Then I asked him if Gwen and the baby were buried together, and if the cemetery was far away."

Sudden-like, Adrienne stared into my eyes, and her voice got quiet. "Are you sure you want me to tell you this?"

"Yes, I want you to tell me."

"Okay. As soon as I asked Benjamin about the cemetery, he edged away from me, then he stood next to the bed. He looked really sad, and also, a little irritated with me. I tried to say something else; that I only wanted to suggest putting flowers on the graves. He got angry with me. I only wanted to be included in this part of his life, you know?"

Adrienne told me about how Benjamin explained his feelings. He hadn't never gone back to the cemetery, not since the funeral. Ever since he lost Gwen and his baby, he didn't want nothing to do with death, or dying. With funerals and cemeteries. That was why his mama didn't have a funeral service.

After Adrienne finished telling me, we both sniffled, and I handed her a little pack of tissues next to my bed. "You know, that time Benjamin and me met at the cemetery, when they took Violet's bones, he was standing so far away from everbody else."

She blew her nose. "After the argument, I went to take a shower. I cried in there for twenty minutes."

I give Adrienne a suggestion that I think she liked. I said we should stop and eat some cookies and ice cream. She said that was a very good idea, since it would take her mind off her troubles.

After a little while, somebody knocked on her door. I knowed it was Tony from the way he pounded hard and spoke ugly to Adrienne. "Are you gonna let me in?" he bellowed. The pounding got louder and louder, but Adrienne hollered at him to go away. Then, there was more pounding, only it was from Adrienne's neighbor in the next apartment. She put her hand on my arm, and told me she was sorry. She said she would get rid of Tony as soon as she could.

When Adrienne opened the door only a few inches, Tony shoved her and stormed inside. Then he turned in a circle. "It's about time you let me in."

Tony's beard was flat on one side, and he smelled like he hadn't had a bath in days. "All that pounding." Adrienne yelled. "I'm sure the neighbors were happy I let you in."

"You wouldn't answer the phone," he said to her in a unkindly way.

"No, you're right. I wouldn't. Ever stop to think maybe I didn't want to talk to you?"

Tony reached into his pocket for a cigarette, but Adrienne said she didn't give him permission to smoke in her apartment. Then, he glared at me. "Aunt Helen, why are you here?"

I didn't want to answer him. I didn't like the way he was talking to Adrienne, all nasty-like. When I didn't answer him, he grabbed the little book from Adrienne's box. "What's all this crap?"

Adrienne snatched her book away from Tony, and pushed him toward the door. "I want you to leave. Now."

Tony just stared at her, then he stared at me. "Is she still dating that old guy?" he asked me.

"Benjamin's not old. And he's nicer than you."

I knowed Tony would never hurt me or Adrienne, but I was still a little scared of him. Finally he left, and Adrienne locked the door and even put on the chain. Then she turned back to face me. "I'm sorry Helen. Sorry you had to see that. He makes me so angry."

I patted the sofa cushion next to my leg and she set down with me, letting out a long breath. After a quiet minute, she started in telling me about the night she seen Tony with the other woman.

"I never told you about that night. I went to his house after dark, but I thought he wasn't home. When I went into the house, it was dark inside, but then I heard a noise from his bedroom. I know I shouldn't have, but I opened his bedroom door and saw him with her. On the way out, I bruised my hip on the doorway, and turned to run outside. Then you know what I did, Helen?"

"No, what did you do?"

"I vomited in the gravel next to the car."

It didn't surprise me none. If I had seen what Adrienne seen in Tony's bedroom, I might of done the same thing.

CHAPTER NINETEEN

Pearl was still at work, and she told me not to take my bath until she got home. I didn't mind so much—I wasn't expecting no company. Since the air was so warm and it was a sunny day, I decided to take myself out to the back porch for a minute. I had me a little trouble with the door, but once it slammed behind me, I scooted to the porch chair and eased myself down into it. Then, I laid the crutches flat on the floor of the porch.

Across the fence in the next yard was the neighbor's dog tied to a chain. Pearl said his name was Bear, and he was a mix between different breeds. From the looks of his broad jaw, I reckoned Bear was part pit bull and part something else, but I didn't know what. He can sure bark, though. Ever time the trash man comes, he barks, and last week, he almost made it over the fence when the gas man come to read the meter in back of our house.

I recollected what my daddy used to do whenever we had a dog to jump the fence and stroll into our property. Daddy would get his rifle and shoot near the dog to scare it away. Then if that didn't work, he would bring out a big bucket of water and a ladle, and try to splash the water on the dog. If he got the dog wet, he would open the gate and let it out. That a-way, we could keep the dogs out of our chickens.

All of a sudden, Bear took to barking and pulling against his chain, straining to reach something by the fence. I called out to him, "What's the trouble, Bear? Did you see a rabbit? Was it a cat or something?"

Then, Bear got to fairly yanking on his chain, just a barking and carrying on something fierce. At first, I reckoned maybe somebody was coming to the front of the house, and tried to scoot myself up from the chair. Instead, the person come around to the back by the fence, while Bear just barked and carried on. Bear didn't like the man.

It was the man with the overalls.

If this man was fixing to harm me, I knowed I couldn't get up and run with my broke leg, so I just set still in my seat and asked him if he was real.

He made him a little hiccup sound, like as if he had too much to drink. "I'm real, all right." He leaned against the porch post, while Bear kept on barking and pulling his chain. Out of the blue, Bear broke loose and climbed hisself over the fence. That man in the overalls just made a little yelp and run out of the back yard, with Bear right behind him, snapping at his heels.

I waited, but the man never come back, and neither did Bear. I set back in my chair and wished I could ask Bear to tell me for certain that was a real man.

#

On Sunday, Benjamin took me and Adrienne to the park in Charlotte. We had one blanket for me to set on, and one for Benjamin and Adrienne, so they could snuggle. I pretended I was dozing off, and just listened and peeked my eyes open.

Adrienne had her shoulder bag on the blanket, stuffed with her things. She was laying on her side facing Benjamin, who leaned up on one elbow, fiddling with the clasp over the zipper. "Ah, the timeless mysteries of a woman's purse," he said.

Then, she touched the tip of his nose. He wrinkled it. "Go ahead," she said. "You know you're dying to see what's in there."

Benjamin snapped his arm back by his side. "My mother taught me never to..." he paused a moment. "I prefer to just imagine what's inside."

"But Benjamin, I don't have a problem with it." She opened the clasp, and held the open mouth of her handbag near his hand. "I mean, at this stage in our relationship, we shouldn't have any secrets." When Adrienne said that, she peeked over at me, but I give her the signal that I wouldn't say nothing about her pills.

"It's not a matter of secrets. It's a matter of...the painful childhood memory of having my hand slapped." Benjamin grinned at her, so's she would know he was just making a little joke. Reaching inside her bag, Adrienne pulled out her wallet and set it on the blanket. Next, she pulled out a little box of crayons.

He lifted them and held them up in front of her. "Crayons?"

She snatched them away. "Yes, crayons." Adrienne was trying to hide her smile. "My weakness."

Benjamin had a confused look to his face. I reckon he wanted to know the story behind it.

"I like to color. In coloring books. It relaxes me." She giggled while she said it.

After staring at her a moment, he took the crayon box from her hand and set it back inside her handbag, but drew his hand out as if he'd been bit.

"Somebody slap you?" she asked, smiling. She lifted his hand and kissed the back, then turned it to the palm, and kissed him there too. "Where else does it hurt?"

Benjamin didn't answer her. He stared across the park.

"What are you thinking about?"

"Just some of the... *other* memories. From my childhood."

Then, he was still. Adrienne's voice got quiet, and she asked him how old he was when he lost his daddy.

"I was twenty-four. He died suddenly when he was forty-five. Same age I am now. The doctors said natural causes, but sometimes I wonder. I helped my mother move into a smaller home after he died." Then with a small shake of his head, he seemed like as if he was clearing his thoughts.

"Have you found out anything more about the radium factory?"

His shoulders sagged an inch or two, and his lips turned down at the edges. Then, he took him a breath and peeked over at me on the blanket. He must have thought I was asleep. "There's one thing I'd like to know, but the only person who can answer it won't tell me."

"You mean why she and Clara kept their job a secret?"

"Yes, exactly. I'd just like to know, that's all."

After a second or two, nobody was talking so I peeked my eye open. Benjamin seen me awake, but he shushed me and Adrienne.

"What is it?" Adrienne asked.

"Shh. ...It's a...no, it's an Indigo Bunting."

"A what?"

"There, hear it? The high pitched chirping?"

Benjamin demonstrated for us. Adrienne giggled at his bird call. "I never knew you were so talented." Then, she buried her nose in his shirt collar and took in a breath.

"I can do more," he whispered into her hair. "Tell me what this one sounds like."

Benjamin made his lips and face look funny, as he did the next bird song.

Adrienne asked me if I agreed it was like being in a aviary—so realistic. "That one sounded exactly like someone squeaking their shoes on a tile floor."

Next, he set up straight, and struggled to keep from chuckling. He couldn't get his lips to come together. "How about this?"

Benjamin did a new one, then we all laughed. "Like a tooting whistle at a ballpark," was my description.

"Now this one."

We was enjoying the game. So much fun to hear Benjamin sound like the different birds.

The next bird call wasn't nothing like the others. Not done with a whistle. It sounded like someone being choked or calling for help. Me and Adrienne didn't like it. "What kind of bird was that, Benjamin?" she asked.

He held her face in his hands. "You don't like that one. I won't do it again."

I stared at a small hole in the blanket, picking at it with my index finger. "I didn't neither."

Adrienne said she didn't like it, but wanted Benjamin to please do more. "Just a more cheerful one," she asked.

He reached for a Pepsi bottle from the cooler. "Mind if I wet my whistle first?" Adrienne didn't answer him. Instead, she kissed him. I could tell Benjamin and Adrienne was in love, and all of a sudden, I was beginning to feel like a fifth wheel.

CHAPTER TWENTY

While I was setting up in bed looking at a Life Magazine about Doris Day, Pearl and Donald was talking. They was trying to be quiet, but I heard nearly ever word. Specially the important ones. They was talking about me.

"Honey, I want her to have that testing. If she's going to get cancer and die, I think we should know as soon as possible."

Donald cleared his throat a little. "Have you approached her again with the idea?"

"Yes, but she says she's too scared. She's worried the testing might hurt, or she'll be too nervous around the doctors."

Pearl had asked me two or three different times to go to Illinois for the testing. Ever time, we get into a argument. When she explained my reasons to Donald, she got the information exactly right. I don't want no doctors poking around me, asking me questions about things I want to forget.

"You can't force her to go," Donald said. "She has to *want* to have the testing done."

For a few minutes, they was quiet, but then there was a little shuffling sound, like somebody moving some papers or magazines. Pearl said she was trying to train a girl at her work to take her job after she quits. The girl was stupid, and she didn't think she was learning everthing too good. So Pearl was going to have to spend more time there training her, and she would need to be at work more than usual. And that meant she would have to get somebody to come in and look after me.

Then, she described how much extra work it was for me to be there with my broken leg. Pearl said she had to bring all my meals in and do my laundry, and she had to wrap up my leg with plastic before I got into a bath, and help me get in and out of the tub. Then she said one time, my crutches slipped and fell to the floor and I couldn't reach them and Pearl had to get up at four o'clock in the morning so's I could get to the bathroom on time.

For a minute, I didn't hear nothing, then Donald said maybe he could hire a nurse. Pearl said that would cost too much because nurses are expensive, and Donald said money would be no object, if it was for his lovey, and he said, "What about Adrienne?" He said he thought she would make a good nurse for me.

Now, I been around a lot of nurses in my time, and I like Adrienne, but I knowed she was learning to be a midwife, not a old folks nurse. But Pearl said she would ask anyway. I knowed what Adrienne would say. She would say no, because she didn't like Pearl none. Besides, Adrienne worked a lot of hours already.

That night, I was setting out in the living room when Pearl was on the telephone in the bedroom saying how exhausted she was all the time. She was talking to Adrienne, but the call was short, and next thing I knowed, Pearl was throwing things and stomping her feet. After a few minutes, Adrienne showed up at the door, and Pearl let her in.

Adrienne was dressed in a sweat shirt and her blue jeans.

"And just what was so damn important that you had to get in your car and drive over here?" Pearl asked with one hand resting on her hip.

While she rolled up her sleeves, Adrienne said hello to me, then she pinched her lips and started in on Pearl. "The reason I couldn't tell you this on the phone, is because I wanted to tell you to your face. I feel sorry for Helen, because she has to live with you. I hate it that she has to be alone here all day with nothing to do but watch TV and read magazines. If you're too lazy to take care of the woman who raised you, when she's sitting here with a broken leg, then you deserve to be exhausted."

While Adrienne was flinging her arms and yelling at Pearl, I was enjoying myself, thinking this would make a good television program. Pearl added some unkind things about Adrienne, such as what Tony said about her. That he never really loved her, but kept her around for her looks. The sparks was flying, and I was right there to see it.

Then Adrienne got tears in her eyes and come over to hug me good-bye. When she got close to me, I smelled the sweat on her. She was fired up hot. She whispered she was sorry, and she hoped I understood what she was saying. Next Pearl told Adrienne the sooner she was out of her house, the sooner she could work on forgetting her. Then Adrienne left, and Pearl hollered at me that Adrienne had bumped the end table and spilled my milk on the new carpet. Now, she had one *more* thing to take care of.

#

Pearl was still upset about not knowing exactly how her mama died. "I wish they could get her test results sooner. It's so hard to have to wait," she'd said.

Violet's bones didn't need to be tested. Too much radium in her body is what killed her. Pearl should of knowed by now, but she wanted to see the official report from the laboratory when it was done. I was with Violet in 1933 when the doctor told her why he reckoned she was losing her teeth. Violet begged her husband Grady to not make her go, but he insisted. He was gone to work, but he told her to make sure she saw the doctor as soon as she could.

"Name please."

"Violet Rodgers."

"Occupation?"

"Housewife."

"Age?"

"Twenty-eight."

The nurse filled out the form for Violet. We set in the waiting room of the Gastonia Doctors Building, while Violet thumbed through a newspaper somebody had left on the table. When the nurse called Violet to see the doctor, Violet said, "I want my sister to come with me." So I did.

The doctor come into the room and smiled. When he seen two patients, he asked if we was going to pay him double. Me and Violet chuckled a little, and told him he was only seeing Violet. He give her a examination, and asked her what was her symptoms. She showed him the two gaps in her teeth, and said her neck was sore all the time. He said this Depression has everbody sick, cause they didn't get enough vitamins. The doctor poked her in the chin, so's he could get her to raise up, cause he wanted to check her pulse in her neck. When he poked her, she moaned and held onto her jaw.

"That's tender there, is it?"

"Yes, doctor. It is. Feels like you knocked something loose inside."

The doctor looked at me, like as if to decide was she just making a little joke, but she wasn't. She was still holding onto her jaw, and she had a pained sort of look to her face. Then, he looked back at Violet. He reached up to her chin again, and asked her to open her mouth. He stuck his thumbs straight inside and run them both up and back beside her gums, with his fingers on the outside of her cheeks and jaw, all the while staring across the room. When he stopped moving, Violet let out a wail. The doctor had to slowly slide his thumbs back out, and he told Violet she would need to get a x-ray. While his thumbs was on the way out, one of Violet's teeth come with them. It didn't bleed. It just fell out onto the table.

The doctor told us he would be back after he got his nurse to set up the x-ray machine. While he was gone, me and Violet whispered to each other about what was likely to happen. She held her jaw and leaned close to me. "You think he'll know?"

"About the radium?"

"It's been in the papers. I bet *all* the doctors know about the symptoms by now."

I stared at the door, wondering how much longer until the doctor would come back. "I reckon he might figure what you've got, but he probably won't know how you come to get it."

In a moment, Violet put her jacket back on. "We need to get out of here." Just then, the doctor come back into the room with the nurse. He asked Violet if she was cold. "No, I'm fixing to leave. I can't afford an x-ray."

Then, the doctor put one fist on his hip, and shifted his weight to the other side. "I'm sorry to hear that. Would you allow me to run some other tests on you? Perhaps draw some blood, or get a urine sample?"

Now, Violet had hopped down off the examining table. She stood me up too, and told him we was leaving, and we would like a bill for the services.

After we got home, I listened to her lie to Grady about what the doctor said. "He says it's just this old Depression. Folks are losing their teeth, and having all sorts of problems. Told me to try to get out in the sunshine ever day and to drink more milk and get some healthy foods once in a while."

Grady frowned. He said he was sorry, wishing he could earn more, so they wouldn't have to worry so much. Then, he reached his hands to either side of her face, giving her a squeeze. Then Violet cried, telling Grady to don't never touch her there again.

#

"Helen, isn't it exciting? We've set the date."

Pearl hopped around in her stocking feet on her new shag carpet, twisting herself into a circle. "I just got off the phone with Donald and we decided it would be after the election. On the Friday after Thanksgiving." She slapped her hands together with her eyes blinking as if somebody had give her a start. "There's still so much to do. That hot water heater mess put me weeks behind. Did I tell you, his mother still wants all of us to go to her house for dinner? We'll be there on approval, Helen, so we have to be on our best behavior. She still wants to meet you. She said she wants to meet the woman who raised me."

I was there for part of Pearl's childhood years, but not all of them. I only filled in in Violet's place.

"Remember we couldn't go last time, because you'd just broken your leg?" she asked. "You'll need to get your hair done, and I'll get you some nice jewelry from my jewelry box."

I reckoned I wouldn't mind meeting Donald's mama. At least I could finally get to see our new house. It was hard to think about what the future would be like, living in Charlotte. I wished I could've had a visit with Madam Langlie in Gastonia, like me and Violet did one day after she started to get more and more sick. We was driving home from the market one day, so we decided to go see Madam Langlie. She was old now, but she still had her a crystal ball and some special cards to tell people what was in their future.

Me and Violet left little Pearl in the car and went inside to have our fortunes told. "We can't stay long," Violet said, worried about Pearl asleep in the car by herself.

"Come in, come in," Madam Langlie said, opening the door wide. In her big room, she had her a entire wall filled with teeny bottles of medicines. Some had little eyedroppers in them, and others had just regular bottle tops. She told us to set together on the sofa, so me and Violet put our handbags on the floor and set down.

"Violet, I'm sorry to hear you're so sick," Madam Langlie said, tilting her head to the side. She wore her silver hair in a loose bun with unruly strands that puffed out above her ears. When she smiled she had her a crooked mouth, with one side up higher than the other.

Violet thanked her, and crossed her arms. She wasn't smiling too much lately, now that she had lost more of her teeth.

I asked Madam Langlie what all the teeny bottles was for. She said she was now studying natural medicines, like in the olden days. She told us they used to use all sorts of herbs and things from nature to cure ills, and they was finding new ones all the time. Me and Violet stared at each other a minute. I knowed we was thinking the same thing... that Madam Langlie might have something that would make cancer go away. But Violet didn't have to ask, because Madam Langlie spoke up first.

"You know, you don't have to be sick anymore, Violet. I think we can take care of you, without a doctor."

"You can?" Violet's voice sounded hopeful, but she was still worried too.

Madam Langlie begin, gazing at her wall of little bottles. "Oh yes, I'm sure of it."

Violet wanted to hear more, and I did too.

"Now, some of these medicines only work when you take them together. In a certain combination."

I knowed what she meant. Like when you mix milk and lemon juice to make sour milk for a chocolate cake.

"One of the most popular cures is for you to take these two together." She took two teeny bottles off her shelf and handed them to Violet. "This one is licorice, and the other is ginseng."

Now, I knowed licorice was a candy, but I hadn't never heard of the other one.

"How much will it cost?" Violet asked.

"Four dollars a bottle. But they only work if you take them together."

When Madam Langlie said that, me and Violet nearly exploded off the sofa. We didn't have four dollars between us even for one bottle. I told Violet we could skip the ginseng and go to the Belmont Five and Dime to get us a dollar's worth of licorice candy instead. We would have to hide it from Pearl, though.

We thanked Madam Langlie and started out the door. "Don't you want to see what the crystal says?"

Violet said no, and even though I was wondering what was in store for my future, I decided instead I was craving some licorice candy for my own self.

CHAPTER TWENTY-ONE

I knowed I shouldn't of listened, but Pearl's voice is so loud sometimes, I can hear her all the way into my room. Benjamin had come to the house, and Pearl met him in the living room.

"How does this thing work exactly?" Pearl asked.

"Well, as I mentioned on the phone, it's a machine that detects radioactivity. It's on loan from a military surplus business in Atlanta. A friend of mine works there."

"Hmm. What's in the *small* box?"

"Just a little something for Helen. Is she awake?"

"Oh, you can wake her. With that medicine they gave her she sleeps all the time."

"I'd rather not..."

"Don't worry," she interrupted. "She'll be happy to see you. Just set that thing down here," she said. Then there was a sound, like somebody setting a heavy object on the floor.

Their footsteps was in the hall. "Excuse the mess, but we're preparing for the move."

"Miserable undertaking, isn't it?"

"Oh yes. I just hate it."

I was just setting up in bed, listening to the radio. Big band jazz. "Helen, you have a visitor."

As Benjamin stood in the doorway, he stared like as if he forgot I had a broke leg. Also, he was staring at my toenails. They was still pink. After Pearl stopped being so nosy, I reached my hand for Benjamin to come on in. Pearl stepped out of the way, then left us alone.

"Benjamin, I'm so glad you come to see me."

He reached his hands to mine, too. Then he told me a little joke. He pointed to my cast, and said, "Some people will do anything to get out of housework."

I chuckled, then asked him to set with me. "What did you bring me?" I reached over for his present, tearing off the wrapping paper.

"Nothing much. Just something I thought you might like."

Inside was a brand new pair of furry, blue slippers. "Thank you kindly. I just love them. See that pair on the floor? By the closet? When the hot water heater broke they got wet. They haven't fit right ever since."

Benjamin told me how happy he was he chose the right gift.

"How are you and Adrienne getting along?" I asked.

"Very well, thank you. I'll be seeing her as soon as I leave here."

I leaned forward and whispered, "I like you better than Tony, even if he is kin to me."

Then Benjamin whispered back, smiling. "Thank you very much."

"Are you able to stay for supper tonight, or do you have to rush off to see Adrienne?"

"I'm here to run the Geiger counter for Pearl. I mentioned I had the use of one, and she asked if we could test some items here."

"What is a...?"

"It's called a Geiger-Muller counter. A machine that tests for radiation. Pearl asked me to go up into the attic and test a few things for her."

I reached for my crutches. "Can I go up there with you?"

Just then, Pearl marched into the room. "Now Helen, you know that's not possible. Not with your leg that way. Besides, once Benjamin and I are up there, the attic will be too crowded. You just wait here."

I swung both my legs to the side of the bed and pushed up. Benjamin stepped toward me and offered to help, but I wanted to show him how good I could get around on my own with the crutches. I told him sometimes it itches like all get-out, and the thigh on my broke leg had made itself a new muscle, from carrying around that cast.

"I wish I could go up to the attic, because I want to find my water color. It's in a nice frame with a blue ribbon. I won a prize for it."

Benjamin said he could be glad to take me up to the attic, and he asked Pearl if there was a place I could set down once

I was up there. She said all right, but she wasn't too happy about it.

Slowly, me and Benjamin climbed up the steps. We was both out of breath, and he placed his hand flat against his chest for a minute. Then he set me into the green wicker chair. Pearl had already took some things from boxes, and then Benjamin said he would be right back with the radium machine.

After he was back, Pearl pointed to the ones she wanted tested. Then she handed Benjamin a yard stick, and said he could use it to move things around without stepping over them.

Holding the Geiger counter in his arms, he told me and Pearl the higher the gauge was, the faster the clicks we would hear. At first, the machine didn't make a noise, then he moved to different spots in the attic and the machine begin to make clicks. He got closer to something leaning against a box, but all I could see was the wire hanger on the back. While the machine clicks got faster, he used the yard stick to lift the wire hanger, turning it to the front. It was my water color. My lovely scene of the park, with the pretty blues, greens, and pinks. I smiled and reached for it.

"Oh, you found it." Pearl said, staring at the picture. "Helen's been asking about it. She painted it when she was young. But why is it... I mean, the clicking is so *fast*."

Benjamin turned his face to mine, and his eyebrows was raised like as if he was asking me something. "My guess is some of the paint used was radium paint."

Pearl sucked in a breath. "You mean that same paint that killed my mother? And it's been in this house all these years?" Her face turned pale, and she stared over at me. "I had that hanging on the wall for years at the old house. Since then, it's been up here." She put her hand on her throat. "Oh, I'm just sick about this. Am I in danger?" Pearl asked.

"I can't say for certain. Even the man who loaned me the machine said there was no definitive level considered too high. He simply said if it clicks at all..."

Staring off in the distance, Pearl exhaled a slow breath. "Helen, how could you? Radium paint? And you kept it even after you knew the dangers? You know, I always wondered about that water color. It was so bright, even at night. It was hanging in the hall across from the bathroom, but I always thought it was reflecting the bathroom nightlight. I never knew..."

Suddenly, Pearl got a serious look to her face. "We'll need to get rid of it. We should burn it."

"No!" I yelled. "I won't let you."

Benjamin took hold of my hand. "Burning it is not an option. It would cause the radiation to dissipate in an unhealthy manner. As I mentioned on the phone, I discovered something in my mother's belongings that also registered high."

"What was that?"

"A plaque. Excellence in Training. We notified the Atomic Energy Commission. They sent someone to the storage unit immediately, with protective gear so they wouldn't have to handle it."

Suddenly, I was sick to my stomach, but I didn't let on. I just set in my chair, hoping there wasn't nothing wrong with my plaque, and the government people wouldn't have to come take it away neither. Maybe I could hide it back in my drawer.

"I'd feel better if the water color was disposed of at once," Pearl said, stepping on the first stair step down. "Helen, that's just the way it'll have to be."

Pearl asked Benjamin if it would be safe to leave the water color in the attic.

"I'm sure that will be fine for now. Is there anything else you'd like me to test?"

She stopped and nodded her head. "Oh, I almost forgot. There are some things in Helen's room."

"Let's get down there."

#

Benjamin and Pearl helped me back into my bedroom and now that it was dark outside, I reached for the light switch in my room, but Benjamin was behind me. He asked me what that was on my nightstand, and I was surprised he could see anything since the lights wasn't even on yet. Then I was surprised too, when the plaque was giving off a pale light. It was pretty, and it glowed in the dark.

As Benjamin stepped closer to the plaque, I wished I could have hid it before he got there, but now it was too late. "Just like my mother's," he said. "Hers glowed as well. I discovered it after she'd passed away, and she'd kept it hidden in a closet, wrapped in aluminum foil and a pillowcase."

Pearl gasped. "Does the Geiger counter make clicks for it?"

Benjamin waved the little microphone part over the plaque. Sure enough, it made little clicking sounds. Pearl was snotty again, saying we would have to get rid of it, just like the water color. "Test her other things too, Benjamin."

When he pulled the first dress out, the little machine made a clicking sound, and then he laid that one on the bed, and took out the other one. It made a clicking sound too. Then, he said everthing I owned from the old days made a little bit of a clicking sound. My new slippers and my white gloves from Mannington was fine. He was glad of that, and said I should wear them in good health.

Pearl stuck her hand on her hip, pointing to my dresses. "You *do* know we're going to have to destroy all these things, don't you?"

My face turned hot, and I thought I was going to get me a headache. "Destroy them? Why?"

"They're radioactive. It's harmful to have these things here."

Instead of looking me in the eye, she looked at Benjamin instead, like as if he had all the answers. Her eyebrows was wrinkled, and she started to pick up one of the dresses, but let it go, like as if it had scorched her skin. Then she wiped her hands on her slacks.

"Helen, Pearl believes it would be safest to discard any items that are radioactive."

"But those are *my* things. They belong to me, nobody else. I don't want nobody discarding nothing of mine. It wouldn't be right."

Just then, Pearl took hold of Benjamin's sleeve, and they left my room. They was talking in the hall, but I heard some of what they was saying. Pearl said she handles all my affairs, and Benjamin said he felt awkward being in the middle of a domestic dispute. Then I couldn't hear the next part, but Benjamin come back and stood next to my bed. "I have to go now, Helen, but I hope to see you again soon."

"Please don't go. Tell Pearl to let me keep my things."

"I'm sorry," he said, squeezing my hand like a friend. Only just then, I felt like as if I didn't have a friend in the world.

#

Now that Adrienne and Benjamin was getting to be so close, I wondered if Benjamin knowed about her taking drugs or not. I know what it's like when somebody has to take a little something extra, just to smooth out the rough edges. Clara Jane was one of those people, at least after she got older. After she got married, and she give birth to her first baby. Benjamin had him a little sister, Iris, and when I seen Clara with her new baby, I seen her take a sip from a little metal flask. I smelled the liquor on her breath.

She asked me to join her to a picture show, while her husband stayed home with the children.

I told Clara I would be happy to go to the picture show with her, and on the way there, she stopped the car and took out her little flask from her handbag. Then, she took a long sip from it, offering me one too. I told her no, I wasn't thirsty.

"You sure?" she asked, swallowing her last sip.

I only nodded. Then, Clara put the lid back on and the flask was gone again. For a minute or two, I couldn't say nothing. Then, Clara told me how taking a sip of gin ever so often can just make her feel better about old memories.

"You mean, about things you done that you wish you hadn't?"

She shrugged and tilted her head to the side. Her breath was wretched, like the gin. "Not only that, but for the past few years, we've heard about so many of the girls dying or getting sick with cancer. I don't like to think about it. Now that I've got the new baby, and Benjamin is getting older, I know I should be worrying about taking care of them, but sometimes I just need a little something to keep the memories from getting the best of me."

I told Clara to be careful, so the gin wouldn't get the best of *her*, neither.

As we was walking from the car to the ticket booth, I stopped Clara and asked her one more thing. "Do you ever go to confession anymore, Clara?"

She told me she went ever Sunday to Mass, and even took Holy Communion. But she hadn't been to confession since she was a young woman. The reason she told me she didn't go to confession any more was she didn't want no more punishment than she already had, ever day of her life.

#

Early the next morning, Pearl woke me up when she turned a bright light on in my room. I made a groan sound and covered my head with the pillow. "Turn it off," I sputtered.

She said no, she wanted me to look at something on her arm. I was still angry with her from when she said we had to destroy my belongings. She said we would talk about it again in the morning. Maybe that would be now. I brought my head out from under and blinked until my eyes got used to the light.

She pointed to something. It was a mole on her arm. Just above her elbow. Grabbing hold of my index finger, she made me rub my fingertip up and back across her mole. It felt lumpy, with a teeny bit of hair. I looked at it too, and she said she thought it might be cancer.

For the next couple a minutes, Pearl bawled about how she could have got cancer from her mother, since Violet was working with the radium before Pearl was formed in the womb, and that was maybe why her twin brother died. Not to mention the water color and all the other things in the house.

"I want to have this ugly thing removed before the wedding," she said, pinching and playing with her mole. "They could do a biopsy on it and let me know. Cancer or not, at least it would be gone from my arm. I don't want to go on my honeymoon with an unsightly blemish for Donald to look at." Then, she put a wadded tissue to her nose.

Since my bladder was full, I told Pearl to please pass me my crutches, so's I could get out of bed. As she reached for them, she had a expression on her face like she seen a ghost, and she looked away from my eyes. "If I was found to have cancer, you don't think I would get as sick as Mama, do you?"

I set up on the side of the bed, sliding my feet into my new slippers. They was on the wrong feet, so I switched them. "How much do you recollect about when your mama was sick?"

She pinched her bottom lip with two fingers and said she recollected her mama laying in bed, stroking Pearl's little girl arm and sending her for a extra blanket or to switch on the radio, so's she could listen to a orchestra.

"I remember when I wasn't allowed to kiss her any longer. I wasn't allowed in her room."

Just then, Pearl's cat run into the room and hopped up on the chest of drawers. Pearl leaned over to hold him in her arms, to be a comfort to her. But he just jumped right onto the floor and flittered away.

CHAPTER TWENTY-TWO

At the doctor's office, Pearl and Dr. Meyer helped me onto the soft chair and got my legs up on the foot rest. Dr. Meyer pulled her white coat around her middle, and set in a swivel chair at her desk. Pearl set in the other soft chair, but she didn't put her feet up. Instead, she set there with her knees together.

First, the doctor asked Pearl some questions from her paperwork, just making sure she had the right address and telephone number, and about Pearl's job at Belk's. Pearl squirmed in her seat. I reckoned she was ill at ease because she doesn't like doctors any more than I do. Also, Pearl doesn't like talking to doctors about when she was a girl. After Violet died and Pearl's daddy left, I had to try and explain to her what happened. Explain that her daddy was a weak person. That when Violet had got worse, Grady took to drinking. Pearl wasn't never close to Grady, but he *was* her daddy, and when he left, it never come as no great surprise to me, but it did to little Pearl.

After she was done with the paperwork, Dr. Meyer put it in a folder on her desk. "Now, Mrs. Velasquez, I asked to meet with both of you together, because it can help to involve the family members in therapy, especially the primary caregiver of our elderly patients."

"Well, I don't mind coming here once in a while, but as Helen has already told you, we'll be moving soon when I get married. She'll be transferred to another clinic nearer our new home."

"Yes, Helen mentioned you'd be moving. Helen, how do you feel about moving to Charlotte?"

Before I answered, I cleared my throat a little. "I can't see no advantage to it."

"Do you mean you'd rather stay in Belmont?" Dr. Meyer asked.

"No, I mean I was happier at Mannington."

Pearl set up straight as a board in her seat. "She doesn't mean that, Doctor. She's just upset with me because, well, I've been so busy lately, getting ready to move, and getting ready for the wedding, and now with her broken leg, I haven't had time to concentrate on much of anything else."

Then, Dr. Meyer leaned toward me a few inches. "Helen, what do you think you and Pearl might do together after she's married and you're all settled in Charlotte?"

"Do together? You mean like go out somewheres, or go on a visit?"

"Yes, what sorts of outings might you take? Or what sorts of activities might you do together at home?"

All of a sudden, my mind just went blank. I couldn't think of no place I wanted to go with Pearl, or nothing I was hoping to do with her at home, neither. Nothing come to mind, except how much I hoped my leg would heal faster, so's at least Pearl wouldn't be so fretful all the time.

"I can't think of nothing right now."

Pearl glanced at her wrist watch. "You know Doctor, Charlotte's a big, exciting city. I'm sure Donald and I will take her lots of places. But for right now, I really don't have the time. Things are very busy at my job, since I'm training the girl who will take my place after I'm gone. I don't even have the time to be *here*."

The doctor sort of nodded her head, then asked me a new question. "Helen, is there anything on your mind today that you'd like to talk about?"

Since the water color and my dresses was heavy on my mind, I answered her quick. "I didn't want to, but I had to allow Pearl to take away my things."

Dr. Meyer stared at Pearl, like as if she was waiting for her to say something. "Her things?"

Pearl sort of frowned and smiled at the same time. "Oh, Doctor, we've had a terrible thing happen at home. It turns out Helen and my mother Violet worked in a factory years ago, and got themselves exposed to radium. A couple of days ago, we found out some of Helen's belongings were covered with radiation. Of course, we had to dispose of them at once."

"My goodness. How did you dispose of them?"

"We asked the sheriff to come pick them up," I said. "But he sent some other men, with gloves and hard hats on. They took them away in a couple of big black bags."

I told the doctor how it made me cry to see my plaque and beautiful water color took away by strangers. The blue ribbon was gone off my picture, too.

A second later, Pearl added that I shouldn't of used that paint in the first place.

I begin to see stars before my eyes, but for some reason, I yelled at Dr. Meyer instead of Pearl. "Violet snuck the paint home with us to Belmont. We never knowed it would hurt nobody. I just wanted some of that special paint on my water color because I reckoned it would look pretty to see it at night too. Over the years, I forgot it had that paint on it."

"I can see this has upset you very much," Dr. Meyer said. She got out from behind her desk, and touched me on the shoulder. "I'm afraid our time is about up. I want to thank you ladies for coming today, and Helen, let me help you out of that chair." She reached for me, but Pearl butted in front. "I've got her, Doctor. We can manage just fine." She handed me the crutches and helped boost me up till I was standing.

Just before we left, I looked again at Dr. Meyer's face. She wasn't staring at me the way she did the first time I met her, like she thought I was stupid. This time, she was looking that a-way at Pearl.

#

After my bath, Pearl said I could read the paper if I remembered to save it after. She wanted it so she could wrap her breakable things for when we moved.

As I looked at the front page, there was a article about a trial in the state of Wisconsin, where a woman said she had caught a lung disease from working in a unsafe place. Back in 1938, Clara sent me a article in the mail, and it was about nearly the same thing.

All along, Clara was keeping up with the other Radium Dial ladies who was trying to get money for their doctors' bills. They was called "The Ottawa Society of the Living Dead." They had been trying since 1934 to get their money, and it took all the way until four years later for the government people to decide the trial. Finally, the ladies would get their money for the doctors' bills and for their lost wages. But the Radium Dial people did a appeal in court, because they didn't want to have to pay. I saved the article, and more like it as the years went by. Other articles said ever time the trial would be decided, the company presidents would file a new appeal. Over and over.

One of the articles was about a real nice lady with a husband and two little children, who had first got a pain in her ankle. Then, it spread to her knees, and she took to limping when she walked. At her trial, she showed them how we was taught to dip the brush in the paint and kiss the brush, but they wouldn't listen. Even though she said she had worked at the Radium Dial, the doctors wasn't sure what was wrong with her, and when she went for her trial, they say she looked like a old woman, even though she was still young.

Sometimes when Clara sent me those clippings, she would send a long letter with them. In her letters, she would first tell me about Benjamin and Iris and her husband, James, and then she would tell me how she was full of guilt and remorse all the time. I wrote her back and told her she didn't have nothing to feel guilty about. Instead, the people who should feel guilty was the company presidents of the Radium Dial, for not helping all those ladies.

I wish now I still had those old articles so's I could show them to Benjamin or Adrienne. But when Pearl and them first put me in the hospital, I lost all the clippings. I don't recollect where they are.

#

Yesterday evening, Donald and Pearl said I could set with them on the back porch, since the temperature was in the sixties. I tucked my sweater around my shoulders, and Donald went into the house and found me a small coverlet for my legs.

"Those are some fine looking slippers you have on, Helen."

"Thank you. They was give to me by Benjamin Reed. He brought them the day he come with that clicking machine."

"Geiger counter," Pearl said, adding a couple more ice cubes to his drink from her ice bucket.

"I'm sorry you had to give up your belongings, but Pearl mentioned they were radioactive. Quite dangerous."

Then, Pearl rolled up her blouse sleeve and showed Donald her bandage. "I asked Dr. Olmstead to remove it. He's sending it to a pathologist for a biopsy."

Donald stared at the bandage. "Did he suspect it was cancerous?"

Pearl took a big drink of her Coke, and her eyes got funny, like as if she didn't want to say what she was thinking. "He said he would check." Then, when she set her Coke back down, she asked Donald if now that my leg was getting better, could we finally re-arrange that dinner with Donald's mother.

He said his mother was fairly busy right now, but he would ask.

After a minute, we set and listened to the outside noises—some crickets, and a far away dog. In the trees out back something was rustling, but we decided it was likely a raccoon or a squirrel. But from the kitchen come a different sound. Tony stepped onto the porch. His beard was trimmed shorter, but it was a might crooked.

He had him a new girlfriend. She had a hard look to her, like as if her face was older than her body. She was wearing more eye make-up than any one girl needed. Tony introduced the girl to all of us. She shook my hand, but only with the tips of her fingers, and they was sweaty and cold. Her name was Bernice Jo Healy, and she was from New Zealand. She had her a funny accent to her voice, such as saying *hid* instead of *head*. She told Tony they had to leave soon because her *hid* was hurting.

"Before you go, Tony, have you found anyone who can look in on Helen during the day?" Pearl asked.

"Well, Bernice just happens to be looking for a job. She's free every day except Wednesday, when she has to go to a... doctor's office, but otherwise, maybe she could help out."

Pearl was full of questions for Bernice. I didn't want to listen no more. It was giving me a headache, just thinking about that strange girl taking care of me. All I wanted to do was to recollect in 1934 when Violet was laying on the living room sofa, so's folks could come by and say "good-bye" to her, just like we did that time with Bess.

I showed Clara to the sofa, and she set on a small wooden stool next to Violet. "I came as soon as I got Grady's telegram," Clara said.

Since Violet's hair was so patchy and dull, we wrapped a nice scarf on her head. Her voice was not as strong that day as it was the day before, because her throat was raw most of the time, but Clara and Violet had them a talk about children and about memories. All around the room, there was other folks who wanted a turn with Violet, but I said Clara was one of our oldest and dearest friends, and could they please allow her a few extra minutes.

Violet asked how Clara's little boy Benjamin was, and her husband James, and then she was out of breath. Clara wiped a few tears from her own cheeks, then told her about little Ben, and how he was interested in collecting bugs of all kinds, specially spiders. When Clara said that, Violet almost smiled, but it was hard then for her to smile at all. She'd lost all her teeth, and she didn't have much to smile about, with her strength gone. Because she always had something draining down the back of her throat, it give her a constant little cough. Sometimes when she tried to swallow, drinks or food would come right back up onto her chin and neck.

When Violet's nose started to run again, I got the soft cloth and wiped it up. Sometimes it was blood, and sometimes it was a sour-smelling pus that run out. Since we had company, I tried to keep Violet wiped up as best I could.

She didn't have too many bad days no more, now that she was on the morphine and close to passing on. Once in a while, she would get to fretting about things that wasn't real, like hollering for somebody to get her blanket off, when she wasn't wearing nothing but a nightgown. Other times, she would get up in the middle of the night with a burst of energy and start mixing up flour and water and get out the rolling pin to make biscuits. Once, she tossed out a brand new jar of Wesson Oil, because she was sure the inside of the jar was full of dirt.

Clara leaned over and patted Violet on the shoulder, asking me if she could have a word with Grady. I showed Clara to the back bedroom, where he was standing by the closet, staring up at the top. He didn't know we was watching him, and he jumped a little when he seen us.

"Excuse me Grady, but you remember Clara. You remember you wrote her a telegram for Violet? She come on a bus. All the way here from Atlanta."

Grady had him a long face. More so than usual. I recollected the time Violet had showed him that poor crumpled little baby chick, and he had all but wanted to run off to be sick to his stomach. Or when his little baby son William died. Grady had the same face now.

He mumbled something about "nice to see you," but I knowed his mind was on Violet. I whispered to Clara for us to leave him alone, and maybe she could talk to him later. We left for the kitchen. Clara set herself down in a chair, fiddling with the edge of the tablecloth. Her eyes was filled with tears, when she gazed up at me. "Where's little Pearl?"

"She's visiting with her girlfriend, Edith Mae, at her home until Violet passes."

I told Clara how one day last week, Pearl run right out into the road when she seen a dark red, oozing boil inside Violet's mouth.

"Are you as scared as I am?" Clara asked.

"You mean about this happening to us?"

She only nodded her head. She told me that so far, she barely had a day yet where she didn't feel as right as rain. Never caught colds, unless it was the dead of winter, and she never had her a loose tooth. Maybe me and Clara would go on to live long, healthy lives.

"Is one of the visitors out there her doctor?" Clara asked.

"Yes, he was the one in the corner by the radio. The man with white hair and a dark brown suit. He's been giving her the morphine to keep her pain down."

Clara said she recollected which man he was. "What does he think it is?"

"He says he knows for sure it's a brain abscess. I even heard him say he wouldn't even need to do a autopsy, because he says he seen this before, and he knows the symptoms. I didn't give him no argument."

Then, Clara got real close to me and whispered. "Don't you think we should tell the doctor what it really is?"

I had already thought up the same idea, but I told Clara it would make Violet unhappy, and therefore, I would not be telling the doctor nothing. Violet didn't want the doctor to treat her. Just keep the pain down.

"Helen, I've been studying a little about the law. If we told, we would only be considered accessories to the crime. Violet would be charged with involuntary manslaughter, but you, Jesse, and I would probably not be in too much trouble."

"Maybe so, but we would be dragged up to Illinois, and we would have to stay in jail until the trial, and we would miss our families and friends while we was there. We would be on the newsreels at the picture shows, and have our faces in all the papers. Your little Benjamin and baby Iris would know what you done. Do you want to have to go through all that?"

She said she reckoned it would be best if she didn't say nothing.

All of a sudden, we both heard a door slam at the back of the house, and then a noisy automobile driving away from the front. Somebody called us to Violet, and she was asking for Grady, reaching her hand out for him. I walked back to the bedroom, where only minutes before, we seen him staring up at the inside of their closet. He was no longer in the room, and on the top shelf was a empty space. I recollected what used to be up in that spot, since I had helped Violet re-arrange some things just the other week.

Now there was two things missing. One was a suitcase, and the other was Violet's husband, Grady.

CHAPTER TWENTY-THREE

It's usually not my way to listen to other people talk, unless I can't help it. When Adrienne and Benjamin was taking me to the hair salon for my haircut, I set in the back seat of Benjamin's car and listened to those two talk. For the whole summer, they have been spending so much time together, and now they was talking about living in the same city, which would be Atlanta, and maybe even in the same apartment together.

Just before we turned into the salon parking lot, Adrienne bent her elbow over the front seat and turned around to me. "Helen, Benjamin and I have been thinking of moving in together. What do you think of the idea?"

Ever since I was a girl, I knowed it was wrong for a man and woman to live together in sin, but nowadays, things was different. It didn't bother me none, so long as the man and woman was in love with each other and treated each other in a decent way. "I think it would be just wonderful. I would be happy for you both."

Adrienne got out of her seat and went to the back car door to let me out, then she stuck her head inside the driver side and kissed Benjamin on the lips. "See?" she said, smiling at him. "We've got our stamp of approval."

Once we was inside the salon, Benjamin drove off to do a errand at the post office, so me and Adrienne set in the waiting chairs and whispered about things. "So, you think Benjamin and I make a cute couple?"

"Of course you do. You're just right for each other. Except for him being a bit older. But that don't seem to matter none."

Adrienne stopped smiling for a moment, and whispered again, while one of the hair dressers sprayed hair spray all over a lady's head. I sniffled and sneezed.

"I'm worried Benjamin will find out about... you know, the pills. I'm wondering if I should tell him before we move in together. What do you think?"

For once, I didn't have a answer right off. I had to think about it for a while. I was being asked to give advice again, and I felt ill at ease being the one to give it. Then, it was time for my haircut. I told Adrienne I would give her a answer later, but she said there was one more thing she wanted to ask. "I haven't asked Benjamin yet, but how would you feel about staying with us, instead of with Pearl? We would take care of you. We already know we get along. All three of us."

Just like with the advice about her drugs, I said I would have to think about it, and Adrienne said she would mention the idea to Benjamin.

"Maybe I could come to Atlanta one time, and see where we would live. Maybe if I see how I like Atlanta first."

It would be a big decision. I would have to move all my things, and get a new doctor instead of Dr. Meyer. But the best reason for me to go to Atlanta is I wouldn't have to go live with Pearl and Donald in Charlotte.

#

Benjamin and Adrienne was painting a bedroom while I was setting out on his little balcony. He had him a nice big apartment with three bedrooms. As soon as they showed me my new bedroom and my big closet, I decided I would like to live with them.

When the doorbell rang, I come out of the balcony so's I could answer it, and a nice older lady with a fancy dress and a pretty hat said her name was Jean and she was Benjamin's cousin, there to see him. Over her shoulder she was carrying a flowered bag with straps, and she hoped Benjamin didn't mind her dropping in unexpected like that. I went to get him and Adrienne, and they washed paint off their hands and come out to see Jean.

After a few minutes of chatting, Benjamin told me Jean was from Southern Georgia, just passing through Atlanta, and she brought the photo albums with the pictures of Clara. While we set in a row on the sofa, Jean reached inside of her bag and took out two big albums for us all to see. Jean opened the first one to a page with a bookmark. "Here's the one I mentioned on the phone. This was your mother with cousin Duke in 1920. We were at the lake, swimming, and that was when Duke put the frog down the back of her suit."

I stared at the photo, with Clara's face only in a profile. Her hands was on her hips, elbows bent to the side. I recollect even as a young teen girl, she was beautiful. The other cousins was splashing in the water. One boy in swim trunks was running off, and his body was in a blur.

"Who took the picture?" I asked.

"Our father did," said Jean "He was the camera buff. Always snapping us in awkward poses. Once in a while, he would catch us in candid shots like this one."

Jean turned the page again. "Here's one Clara sent me when she was older."

This photo was a close-up of Clara standing with Violet, their arms linked together. Both of them was smiling, and of course Violet was taller, with wavy hair. "There's something written on the back, if you'd like me to take it out of the album."

"Yes, please," Benjamin said.

When she flipped the photograph to the back, the words had been wrote in ink, but had yellowed and smeared over time. "Clara and Violet, June 1920. Friends for life."

Jean stared at the picture again. "I don't recall who this young lady was with Clara. The one with the dark hair."

I knowed it was Violet. That was her handwriting on the picture, but I got a funny feeling in my stomach that I didn't recollect the day we went swimming with Clara and her cousins. Why wasn't I in the picture? The girls seemed close. Like as if they was the best of friends. I started to get a feeling again that Violet had her a secret life. Secrets with Clara.

I cleared my throat. "This is Violet Rodgers. She was my sister. The one who died in 1934."

"I'm so sorry. You know, I still can't believe all this," Jean said. "When I look back at these old photographs, and think what a vibrant, beautiful young woman Clara was..."

Benjamin asked Jean to tell him more about his mama when she was young. Jean stirred in her seat, then took her a deep breath. Then, she let out her breath, speaking to Benjamin. "Before your mother married your father, she was never without a date for a Saturday night. People used to tease her, saying she was an old maid, but she was just choosy. She loved to dance. She would even dance when there was no music, just humming to herself."

Of course, I wanted to know if Jean knowed when Clara and Violet went swimming without me in 1920, but she said after Clara moved back to Illinois with her family, she didn't get no more letters from her. "After we lost touch, we only corresponded once or twice per year, and occasionally she sent other photographs." She flipped to a different page in the album. "This one is you, Benjamin."

Jean showed us a snapshot of Benjamin as a eight-year-old, in 1935, dressed for a pageant at school. He was a bald eagle. After Adrienne said how darling he was, Jean recollected one thing more.

"You know, there was one letter I received from Clara around 1925 or 26. I remember it because she didn't seem to be herself any longer. I suppose that was why we lost touch. You see, I'm a very happy person by nature. I enjoy being around other happy people. I wish you could come to our home and meet Fred. You'd like him."

"I'm sorry I won't get to meet him this time either," Benjamin said. "Perhaps I'll visit again another time, when he's home."

Then, Adrienne said she forgot her manners and went to the kitchen to get lemonade for everbody. While she was gone, Benjamin asked if Jean remembered anything about the letter from his mama.

Jean interlocked her fingers on her lap. "It's been so many years since then, but I remember her saying she felt as if her life was not turning out the way she'd hoped. Failed relationships with men, and that she so desperately wanted to have children and forget her past. I wrote her back and asked her what she meant by "her past," but she never responded. Then years later, we both attended the wedding of another cousin, and she gave me the picture of you."

I reckon Benjamin was trying to imagine why his mama said that in her letter. What would have sent her into a deep depression?

Later in the afternoon, Jean left and we had us a pizza for supper. They was in the kitchen, and I was laying down on the sofa in the living room, resting my eyes. Adrienne asked Benjamin how he felt about the visit from Jean.

"I guess I was a little disappointed. I was hoping she might have known more about my mother or the dial factory. But at least, it was good to have met her."

"Yes, she was very nice."

"The only thing is..."

"What?"

"Right now, I feel like I have more questions than answers."

#

Once I decided to go live with Benjamin and Adrienne, I felt a lot better. I think Pearl did too, maybe even happy to have me go. Me and Adrienne had packed all my things and then she went home. Benjamin was to pick me up in a U-Haul truck. Once he got me, we drove together to Adrienne's apartment to get her things too. On the way, he said everthing was arranged in Atlanta. All I would have to do was sign my name on the papers for the lease.

"Is Adrienne all packed?" Benjamin asked me. I told him Adrienne had already packed about 14 or 15 boxes and stacked them by the door. She left some things for Benjamin to help her with, like taking down some hanging pictures and some of her big furniture would go into storage.

At Adrienne's apartment, her door wasn't closed or locked. Out of the blue, my arms took on a chill. We stepped inside, and at first, everthing looked all right. Her boxes was by the door. Then, I looked up from the boxes, and there was Tony coming from the hallway.

My heart was thumping in my chest, and Benjamin called Adrienne's name. Tony said the same thing to me he said that other time. "Aunt Helen, what are you doing here?"

He said he already knowed why Benjamin was there, but not me. I reckon I was always confusing him.

Soon, a different man come out from the hallway, and Adrienne was right behind him. When I seen the expression on Adrienne's face, I knowed Tony and the man had been there long enough to upset her, and I clenched my teeth.

Benjamin got fidgety. "Adrienne, everything all right?" He snuck close to her, and held her arm in his.

"Fine," she said, "Tony was just leaving."

"Not without my albums."

Adrienne spit her answer, getting her point across in a instant. "Take whatever was yours Tony. Just get out. Both of you."

The other man had him a dark goatee and long sandy brown hair. His eyebrows was raised like as if he wanted to know what was going on, and he wore him a crooked smile.

Benjamin squeezed Adrienne's arm and he backed away from the two men, bringing Adrienne along with him. Tony chuckled. "Relax old man. We just came here to give Adrienne a little going away gift." He made a gesture toward the other man, who then took a little bottle of pills from his jeans pocket. He held the bottle in the air and shook it, making the pills rattle. When he stopped, Tony chuckled again. "We wouldn't want sweet little Adrienne's supply to run out while she's in Atlanta."

Now, Benjamin would know. He would recollect all the times Adrienne was full of energy, and at other times, depressed and moody. Tony got ugly with his next question. "You knew she was a junkie, right?"

Letting go of Benjamin's arm, Adrienne lunged toward Tony with both arms. "Get out. Get out of here." Her voice broke into sobs, and Tony strained against her. "So, I'm guessing she didn't tell you. Has she ever smoked a joint before bed? Gets her horny as hell. She'll…"

Adrienne didn't allow him to finish his sentence. She hollered at him, then at the other man to leave her home.

"What about my albums?"

"You'll get your albums, Tony. When I'm good and ready."

Tony begin shuffling around the room, moving toward us and away. Then, Benjamin got his courage, and his voice was strong. "Adrienne doesn't want either of you here, and she's asked you to leave. Your albums will be returned to you by mail in a few days." Tony snickered, but he understood Benjamin's message, pulling his friend out the door with him.

I was out of energy from all the excitement, so I set in Adrienne's rocking chair, fanning myself with my hand. Adrienne buried her head in Benjamin's chest, still crying. "You weren't here yet, and they both drove up in Tony's car, and…"

Benjamin told her to shush, and stood with her in front of the sofa. "They're gone now."

After only a few seconds, Adrienne stared at me, this time with fear in her eyes. Then she threw her arms around Benjamin's neck, still crying, but her voice was calm, like a youngun who done wrong. "Don't leave me, Benjamin. Please. *Please.*"

He didn't answer. I reckon he *couldn't* answer. No words seemed to be forming on his lips. All that come to his mind was a question. "What just happened here?"

"I'm sorry you had to find out this way. I wanted to tell you. I just didn't know how. You know, most of the time I'm fine and I don't need anything. Isn't that right, Helen?"

Just then, he moved away from Adrienne and faced the door. "I should go."

"But my things are packed. Can't you stay a while? We need to talk about this."

He told her he needed to be alone. That he wasn't ready to talk yet. As he walked out of her apartment, he mumbled something about being the biggest fool that ever lived.

Adrienne let out all her breath and set again on the sofa with her arms by her sides. "Helen, what should I do? How can I fix it?"

I told my friend Adrienne that some things can't be fixed by others. Sometimes, things just find a way to fix theirselves.

The important thing I didn't tell Adrienne was just before Benjamin left the apartment, I seen something I won't soon forget. The thing I seen was Benjamin had him a cloud around his head.

#

After the night Adrienne and Benjamin had the argument about her drugs, there wasn't no reason for me to stay with them in Atlanta. I had to go back to Pearl's and I wasn't happy about it. I don't think Pearl was neither.

They still wanted Bernice to come to the house to check on me, but I really didn't need her. Ever time she comes, she just sets on the sofa listening to rock and roll music on the hi fi. She also does a lot of crossword puzzles, but she's not very good at it. She asks me questions like what's a three-letter-word for a grown kitten. Now, I like puzzles too, but where's the fun if you don't do it all by yourself?

I don't need help. I can get around fine by myself now with only one crutch and I can fix my own meals and tend to myself just fine. I remember to take my own pills, because ever day at four o'clock I watch *General Hospital*, and it reminds me.

A couple of days ago, Adrienne telephoned me. She cried a little while about Benjamin, and then she apologized about being so silly. I told her not to give it a second thought. After that, she said she had her some good news. Her brother Ron was done with his surgery and his leg was better. Now that Ron could walk, the doctors told him he wouldn't be handicapped and he would have to get a regular job. Adrienne said Ron was getting him a ride out to North Carolina with his friends Richie and Neil. "I am so excited, Helen. I can't wait," she told me, with a smile in her voice. "It's been four long years, and I've almost forgotten what he looks like."

I told Adrienne I was looking forward to meeting Ron. It would be good for Adrienne too, to have somebody visit from her family after parting ways with Benjamin. But I didn't think it would matter if she couldn't recognize her own brother right off. War changes a person.

In Ron's case, he had him a different leg than before, and because of how he got that different leg, he was changed, inside and out.

A whole person's life is something like a war. After you fight in a war, you can't help but be different in some way, but folks change just from living through hardships and sorrows and angers too.

Also, like a war, nobody really wins, but life goes on anyway.

#

Just after Bernice drove away, Adrienne come to the house. Bernice had left the light on in the dining room again—the one over the dining table. Even though Pearl asked her a hundred times not to. I stood up with my one crutch when Adrienne come in, so's I could give her a hug. I knowed she was still tenderhearted about Benjamin, and sure enough, while I was hugging her, she sniffled a little bit.

Soon, Adrienne tried to smile. "You're getting around so well now with just one crutch. I'm proud of you."

"I can't wait to get this thing off," I told her, easing myself back down on the sofa.

She was still teary eyed and sniffling. "You know Helen, I wonder if Benjamin and I will get a chance to really talk things through, the way many couples do after they break up. I mean, even with Tony, we at least had a few words with each other, and more than once."

A minute or so passed before I said anything. I was busy thinking about Jesse. Most of the time we had only *good* words with each other. Words of love.

She shrugged a little. "How's that nurses' aide working out for you? Isn't her name Bernice?"

"She's not very smart. Sometimes I have to tell her the most simplest things, like to clean out the lint before she uses the dryer. Things like that."

Adrienne said she wondered why Tony would date somebody like Bernice. She added she would never want to be with him again. She also said she was going to try to get off drugs permanent.

"For fourteen years, I was on that Thor'zine at Mannington. Kept me asleep most of the time. I had me the most fretful dreams." I chewed a little on the inside of my lip when I told her that. Then, I recollected I hadn't seen the man in overalls for a time, and I wondered if I would ever see him again.

"You know what we should do, Helen?"

"What should we do?"

"You know that letter about you going to Illinois for the testing in the lab? At Argonne?"

Out of the blue, I started breathing double quick and my heart hurt. "I...I don't think I want to go." I knowed I should be going, but I was still scared of the whole idea. Also, I wanted to wait until my leg was all healed. "Can we wait until I can walk better?"

"Of course. Let's plan it in a couple of weeks after your cast is off. I'll be with you for the bus ride, and I'll help you every step of the way."

I recollected the letter said the person going for the test could bring somebody with them, and the laboratory would pay. And Adrienne wanted to take me there, because she thought it would be important. Also, she said she wanted to give me some time away from Bernice and Pearl.

Then she got real quiet, and asked me why I never told I worked at the factory.

"It was because of Violet. Because of something bad she done." Something we *all* done.

Adrienne set still for a minute, like as if she was recollecting something from long ago, when *she* was young. Then she tilted her face to mine. "Everyone has things in their past... It might do you some good to talk about it."

I reckon Adrienne was a good nurse, and it was just part of her nature to help folks talk about their feelings. But I just said I would tell her the rest after the testing was over, and she agreed that might be a better time.

#

While I was setting with Pearl at the doctor's to get my cast off, a woman across the way was shushing her infant baby. He didn't want to go back to sleep, and it reminded me of the day we buried Violet.

We was standing at the cemetery, waiting for the preacher to walk to the grave. He was a old man and couldn't walk very fast. Jesse held my hand, squeezing it now and again. One of our neighbors, named Margaret, held her baby boy in her arms, and tried to get the boy to stop crying. She tried having him suck on the end of her finger, but the boy had him some little teeth, and that made Margaret pull her finger right out.

Soon, other folks joined us at the gravesite, and we all stood holding hands around Violet's grave. I knowed there was no chance I would keep from crying, and soon, Margaret had her arm over my shoulder. I asked her if I could hold the baby, and she said of course. Then, she handed him to me. I fiddled with his little blanket, accidentally dripping a couple of tears on it. I brushed them away.

Walking behind the preacher was our daddy, his face drawn. He stood across from me and Jesse, with Margaret waiting for the preacher to begin, then she planned to take her little son back. I cuddled against him, because he was the only person who was giving me any comfort. He was just a baby, with precious eyes and a petite nose, but when he cried, he made no tears. Just his voice. He got me to stop sniffling and I kissed his face hard, squeezing him tight against my chest. I couldn't help recollecting Violet's little baby William, and how he was so sickly.

Margaret wanted him back, but I wouldn't let go. The preacher was about to begin, but I was still clutched onto the baby. Soon, all my memories come rushing forward, how I couldn't have no babies of my own, how Violet had got so sick from the radium, how baby William wasn't able to live more than a few days, and how Bess had died a horrible death. I sobbed over that little baby, my lungs trembling with ever breath.

Finally, I reckoned I would have to allow Margaret to take the baby from my arms, and I let go. I kept my eyes on him until she wrapped him tight against her. Now my arms was empty, and so was my heart.

CHAPTER TWENTY-FOUR

Over the years, me and Jesse didn't have many arguments. Sometimes we would argue about little things like what color curtains we liked, or whether to get a new toaster. One thing we did agree on was to never talk about that night of the fire. Even if we didn't never talk about it, sometimes it was on our minds.

What used to be a scary thing had turned into a dismal thing. A ugly sore nobody wanted to tend to. Specially late in the night, when Jesse would wake up suddenly and get out of bed. He would have bad dreams and go out to the yard, looking up at the sky.

I reckon it was hard for him to have a wife who was all the time scratching herself and looking for cancer. And since he always wanted a son, and ever time we tried to have us a baby, we couldn't, I reckon that that made him fretful too. I recollect one time, a few months before he went off to war, we was fixing to go to bed for the night. I asked him to kiss me before we got under the covers, and Jesse just set still with his feet on the floor. His head was down, and his hands was rubbing his cheeks, like as if he couldn't think of what he wanted to say.

"Jesse, are you coming to bed?"

He let go of his head, and turned his face part way to me. "I'll be in bed in a little while."

"Is there something wrong?"

He said no, there wasn't nothing wrong, but he would just be in bed in a little while. He turned out the light as he left the room, and I fell asleep wondering what was the trouble.

A little while later, I woke up and Jesse was still not in bed. I tiptoed out of the room and found him in a lounge chair, asleep, with a pad of paper in his lap. A pencil had rolled to the floor, and Jesse was slouched down, like as if he had fell asleep that a-way. Instead of nudging him in the shoulder and whispering for him to wake up and come to bed, I leaned over and took a look at what he wrote. It was a confession letter, and he was writing it to his mama and daddy in Illinois. In the letter, he wrote all about what happened that night and how we had promised to keep it a secret. He said he wished now he hadn't never left home and married me, because I was mentally confused and he didn't think he could love somebody like that.

I just stood next to Jesse and my eyes was filled with tears. Even if I knowed it in my heart, it was still a sad thing to read on a piece of paper.

Soon after that, the night before he got called up to war, Jesse got him a telegram about a lady he used to know from high school. The lady's name was Alice, and she had worked at the Radium Dial a little while after me and Violet. Also, Jesse remembered her from when they used to take U.S. History together. She had died from cancer, just like Violet. Even had the same thing happen to her jaw, and her teeth fell out the same way too.

When Jesse seen the telegram, it was his last night before he went to war. He broke down and cried. He grabbed hold of me and hugged me tight, like when he used to love me so much. Like before we was even married, and before I started to get the itching. He held me tight and said he loved me, but our love had changed now. Instead of being "in love," I was his responsibility. He would always take care of me, as long as he lived.

We cried together that night, and he promised as soon as he got back from the war, we would get me a good doctor at a good hospital, to make sure everthing was all right. "I don't want to lose you, Helen."

I reckon that made me feel better for a time, knowing that he would come home from the war and everthing would be all right again. But when the day come six months later, and I got the telegram telling me he had died, I felt like as if I was dead too. They brought his body back to the United States, and back to Belmont. We had a service, only with a closed casket, and that was when I had to go to Mannington.

I sometimes wonder if Jesse hadn't never got the news about his high school friend, if he would of realized he still loved me and wanted to take care of me. But just like many things in life that went some way different from what we planned, I won't never know.

#

Now that I got my cast off, I have me a little Ace bandage, and I can get around with only a cane. I got to go to Adrienne's apartment and see her brother, Ron. He was a short fella, with skinny arms and legs, and a bigger stomach than he should of had. He limped a little just like me, and his breath smelled like a bitter medicine, but he was friendly. His friends dropped him off to stay with Adrienne for a few weeks.

Yesterday afternoon, I was setting out on the back porch at Pearl's in the middle of the day, when I heard the sound of the metal gate on the side of the house.

I gasped a breath when I seen the man in overalls again. I squinted at him, wishing I had somebody with me, so's I would know he was real. "Didn't you come to Mannington a time or two?" I asked him.

He tipped his hat a second, then he took it off and held it in front of his belly. "Yes... I did." He had him a accent to his voice, so I knowed he wasn't from Belmont.

"Well, who are you?"

The man walked closer to the porch and asked if he could come in and set down with me. This time, Bear wasn't in the yard, tearing up the grass. I told the man to please join me.

"Thank you," he said.

He held onto the side railing as he stepped up into the porch. When he did, he groaned a little, like as if he had him a bad knee. Up close, I could see his face was tanned and his teeth was stained yellow. Beneath his overalls, he had on a short sleeve, plaid shirt. Next to the chairs was a little side table, and he set his hat on it.

Just as he set down, he seen my cane and my sore leg, and his eyes got big. I seen a genuine look of surprise on his face, and also, he was sad. "How did this happen?" he asked me.

"First, why don't you tell me your name, and what you're doing here on Pearl's porch? Then I'll tell you about my leg."

"I'm sorry. You're right. You're absolutely right. My name is Everett Calder."

For a little minute, I just blinked my eyes and stared ahead. Then, I let him finish what he was saying.

"My grandfather was Andrew Calder of Ottawa, Illinois."

Inside my chest, my heart was thumping double quick, and I lay my hand across it to settle it. "I see."

"And I know all about the night he died."

I wondered just how much Everett knowed about that night in 1923, but first, I had to wait for him to say more.

"About two years ago, I received this letter in the mail." He reached inside one of his overall pockets and brought out a folded letter. The edges was frayed and wrinkled. He unfolded it and showed it to me. At the top, it said, "Mrs. Clara J. Reed," with her address in Atlanta. Then, the letter begin with "I am writing you this letter because I have recently learned I do not have long to live."

Then, it went on to say how me and Violet and Clara and Jesse had drove to Mr. Calder's house that night and how we promised to keep the secret. But the letter said straight away that it was Violet who done it.

"I waited to find you. At first, I was angry with the authorities for not doing a better job at the time. When my grandfather died, I was only a boy, but I spent many years worrying over his death. It haunted me. My mother kept me at home instead of sending me back to school with the other children, because I was continually fretful and worried. Then again, I was always like that. His death in the fire just made me more worried—about the gas burners in the kitchen, the farm machines. Anything that could catch fire."

I hadn't never thought about the family of Andrew Calder. I had done such a good job of forgetting, I put all that out of my mind. Now I felt bad for the boy who become a grown man, still fretting over how his grandfather died.

"When I got the letter, I wrote back to Mrs. Reed, but she never answered. I went to the Ottawa police, and they said the death was such a long time ago, they didn't think they could devote any time to the case, and if I wanted to, I could go out on my own and try to find you."

"Well, when you come to Mannington that first time, why didn't you just walk right up on the porch and talk to me?"

Everett hung his head and leaned forward. He intertwined his fingers between his knees. "As much as I wanted to find you, I felt ashamed for coming. Like I was stirring up old wounds. So many ladies in our town have died from the radium. You see, I...I'm afraid I'm not a very strong person."

I could tell Everett was ill at ease, with his foot twitching, and there was a little sweat above his lip. "Clara's letter said the two of you stood by and didn't participate, and that you'd kept the secret all these years." Then, he gazed up at me, staring into my eyes. "And now I see you hurt your leg, and I feel worse about being here."

I just smiled at Everett. "Would you like me to tell you how it got broke?"

His body relaxed just a little. "If you'd like to tell me, I'll be glad to listen."

I told him all about my great nephew Tony and how he didn't see me in the driveway. I also told him how much my leg hurt, and how hard it was to walk around having to lift the heavy cast everplace I went.

"I'm so sorry to hear about your accident."

"I got to be sixty-five years old, and I hadn't never broke a bone before."

For a while, me and Everett just set and talked about things. I told him how sorry I was about what Violet done, and the part I played. He told me he knowed Jesse's family, and recollected when they heard about him dying in the war. He explained about when they closed the radium factory for good. He told me how much Ottawa has changed and I told him about Pearl.

Later, he said he had to go, but he would write to me from time to time.

"How did you ever find me?"

"Oh, just by asking people. You'd be surprised how easy it is to get information about a person, just by asking."

"You sure you can't stay for supper with me and Pearl?"

"I'm sure," he answered, checking his watch. "It's time I started back home. Got a long drive ahead of me."

"You still live in Illinois?"

"No, I live just over the state line, in Tennessee." He stood and when I started to get up, he said, "Please, let me help you."

Once I was to my feet, and standing straight, Everett reached into his other pocket and give me a photograph. "You may have this. It was cut out from a photograph we found in some old papers of my mother's. From the Radium

Dial. I guess somebody took a group picture. Do you remember it?"

I told him I recollected the day they took a picture of us setting at our desks and it was in the Chicago Tribune.

I was sorry to see Everett go, but glad now that I had the photograph, I could be assured he wasn't part of my imagination. Now, Dr. Meyer wouldn't have to change my medicine, and I could stop worrying over who the peculiar man was. Only now that I got to know Everett, he didn't seem half as peculiar no more.

#

Adrienne wanted to cook a nice supper to welcome Ron home. While I was there, Adrienne asked me to tell her if the rumor was true.

"What rumor is that?"

"The one about Pearl and Donald and how Donald broke off the engagement."

I told Adrienne I only knowed a little about it. After Donald lost the election, him and Pearl decided to "postpone" the wedding, then they decided to call it off.

"What happened?" Adrienne asked me, tapping her fingers on the table.

"I heard her and Donald talking about her mole," she said. "The doctor told her it was cancer, but only the kind that never spreads."

Adrienne told me it was called basal cell carcinoma. Then I continued. "Pearl and Donald got into a argument because she was just so sure she was going to die from the cancer, and Donald said she was getting herself all riled up over nothing. In fact, he couldn't stand her no more."

Ron just chuckled and left to answer a telephone call.

"How is Pearl taking it?" Adrienne asked.

"She's been on the telephone with one of her close girlfriends, but she won't talk to nobody else."

In a way, I reckon I felt sorry for Pearl. She had tried so hard to improve her lot in life, something Adrienne had been trying to do too. Only not by marrying, the way Pearl wanted, but by becoming a nurse.

"Pearl is sure troubled by it. She done so much packing, and now it has to be unpacked. She had already made her the appointment with the movers."

Adrienne set her napkin on the table, and looked me right in the eye. "Helen, I want you to know, I made an appointment with someone. For my... problem. He's a therapist in Gastonia. He sees people on a sliding scale."

"That's just wonderful, Adrienne. I hope he's a great deal of help to you."

She told me how wearisome she knowed it would be. I agreed. "Anytime you need to talk, and you can't get ahold of that doctor, you just come and see me, all right?"

"I will, Helen. And thank you for being such a good friend." She squeezed my wrist.

"The reason I'm your friend is not for any sort of thanks. I'm your friend because good-hearted folks *should* be friends. So's we can stand up to the bastards."

"Helen, next time you see Tony, will you lock him up in a closet until I get there? Between the two of us, I think we can take him."

#

Adrienne said she had some news for me, and it was good news. "Benjamin called me."

"He did? How exciting." I truly was excited. I hoped maybe he could find a way to forgive Adrienne for keeping her drug problem from him. "What did he say?"

Adrienne told me lots of things Benjamin said. He had did a lot of thinking. He had been missing Adrienne. The most important thing he said was he drove to the cemetery where his wife and youngun was buried.

"He told me he took a shortcut he hadn't taken in years, and without thinking, he turned into the main entrance of the cemetery. It took him five or six minutes to remember where the graves were. Then he parked the car, just sitting for a moment, trying to screw up his courage."

I reckoned it might of been one of the hardest things Benjamin ever had to do.

Adrienne continued on. "After a short walk, he entered the wrought iron fenced enclosure where Gwen and the baby had been buried. He said he fell on his knees and wept."

"Of course he did."

"You know, Helen. I'm just so proud of him. As a friend. I don't know if we'll ever be able to get back together, but I just feel better knowing I helped encourage him to do something he needed to do."

I knowed exactly what Adrienne felt, because when I lived at Mannington with Neely, I was always trying to get her to do things that would be good for her. Sometimes we would talk, and I would try to get her to do things on her own.

Sometimes, people worry about bad things that never happen. I tried to tell Neely, that just because something bad *might* happen, it doesn't mean it will.

CHAPTER TWENTY-FIVE

In the middle of supper, Pearl got her a telephone call. She stood in the kitchen and listened for a while, and then her face turned the color of egg shells. She only said short sentences, like "When did this happen?" and "I'm so sorry."

At the end of the call, she said "thank you" to the person on the line, but I could tell it was news she didn't want to get. Pearl's eyes was wet, and the edges was pink.

After she hung up, Pearl said she didn't feel like finishing her supper, because Benjamin's sister Iris was on the telephone just now.

"What's wrong, Pearl?" I asked her.

She give herself a little hug around the middle, and her voice got quiet. "Iris just gave me some bad news. She just told me Benjamin... well, he died."

When somebody gets to be as old as me, they hear about people dying all the time, but when Pearl told me about Benjamin, I just set in my chair and forgot to breathe. It couldn't be true, but it was true. It would just take me a little while to believe it.

I asked Pearl what happened, and she told me it was his heart. Iris had told her Benjamin come home from work and when the landlord found him, he was on the apartment floor, from a heart attack. Now, Iris was planning a funeral, and asked Pearl to let the others in Belmont know about it. That meant Pearl would have to call Adrienne.

Some tears fell to my cheeks. I wanted to tell Adrienne myself, but I would have to get Pearl to give me a ride to her apartment. "Is it okay? Can you take me?" I asked. I didn't think Pearl would be too happy about telling Adrienne, and I was right. But at least Pearl said she would drive me over and help me inside. She did, and for a little minute, I was proud of my niece. She left and waited in the car.

Together, me and Adrienne set on her sofa. She wrinkled her eyebrows. "Something terrible has happened. That's why you're here, isn't it?" It was news I didn't want to give her, but I knowed I had to.

After I told her, her head fell into my shoulder, and I stroked her hair. She cried for a while, telling me things I already knowed, like what a good person Benjamin was, and how she really loved him. I reminded Adrienne how even though God took Benjamin early, he was with his wife and baby daughter now.

A little while later, I told Adrienne Iris had invited her and Pearl to come to the funeral, but Adrienne said she didn't think she wanted to. She didn't know how she felt about everthing just yet.

Maybe she didn't know now, but I reckoned Adrienne would be crying for quite a long while. I told her how sorry I was, and truly it was the saddest thing I ever heard, since I hadn't never knowed nobody like Benjamin my whole life. But right now, I was being a good friend, which is something we all need.

#

Sometimes, you can just set with a friend and not talk. I reckon that's how you know you have a good friend, because you don't have to say nothing. You can just visit and thoughts can pass between you without a single word.

Me and Adrienne was like that. We could set and watch a television program together or a Saturday night movie. We had a memory or two between us. Things we could share when the time was right, or we could just keep the memories to ourself and know we shared them when they happened.

When I thought about everthing that happened since I come home to live with Pearl, I reckoned Benjamin would of wanted me to go to get that testing done. Also, it was something Pearl kept asking me to do, and I always said no because I wanted to be ornery.

As Adrienne was setting next to me on the sofa in her apartment, I asked her to turn off the television for a minute.

"There's something I want to say to you," I said, trying to sound as serious as I could. "I think it's time now."

"Time"?

"For me to go to that testing at the laboratory. Would you take me?"

I held my breath a minute, hoping she would say yes. I couldn't even think what it would be like to go with anybody else.

Adrienne hugged me and sniffled. "Of course I'll take you. If you promise me one thing."

"What is it?" I would of promised her anything.

"Promise me you'll let me take you to Belk's Department Store and get you a nice new suit to wear when we go to the laboratory."

"We'll have all the doctor's heads turning."

Adrienne had her such a lovely smile.

#

Just as Adrienne come to pick me up for the bus station, Pearl got her a telephone call. She was only half dressed for work, standing in the kitchen in her robe. Me and Adrienne both listened from the living room. "Tony, make it quick, I'm trying to get Helen out the door, and I'll be late to work as it is."

Then, she was quiet for a little minute, and she hollered into the telephone. "All night last night? ...Bail you out?...No, you'll have to wait until the bank opens... No, I don't want to use a bail bondsman. The interest is too high." Me and Adrienne stared at each other, both coming to the same idea at once—that Tony got caught with his drugs, and he spent the night in jail.

After Pearl hung up, she come to the kitchen and stared at me and Adrienne. Her face was pale and she buttoned her robe up tight. I wasn't sure if she was fixing to ask me and Adrienne a question, or if she was going to set down and cry, but in a minute, we knowed just what it was. Pearl turned around and sashayed down the hall, like as if nothing was wrong. Then she shut her bedroom door and hollered out the biggest "damn it" I ever heard in my life.

#

Our first morning in Illinois after the bus ride, Adrienne finished fixing up my hair with hair spray, then she got the hotel room ready for us to leave for the laboratory. She hung up my robe and stuck my blue slippers on the floor of the little closet.

So's I would look nice, I was wearing the new suit she bought, with a soft gold colored skirt with black trim, and a matching short button-up jacket. I was glad I recollected to bring my nice white gloves. I put out my cigarette in the tin ashtray and Adrienne pulled on her coat. "I know they won't be here till eight-thirty, but I want to have everything ready. I hate coming back to a messy hotel room."

My stomach was too jittery to eat breakfast, but Adrienne went down to the office and got her a cup of coffee and a sweet roll, then brought it back up to the room. I didn't mind none that she ate it in front of me.

I reckon I was nervous and jittery because I didn't want nobody to be mad at me, about never telling I worked at the Radium Dial, and also, because tests from doctors I don't know always make my stomach jittery.

In a minute, there was a knock on the door, but instead of the automobile to take us to the lab, it was a young man with a white shirt and crooked necktie, handing us a bouquet of flowers. There was carnations and daisies in there, different colors. Adrienne tore the envelope open, and read the note inside to me. "For a very special lady. To Helen, from the staff at the Center for Human Radiobiology." Adrienne said how nice it was for the folks at the laboratory to send me flowers, and she had to stick them in the bathroom sink full of water until later.

The next time somebody knocked, it was a nice lady from the laboratory, there to take us for the testing. She helped me into the back seat with my cane. With my cast gone now, I still wobble a little, because my leg feels light as a feather. It still itches sometimes too, just as if the cast was still there. Adrienne set on my other side. After a short ride, we was inside the big government building, and we waited on a small sofa for somebody to tell us where to go next.

A nice lady with a sort of short doctor's coat come over and asked if I would like a wheelchair to ride in instead of all the time using my cane, and I said yes, and she left to go get one. While she was gone, a pretty young lady come into the lobby holding her little girl's hand. The little girl let go of the mama's hand while she talked to the woman behind the desk. She stared up at me, then at Adrienne, and asked, "Is she your grandma?"

Adrienne explained, no, that I was simply a close friend. Then, the little girl tugged my sleeve and whispered, "When my daddy's at work, he cusses sometimes."

I wanted to hear more, because the little girl was taking away my worries for a few minutes, so's I wouldn't have to think about the tests. But, soon, the other lady with the short white coat come back with the wheelchair and I climbed in. She said her name was Teresa Jones, and she would be with me for the rest of the day.

Everwhere we went, the doors was locked. Sometimes single doors, sometimes double doors, and Teresa had to use a key for ever one. Soon, we come to a cold, bright room with little doorways with curtains in place of the doors. Everbody was as nice as they could be, saying, "Mrs. Waterman," and "Would you care for anything to eat or drink?" One nice girl asked if I wanted a bagel or a piece of toast with jelly, but I told her I was too nervous to eat.

She stood up next to me in the wheelchair, and set her hand on my shoulder. "There's nothing to be scared about, Mrs. Waterman. We won't do anything until we explain it first. If you feel uncomfortable in any way, we'll stop."

I took me a deep breath and felt my shoulders drop when I blew out the air. "Thank you kindly. This here's Adrienne. She's here to make sure I get here and back home safe."

Teresa talked to Adrienne a minute, then her voice turned serious and she spoke to me. "Now, I'd like you to please go in one of the changing rooms, and put this on. It ties in the front."

Adrienne helped me get undressed and into the little green gown. It was like the ones I used to wear back at Mannington, but the fabric was thinner. I got a chill, so after I set back in my wheelchair, Adrienne arranged my jacket over my shoulders like a drape. I clutched on it up to my neck. I was shivering from nerves, *and* from being chilled.

Adrienne asked if she had time to go to the ladies' room, and Teresa said it would be okay. After she left, a lady in a green gown set across from me in a chair. She had her a pinched up little nose and round cheekbones, only the place under one of her ears was sunk in, like as if part of it was missing. I twitched when I seen it and sucked in a breath. Her hair was streaked gray and white. She said hello to me and I said hello back. Then she asked if I was there to get the testing done. "Yes. I am. I'm scared to do it, though."

"I just finished, but I'm waiting for the nurse to double-check one of my tests. Then she said I could go."

I stared into her eyes, which was darting around the room, like as if she was thinking hard about something. Then, she looked at me again. "Most of it's not too bad." The lady reminded me of somebody I seen before. Then, I knowed who she was. She was Glenda, the girl who punched Bess in her back all those years ago.

"I think I recollect you from the Radium Dial," I said to her. Then, her eyes stopped darting around the room and she got a good look at me for the first time. Her eyebrows went from wrinkled to relaxed. "Helen?" She smiled and come across to set next to me. She put her hand on my arm and give me a little squeeze. "I remember you and your sister. What was her name? Victoria?"

"It was Violet. She passed in 1934."

"Oh, I'm so sorry," she said, with a quiet sound to her voice. "You know, so many of the girls are gone now. They had quite a time finding us, since back then they didn't keep very good records. At the end of my letter, they asked if I knew the whereabouts of three or four girls. I didn't have any idea how to get in touch with them."

"I know. I reckon there aren't even too many of us left to get tested."

We talked a minute about Bess. Glenda had went to see her too before she died. She said she apologized for being ugly that day about Mr. Calder.

"Did you know I married Jesse, the custodian boy?"

"You did?"

"Yes, but he's been dead since the war."

I told her me and Jesse never had any children, and Glenda said she had four boys, all as big and strong as giants, each with younguns of their own. Now that I was up close to Glenda, I seen the scar under her ear. Her hand went to her face. "I had a tumor. They took it out, and it never came back, but now part of my face is gone. I know it's unsightly."

"Oh no, I barely noticed," I said. She told me the doctors said the tumor had nothing to do with radium. "Just a coincidence."

Just then, Teresa Jones come back clutching onto a clipboard. "We're going to put you into the iron room now, Helen. This is so we can get your whole-body count."

First, I asked if she had her a piece of paper, so's me and Glenda could switch phone numbers and addresses. Teresa give us what we needed, then Glenda hugged me and said she had to leave. The other nurse come by, but she waited until we was ready. Glenda hugged me again and I hugged her too before she left with a nurse.

"So you two knew each other?" Teresa asked.

"Yes, for a time. I didn't work very long at the factory, but I recollect her because she was so young. Only 14 at the time." It didn't seem right to tell Teresa that Glenda had punched somebody in the back, so I left that part out.

Before I seen Glenda, all those girls at the factory was in my mind as sweet young women, with rosy cheeks and clear skin and pretty blonde or brunette hair. Now, I had to get used to the idea they was old women like me, or sick or dying. It made me feel like as if my whole life was flurrying right past me.

Soon, Teresa wheeled me closer to the iron room. I asked her to explain it so's I could decide if I wanted to or not. She said, "It's called a counter because it counts the amount of gamma radiation coming off your body."

She showed me a giant metal door, and she said it weighed several tons. At the top of the door was wheels, so's it could roll closed. I walked into the counting room where they had lead on the walls and she told me it was filled with special air, with no radon in it.

"Now, we need you to sit in this chair for about twenty to thirty minutes. Do you think you'd be able to do that?" She pointed inside to the sort of reclining chair made of steel. I got into the chair and set for a little minute. Since I was so tired, I decided to just lean back and rest my neck.

"Are you comfortable, Helen?"

I told her I was fine, and she pressed a button and the heavy door slowly rolled closed.

All the while I was inside the lead room, my eyes was closed, because I didn't want to see where I was. It was making me jittery again. Out of the blue, my heart commenced to flipping. I wanted to know, if I needed to, would I be able to get out of that room. "Hello? Can anybody hear me?" I called out. Then, there was a crackle sound, and it was Miss Jones' voice. She said, "Yes, we can hear you. Remember, if you get worried or nervous, just speak up."

After that, I felt a little more relaxed. I set in that chair and tried to think about quiet thoughts, like puppies, or flowers.

When my time was done in there, Miss Jones asked me did I have any children. I told her no, I was never able to have children. "Do you think it was because of the radium paint?" I asked her.

"I'm not sure. You should ask your doctor after he receives the test results." Right after that, Miss Jones looked at my chart. "However, it says here on your questionnaire you didn't often lick the paint off the brush, so that is probably a good indication we won't find much radium in your bones."

For the next hour or so, the doctors examined ever part of me, inside and out. They listened to my heart, took my blood, x-rayed ever bone plus my chest, and asked me to walk up a hall and turn around to walk back. I asked how long it would take to get the doctor's reports after all these tests, and everbody told me I would get a letter in a week or two, but it would just be "preliminary."

After me and Adrienne got back to the hotel room, we was both exhausted and we stayed in bed until supper time. Then, she took me to a nice restaurant close to the hotel. When the next morning come around, I got out of bed. My bad leg was feeling better, but the rest of me felt like I had been dragged through a knot hole.

#

On the bus home, we had us a crowd until we reached Statesville, North Carolina, where a group of them got off. This stop would be for twenty minutes, so me and Adrienne decided to stretch our legs. First, we walked to the ladies room, which was big inside, with about ten stalls. The floor was sticky in places, and the air smelled of ammonia and lemons.

Adrienne finished first, and after she flushed, she chatted with me from over by the sinks. "I can't wait until we're home," she said. "I want to take a good long soak in the tub."

I didn't answer her, because I felt something crawling under my skin. Like little ants.

"Helen?"

"It's itching." I flushed, then opened the door to my stall. "My skin is getting that itchy feel again." I started in rubbing my hands all over my arms and inside my blouse sleeves.

"Really? Like you used to at the hospital?" she asked, while rolling up my sleeve to check an arm. "No rash or pink bumps. Only scratch marks." I didn't mean to, but I snatched my arm away, and begin rubbing my arms and legs fast like.

"Helen, please try to keep still." Just like always, other ladies was starting to stare. I tried to keep a smile, but before long, I lost my good mood. Then, Adrienne got her a startled look to her eyes. "Oh my God, Helen. We forgot your Haldol." We had missed my last two doses of medicine. We'd been in such a frantic state, with the trip and the hotel room and the laboratory, I'd forgot to take it. Soon, more and more ladies come in to gawk. Quick-like, Adrienne give me one of my pills.

"What's wrong with *her*?" I heard somebody ask. Other voices mumbled words like psycho, nuts, crazy, and I reckon they was right. But Adrienne stayed right up next to me, telling me how sorry she was about forgetting the medicine and so forth.

She told me not to worry, and the trip may have been a extra stress on me, along with missing my medicine, which was causing the "psychotic episode."

For some reason, I just stopped scratching my skin a moment. My fingernails had left red and purple scratch marks up and down my arms. Instant tears filled Adrienne's eyes. "Oh, Helen, look at what you've done." I felt as if I was a misbehaving youngun and Adrienne was scolding me. She asked one of the onlookers to get her some help.

A minute or two later, I started in scratching again. Then, a older blonde lady dressed in a nice tailored suit and a colorful scarf around her neck tapped Adrienne on the shoulder. The lady had a *Trailways* badge with her name on it—Mrs. Lois Chilton.

We followed Mrs. Chilton to the main office and set on a vinyl sofa where Adrienne told her our names. I kept on scratching, but Adrienne tried to get me to stop again. Mrs. Chilton asked if there was anything she could do, and Adrienne answered right away. "Yes. I need to stay with her, so I'd appreciate it if you'd call this doctor for me."

Adrienne searched through my handbag until she found my pill bottle with the doctor's name on it. My stomach was tied into knots. Mrs. Chilton said she'd get right on it, and after only a short time, two big-boned men come into the office, stared at me, and asked which of us was Adrienne Connaway.

Letting go of my arm, Adrienne answered who she was.

Then right behind them, a female police woman stepped into the office.

"You Miss Connaway?"

"Yes. I'm terribly sorry this has happened."

"Yes ma'am. We'll need to get her to the van, so she can be evaluated." I reckoned they would be taking me to Mannington anyway. The officer asked if we was a passenger on one of the buses, and Adrienne sucked in a quick breath. "Oh! Our things!"

Adrienne told me a bus station worker would get our suitcases and so forth. Also, they would explain to the driver that we would not be returning. Soon, the itching got worse, and I knowed it was cancer crawling around inside my blood. On the way outside to the van, the ambulance workers held down my arms by squeezing them so tight, I thought they would turn purple and fall off.

CHAPTER TWENTY-SIX

On the way to the hospital in that van, Adrienne wasn't with me. The ambulance worker said she would be along after. As I was laying down on that gurney, they strapped me down again, just like at Mannington. They strapped me so's I would stop itching and scratching myself. I knowed I somehow got my cancer back. It was from that trip to Illinois.

The two men in the van was fussing over me, and I got nervous and then my urine run out of my underpants. They got busy and cleaned me up right away. By now, I was sobbing and crying. "Where are you taking me?" One of them held a tissue to my nose and told me to blow.

Soon, we was driving up the road to the front of the Avery building. The leaves was off the trees now, and the sky out the van window was full of light and dark gray clouds. I thought of God's face and his beard with the two shades of blue and white. The itching got worse, and I started to wiggle. It was like being back in the tunnels again, but with no way out on either end. I started breathing fast, worried about what they might do to me. I should of been glad to be at Mannington, but until the itching went away, I wasn't going to enjoy being back.

Once we was inside the building, they didn't even get me out of the gurney. They just stuck me with a needle again, and I felt warm all over and everthing got dark.

\#

A nurse come into the room, and even though I tried, I was still too tired to stand. She handed me a glass of water and a pill. I felt like crying again. "Where am I?"

"This is the new infirmary. Things have changed since you were here last."

"How long have I been here?"

"You've been here two days now. Your old doctor, Dr. Stokes is on his way."

I swallowed the pill and water. "Where's Adrienne?"

The nurse pinched my wrist with two fingers while staring at her wrist watch. After a minute, she answered me. "Where is *who*?"

"Adrienne. She was with me at the bus station, and they said she would be along."

"I'm not sure," she said. "But if anyone comes to visit, I'll let you know. You just lie back and rest right now, okay?"

When Dr. Stokes come into the room, he looked different too. He had him a thin mustache, and I told him he looked silly. "Helen, we thought we might never see you here again. What happened?"

"Well, I think Adrienne forgot to give me my pills, so I got to itching again. Can I please have my old room back, Doctor? Can I be with Neely again?"

"Now Helen, we're not asking you to stay more than a few more hours. We feel you've just had a minor setback, and you'll be ready to leave as soon as we finalize your discharge. Then you can leave as soon as your niece arrives."

Pearl. I would have to go with Pearl all over again. I clenched my teeth together. I thought real hard about how I could still be able to stay at Mannington until Adrienne come for me. I decided I would give them a reason. I stood up from the bed, and started screaming. "I won't go! I will not go home with Pearl, not never!" I stamped my foot and my arms went rigid and straight. I did my best to make my eyes bug out too. Then, with ever last bit of my energy, I cried into my hands, until they decided they would wheel me back up to Ward Six-A in a wheelchair.

As I was leaving, I heard a nurse ask, "What on earth do we tell her niece Mrs. Velasquez when she gets here to take her home?"

The other one said, "I don't know, but it won't be me. I can't stand that woman."

CHAPTER TWENTY-SEVEN

As I entered the hallway of Ward Six-A, I felt like as if I was finally returning home. Nurse Flora took over from the orderly, pushing me in the wheelchair. Half way down the hall, she stopped. "Helen, can't you walk the rest of the way? My arms are getting tired."

I told her I reckoned I could try to walk tomorrow, but I couldn't today. As we continued down the hall, I seen other girls I didn't know. And some of them was dressed in their street clothes instead of gowns.

"Can I still stay with Neely?" I asked Nurse Flora.

"No, she's no longer in this ward. She had to go to acute for a while."

Whenever somebody went to acute for a while, that usually meant we wouldn't see them again for a long time.

"Soon after you left, she got a new roommate, but they didn't get along. Neely received more therapy, but it didn't help. Finally, she just snapped."

I told Nurse Flora that was too bad. "Maybe I can stay with Neely's roommate."

"We have an extra bed down the hall. Other side, across from your old room. You'll be with Mavis Payton."

I swallowed a lump in my throat, thinking I would be with rubber-band Mavis. With my shaky hand, I squeezed the back of my neck. Flora turned the corner to the room, and Mavis was setting up in bed looking at a magazine, chewing her gum. She was wearing a orange gown with the sleeves tore off. Most people wouldn't wear the orange gowns, because they fit funny in the hips, like as if they was meant for a man, but it fit Mavis just fine.

When she seen me, she made a furrow between her brows. "She's not staying here with *me*, is she?"

"Now, Mavis, that's no way to talk to Helen. She's been sick for a couple of days and she just needs a place to stay until she's well. Try to get along."

She stared at my wheelchair. "What's wrong with you? Can't walk around no more?"

Flora set the brake and I got out of the chair by myself. "I got hit by a car. My leg was in a cast for a few weeks. It's better now, but sometimes I can't walk for a long ways without getting tired."

Mavis just went back to her magazine. While Flora was getting the sheets for my bed, I asked her if there wasn't a different room I could stay in. "You'll stay where we put you. This isn't the Ritz Carlton, you know."

I crossed my arms and waited until Flora got the rest of the blankets and got me a pillow. Just then, the radiator in the room give off a loud clang. I jumped and Mavis laughed at me. Then she choked on her gum.

#

For the past week or so, I've been living with Mavis. We finally got to where we could tolerate each other. Course, I'm down in the art room most of the time anyway, still trying to paint God's face. Just last Tuesday, I got the face right, but instead of Roman numerals around the face, I painted a cloud. Just like the one around Benjamin's head before he died. I recollected all the times I seen a cloud or a halo around somebody's head, and now I knowed ever time it happened, it was just before they died. I just never noticed it before.

Nurse Flora come into the room. "Helen, there's someone here to take you home."

I was lying on my side in bed, facing the door, and I seen Nurse Flora standing in the doorway, with her arms crossed. Then, she stepped aside, and Adrienne walked into the room. Adrienne stood still, and Mavis made a little "huh" sound, and left us alone.

Slowly, Adrienne inched forward and give me a hug. I set up straight in the bed, and Adrienne set next to me. "Are you angry with me?" she asked in a quiet voice.

"No, I knowed you must of had a good reason for being so late."

She started to cry a little, but she shook her head and stared up at the ceiling. She whispered, "I will not cry." Then, she hugged me again, tight. "I feel really rotten for not coming sooner. I wanted to make sure everything was... all right."

I reckoned maybe Adrienne needed some time away from me. Maybe she felt bad about what happened at the bus station.

"I've been seeing the therapist. He's helped me realize a lot of things."

I told her I was happy she was trying to get herself off drugs. She stared away for a minute, thinking about something, then she continued.

"Helen, I've arranged a surprise for you. Pearl has agreed to hand over your Social Security check and you can come stay with me and Ron. You can have my room and I'll stay on the sofa in the living room. That is... if you think you'd want to."

Before I could say nothing, I started to cry, but I wiped my tears with my palm. "You won't forget to give me my pills?"

"I will *remind* you to take your pills."

"Can I get some water colors and paint what ever I want?"

"Of course."

I told her I would like to live with her. For a minute, she was quiet. Then she told me she would keep on seeing the doctor for her problem. I told her I was right proud of her. When somebody has to do something that's hard for them, they feel good after they done it, just because it's over. But I knowed, even if she kept on seeing that therapist, it might be some time before she felt good.

"I wanted you to know a letter came about your lab tests. They said the final report would come in a few months, but the preliminary results show you probably do not have enough radium in your bones to cause cancer."

I let out a long breath and smiled. "It seems that trip we took on the bus was worth all the trouble."

"I agree, although I'm still sorry you *had* all the trouble."

I patted her arm. "Adrienne, there's one more thing I'd like to do."

"What's that?"

"After we get home, I want to tell you the secret. Of why I didn't tell nobody about the Radium Dial."

Then, Adrienne smiled and closed her eyes. For the first time in a long time, she seemed to relax her cheeks and mouth. I reckon it meant a lot to her that I would finally tell her. She'd been waiting to hear it, and maybe she felt if I come to live with her we could both start us a new life. She leaned her head over on my shoulder. It reminded me of all those days and nights I held Neely, helping her and taking care of her. I reached tighter to Adrienne.

With my eyes closed, I held her and whispered to her, while I gently rocked her in my arms.

EPILOGUE

After years of failed legal battles in the lower courts and the Illinois State Supreme Court, the women who suffered from radium poisoning, known as the "Living Dead," found a champion for their cause. Leonard J. Grossman (1891-1956) was an attorney from Chicago and a specialist in workmen's compensation cases. He was hired by the women in 1937 to represent them before the Illinois Industrial Commission. William Ganley, president of the Radium Dial Company suggested the claims made by these women were "invalid and illegitimate," asserting that radium was not a poison.

The chief plaintiff in this case was Mrs. Catherine Wolfe Donohue (1903-1938). A dial painter at the Radium Dial Company since the age of 19 in 1922, Mrs. Donohue had worked for the company for nearly nine years. After two years with the company, she began developing health problems, including joint pain, fainting spells, and disintegrating jaw bone.

During the trials Mrs. Donohue's health continued to worsen, and some of the testimony took place in her home. Appeals by the attorneys for the Radium Dial Company caused the litigation to extend on into 1939. Mrs. Donohue passed away at the age of 35, before the courts had rendered a final decision.

In the fall of 1939 the U.S. Supreme Court rejected the last appeal by the defendants. $10,000 was ultimately awarded to the remaining dial workers. Although this sum scarcely compensated them for their legal and medical expenses, the women had won in another sense. Now the world would know how the Radium Dial Company had deceived and mislead its workers, and women's rights in the work place were significantly enhanced and protected.

Author's Acknowledgements

I could never have accomplished the daunting task of writing a novel without the assistance, encouragement, suggestions, and generous time from the following wonderful people.

First, I would like to thank the following individuals for assisting me with research and historical accuracy: Aaron Lewis, Rip Barrier, and Robert Rowland.

Thank you to the many test-readers who offered suggestions and encouragement along the way, through numerous versions and revisions, including Jennifer Pooley, Roberta Lonsdale, Rob Widdicombe, Linda Pond, Paula Widdicombe, Sandy Buffie, Lisa Kline, Joan Merritt, Susan Welch, Beverly Compton, Barry Gilmore, Linda Sienkiewicz, Diane Crisp, Kathy Bower, Marshall Bocher, Kelly Ridenhour, Alli Ringenberg, Ron Packard, and Katherine Fitzgerald. Thanks to Sheila Acosta, Nina Cartee, Vicki Dykes, and Trish Thompson for their continuing support.

Special thanks to Bob and Shirley Widdicombe for their tireless and multiple readings, proofreading, and editorial assistance.

I would like to express my appreciation to Laura McDonald for including my novel on her website. Second, I may have never connected with Laura, if not for my diligent and devoted editor, Sandra Spicher. Thank you Sandra, for believing in Halos and believing in my abilities as a writer. You gently nudged me to stretch my skills and improve the novel beyond what I thought I could ever accomplish.

Thanks to my sisters and my brother for being the best siblings anyone could ever ask for.

Finally, I would like to offer endless gratitude to my sons Gary and Josh for sharing the family keyboard with me, while I wrote and revised hundreds of thousands of words over the past decade.

ABOUT THE AUTHOR

 Originally from Annandale, Virginia, Shelley Stout resides in Charlotte, North Carolina, where she enjoys spending time with her two grown sons. She also enjoys volunteering at a local homeless shelter. Shelley has been a contributing writer for Charlotte area magazines and her award-winning fiction has appeared in anthologies, *The Storyteller Magazine* and online at WordRiot.

Made in the USA
Charleston, SC
11 January 2016